CANDLELIGHTER

LEGENDS OF CRUXIA
BOOK 1

CARTER REYNOLDS

This one's for you mom,
you read all the ones that came before.

ACKNOWLEDGMENTS

I first thank my wife and daughter for supporting me through all the highs and lows over the years of this novel. Also Fat Heads Brewery in Middleburg Heights for letting me stick around and write for hours, even when it was busy. Thanks to Nathan Kingery for always being on the other line when I needed to call about plot or characters, and Matt Helfgott for telling me I could make it.

1

Roisin hung suspended, her legs wrapped in the rafters. She held her tunic close while reaching for the candle. She wasn't modest, her clothes were dyed cheap, one wrong move and she'd catch flame. The Lamplighter's Guild is not safe work.

She dangled above the chandeliers in Her Sacrament of Veridaan, a marble temple built to honor Sister Spring, goddess of birth. Lamplighters were responsible for all the street lights, Candlelighters got the more prestigious work inside.

She worked hard for her new position, head Candlelighter on the Gods' Way. She took her knocks on the lamp posts working the Mule Quarter, lighting the taverns and brothels. Sure, it was her home, but it was also the most dangerous burg in all of Cruxia. Once the sun set, out came the pimps and the slavers all looking for some sweet young thing to visit horrors upon. Worse were the Moles, mutated half-men that lurked in the city's sewers. Roisin thanked Auron she was born a girl for once. Young boys were all the rage on the red market anymore.

Growing up in the Mule was her saving grace, she knew which streets to stay off, which inns were safe, territories that shifted like the tides from day to day, week to week. She was smart too, thanks to her da'. A school teacher, he taught her how to read, write, and count before consumption took him to Sister Mortia. Siblings bless his soul. Amen.

He said Roisin got her smarts from him, and her prudence from her ma'. Roisin never met her mother, complications in childbirth. It cost da' all his savings to hire a medicer so that Roisin would live, but she was worth every silver, he used to say.

Roisin smiled a sad smile, upside down, looking at the silver ring on her thumb. Her da's wedding band. His last gift to her.

But she daydreamed on the job. Gods knew she did enough dreaming when she slept. Daydreaming didn't get her this position, nor her savings, nor the room she rented. Her very own room, not some rope slung in the middle of a shanty tenement for her to slump on with the other poor wretches. No, a room with a bed and desk and a candle. Beneath her floorboards were nineteen silver pieces she saved over five years as a Lamplighter. Her ticket out of the Mule.

Time to focus on the goal. Millions of candles to light before she saved enough. So there she hung in the rafters of Her Sacrament of Veridaan, the greatest temple on the Gods' Way. Veridaan was the Sister of Spring, goddess of birth, protector of the lost. It was here Roisin spent her first year as an orphan.

The temple was carved from one great block of limestone, wide steps and tall columns marched up its entrance. Inside was a dazzle of marble floors, mahogany pews, and a dais fit for the gods. Roisin looked at the towering stained glass window facing north. Veridaan in sparkling blue and white bent over a congregation of children. The Sister of Spring was the closest thing she ever had to a mother.

She scratched her pitch-stick on the sandpaper bracelet she wore, sparking the alchemicals at its tip. These would burn blinding then slow on tallow, giving her time to light all forty candles before moving to the next chandelier. Eight chandeliers in all, Veridaan's temple was the largest on her route by far. Candlelighters started their shift at the fifth bell, finishing their route by eighth toll so the whole city glowed through the night. Dousers came through just after sunrise to put them out, Roisin's least favorite shift. She could stay up all night but waking up early was a different animal entirely.

Roisin stretched her arm, brought the pitch-stick to the last candle on the chandelier, then pulled herself back up to the rafters. She risked a glance to the floor some eighty feet below. A figure, small as a doll, bent at the statue of Veridaan behind the dais. Father Alonso was High-Father and caretaker of the orphans. A jolly, ruddy-faced man who let Roisin in every night and locked the doors behind her when she left. A good man, in the darkness following her da's death the High-Father finished her education.

Knock, knock. Roisin shivered and pushed down the door.

Instead, she smiled and blew the High-Father a kiss far below, then monkeyed up the higher catwalks. A spider web of rafters spiraled off the main dome, wending and winding to every corner of the temple. She inched along, wrapping her legs on the next strut before working her arms forward. Roisin was ever careful, prudence from her mother.

She had flown in these rafters, sailed around them like a bird in her dreams. When she first came to this temple she would not speak, grief a cancer bundled behind her eyes. Father Alonso was the only one who cracked through to her. He set a book on her bed stand before leaving her to catatonia. Reading was the only thing that made the pain go away, the gift her father left her, literacy. Alonso didn't push her to open up, he just came on the last day of the week and set another book on her bed stand. Finally, after six months he spoke to her.

Roisin crabbed over the rafters to the next chandelier lighting another pitch-stick while she thought back to that day. Father Alonso's face was a map of burst blood vessels leading to a bulbous potato of a nose. His white hair hung in wisps around a bald pate and if he wasn't up at the pulpit in sermon, there was a wine goblet in his hand. He knocked twice, then entered her room with his wine and a book.

She brought her knees up to her chin and pulled away into the corner like she did with any visitor back then. He just smiled, sat on the edge of her bed, and picked up the book from last week.

"*Mediations on Humanity*? Hmmm, you surprise me again, little Rose. Galvin Mechino is tough for most scholars. Was it difficult?"

Her only answer was an animal stare.

"Yes, yes, well, this book is different." He flipped open the new one and sprayed through the pages with a thumb. "It's empty. This book is for you to fill." He set his goblet down with a sip and pulled out a feather-pen and ink well. Roisin's eyes widened, they belonged to her da'. "What I'd like you to do is write down your dreams. Would that be okay?"

She worked over to his side, took the pen, and held it to the candlelight.

"Grief is a deep ocean, little Rose, there are few vessels to traverse it. I find dreams to be the soundest ship."

"I don't like my dreams," she rasped. Her first words since her father died. **Knock.**

His green eyes sparkled. "But you could. Dreams come from here," he tapped his temple, "which means no matter how scary, or angry, or sad they are, they come from you. When you realize this, you can shape them and eventually shape yourself.

4

Next time you awaken, immediately take up this pen and write down what you saw. No matter how hard it is to face, no matter how much you don't want to, write down the truth of what happened. The brain is a marvelous and terrible tool. The recollection of your dreams leads to awareness. Inside the dream you will have control. And Veridaan's truth is found there, 'control within begets control without'."

He patted her head, drained his glass, and stood to leave.

"Thank you," she whispered.

"Thank the Siblings for giving you a father so special."

She grabbed his waist and cried and cried and cried.

Roisin wiped a tear as she crawled to the last chandelier. Some wounds still hurt no matter the gulf of time. She thought about how far she'd come. Her position, her savings, her room, all because Father Alonso guided her through that darkness. She still kept her dream journal tucked away with her silver. It was tough at first, but as the pain subsided, she found the control Alonso spoke of. In her dreams she soared these rafters, soared above this city, soared across the oceans to distant lands of wonder. She was utterly in control of her dreams; any fancy, any fantasy, whatever she wanted.

Which is why she didn't need to waste time on the job. She dreamed enough at night, and she must focus or—

Shit!

She watched the candle spin in slow motion. Falling, falling, falling to the floor far below. Stupid little girl, stupid Mule wench. She'd been wrapped up in dreams, and look what it cost? She knocked a candle with her foot like a common urchin on the lamp posts. Krentor's Bell struck ninth toll right as the candle shattered on the floor. She was behind already, and this made it worse. Father Alonso wouldn't mind the mess, but her superiors would have her tongue for tardiness on her first night as Candlelighter. She scampered around the chandelier, hastily lighting the last candles before heading to the floor.

In her hurry, she didn't notice the four figures creeping through the cathedral door.

Maharez hated the next part most. He and his sister would rush in from both sides and grab the target's arms, locking them in place until Hook could work his sorcery. Or just cut their throat. Polo watched. Always. Polo liked to watch.

To Maharez, it wasn't the killing, it was the bit right before. Right when they grabbed his arms. The anticipation, the shaking, whether they shit themselves or not. At least Hook wasn't a sadist. All business. He got in fast and finished them off. Those seconds took ages.

Maharez hated the life; sneaking, sulking, nights crammed in the worst part of the city. All four of them stinking up an inn like common beggars. He hated killing. But it was the job. He would not think about where it placed him next on the great wheel of stars. Halladar has no time for killers.

Still, was it worse than the slave galley? Chained to five other people, stinking skin sloughing off around the cuffs. An eternity of push and pull? He shivered.

And there was Polo's cane to the back of the head. Smack.

"Focus," the Mole whispered in his ear. Great Halladar, he hated Polo more than anything. Everyone hated Polo and Polo hated everyone, a wrinkled and pustule-covered Mole with two great cataracts for eyes. He was ugly even by Mole standards, hunch-backed and liver-spotted.

The four crouched behind a pew in some temple devoted to some god of these white people, Verra or something. Another temple on a block devoted to them, nothing special. These Cruxians had so many gods, too many gods. The temples of Halladar were a thousand times more beautiful; mosaics of gems and gold spiraling up the columns. Maharez missed Hanrabi.

Bent at the dais was their mark, some bald, fat priest. Polo claimed it was a political job. Maharez didn't care. It was just another notch on his debt.

The Cazzaratti: largest crime syndicate in Cruxia spanning two continents and all their former colonies. They saved Maharez and Fatima from a Turvaali slave galley, the Cazzaratti told the siblings they owed them. Three years of work, three years of crime in Cruxia. Maharez was agile, strong for his size. Fatima was better. They excelled early and got promoted to Polo, top sweeper for the Cazzaratti.

Maharez tensed his fingers into a fist then spread them out. Fatima drummed on the marble floor with one hand, her pre-job tick. Behind them, Hook sat with eyes closed, feeling the room with his sorcery. Or Maharez assumed; he thought Hook made up half the shit he claimed was magic.

Hook was a white man in his forties, receding hair and more of a boxer's build than a wizard's. A beer belly hung over his black pants.

Hook leaned forward and signed in army signals he'd taught them. "Alone. Be quick. Expect magic." Polo nodded and signed for Maharez and Fatima to engage.

They darted from the pews, Maharez left, Fatima right. Their slippers made little sound on the marble. Quicker, Fatima bound up the dais to snake the priest's arm. He whirled around as Maharez arrived. They braced his arms behind him. He gasped once then prayed in an ancient tongue.

Nothing happened, no Hook with the knife and magic like usual. Maharez didn't have to strain, the man pushed seventy and was not in any sort of shape. He risked a glance towards Polo and Hook. Both writhed on the marble, spasmed under the priest's sorcery. Hook pushed his fist through a hurricane of force. "Expect magic!" it said.

"Halladar protect," Fatima swore. Maharez didn't appreciate the use of their god's name in this work.

She pulled out a curved blade and stabbed; once, twice, three times in the priest's chest and stomach. He collapsed between them bubbling and wheezing prayers in his alien language. Blood pooled. Fatima crossed her arms and leaned against the altar.

"That's not enough," the wizard Hook shouted. He tried to stand up.

Maharez and Fatima bent down to check. Blood ran back into the man, skin sewn back together.

"Hallad—" a concussive blast of white light cut her off. She skipped on the floor like a stone across water and smashed through the first two ranks of pews. Maharez managed to cross his forearms in a block but the light blasted him over the three-step dais in a heap. Hook bent low; he closed the distance in less than a second. Maharez's vision spiraled like a carousel.

The wizard blurred in heat haze. His knife swung in quick-silver arcs. The priest recovered from his initial wounds and blocked the blade with open palms. Defensive wounds closed as fast as they were torn.

Hook's knife flashed; the priest's throat opened. He dropped to his knees, tried to shove the blood back in. The Hanrab siblings found their legs and limped over. Hook breathed heavily and wiped blood from his face. He was diminished like he'd been up for two days straight. Maharez did not like the man but put a hand on his shoulder. Out of respect. "Well fought."

"Aye. Haven't moved liked that since the army. Mortia's cooter."

"Look, you dimwits," screeched Polo.

Flat on his stomach, shaking, the priest drew symbols in the pooling blood. His throat closed.

"All the gods above and below," Hook swore. The three drew their knives and fell on him. Close work, brutal, streaked in blood. After, Maharez sat on the dais in a slump, stared at his sticky hands until they stopped shaking. It was never that bad. Not ever.

Polo limped over, his cane cracking on the marble. Fatima cleaned her blade on a hanging curtain behind the pulpit. Hook caught his breath like he'd run six miles.

Polo reached them and opened his mouth to say something, but Hook cut him off. He pointed. "There's a girl over there watching us. Look."

2
———

antry walked down the cobblestones of Helinger Way, breathing in the cool sea air as the last of the morning mists faded. This early the city of Cruxia hung in strange limbo, the only other people up and about were linen-clad urchins on the lamp posts dousing lights for the incoming day. By twelfth bell, the air would hang stinking and muggy, the streets clogged with some thirty thousand citizens beating away at their lives. Gantry liked this hour, after the evils of night had finished but before the drudgery of the day had begun.

He walked through the residential district of the Promenade, the palace cutting the sky to the north. The streets were packed with neat little rowhouses no wider than three mule carts side by side. Each had a tiny, manicured lawn, and red brick was everywhere. This is what money looks like he thought to himself as he always did when he was heading to the Inspector General's house. The Promenade was raised above the rest of the city, closed off with limestone walls and turrets above iron gates. Here were the homes of the magistrates, Parliament clerks, and high-ranking officials. Those with even more clout lived in the Palace district itself, raised even higher with taller limestone walls and thicker gates.

Gantry wound past a café and made it to the very end of Helinger wedged between the district walls and a warehouse. The houses were still neat and tidy, but the shadow of the wall made it grimmer. The Inspector General lived on the cheapest block of the Promenade, much like Gantry lived in the best part of the Mule Quarter. Well, Mule adjacent, at least. His tiny apartment sat above a cobbler's shop on a clean merchant block, but the smell of stables and rendered fat still made it to his window every night.

His parents were so proud of him, even after seeing the meager dwelling he inhabited. Farmers from far past the Horn Forest, they were just delighted to have a son who lived in a city; the city. Cruxia, capital of the Empire. They gushed over having a wizard as a son, a professional wizard. Never mind that Gantry was mediocre at best, had failed out of the Mage Corps twice, and would never rise above Assistant Inspector. Never mind any of that to his parents who hadn't been within fifty miles of a college in their whole life. He sighed and lit his pipe with a pitch-stick in front of the Inspector General's narrow red brick house. Fifth bell would strike any moment, and he would give her that much more sleep.

After a moment of watching the urchins monkey up the lamp posts and the horse-drawn carriages start the morning traffic, he took out his key ring and let himself in her front door. Her house was immaculate and barren, every piece of furniture wooden and utilitarian. In the foyer, a coat rack sat by the door, a table alongside it with her sword belt and instrument pouch. A brown, lifeless carpet ran across the room meant only to catch the dirt from your boots. The kitchen was built into her dining room, a table set for one. A single portrait of the Emperor Sentelpedeo Cruxis hung over the small dining room table. Gantry walked past all this and knocked once at her bedroom before entering. It wasn't presumption her orders were to come wake her when a case arose.

Bottles sprawled on every surface, some cluttered the floor. A particularly tough week for her. He picked up an empty and cringed, harsh whiskey from the Rock Coast. Too strong for his blood, Gantry preferred a nice lemon wine, or maybe a stiff brandy if he was celebrating. He could hear her soft breath from under the blankets and tried not to look at her. He sighed and sat down at her desk, neatly stacking all the bottles in a rubbish box. Gantry sighed a lot around Sariah Sternwood.

With the last clink of bottles, she grunted and sat up. "Inspector Willow, good morning." Her features were sharp and lined slightly on a face the color of coffee and cream; her black and grey hair weaved around her scalp, barely feminine in its cut. Her frame was slight, wired in muscle, and she wore a cotton jerkin with a dagger at its belt. She was always on the job.

"Morning, Sternwood, got a live one down the Gods' Way."

She rubbed her hangover and hummed low, all part of the morning ritual. "What have I told you about humor?"

"It is an ostentation of the less educated. It's the only thing you're wrong about."

"Nevertheless, please refrain on duty," she stood and stretched. She took a dip of water from a bowl and wet her face, then sipped some from her cupped hands. "What have we got?" She went behind a wooden partition and urinated into a bedpan. Gantry stepped awkwardly and lit his pipe.

"Temple of Veridaan saw some action last night. A sister of the house found a stiff on the pulpit when she came in for morning prayer. Rang all the bells and got the constables in right quick. Medicer Inspector is down there already. It's bloody."

"When isn't it? Where were the constables last night?"

"Put to sleep."

"All sixteen patrols on the Gods' Way?"

"Sorcery is my guess. Must've been expensive," said Gantry.

Her night jerkin popped over the partition. He heard the ringing clink of chainmail and tried not to imagine her getting dressed on the other side. He could take an ethereal peek behind the curtain at her naked frame. But he wouldn't, couldn't. Gantry Willow's sorcery was an empathetic divination, and he didn't abuse it in such ways. It was why Citywatch kept him on the payroll. He wasn't a powerful wizard but he was an honest Inspector. The latter is rarer than the former in Cruxia.

"Which Medicer did they send?" she asked. Her blue uniform slipped over the side of the partition.

"Vincezzo."

"Well, he's thorough, if less than agreeable. Have they identified the body?"

He pulled long on his pipe and sent a blue plume drifting over the room. "They did. The High-Father himself, Alonso."

She crashed out of the partition clasping the last silver button on her tunic. "What are we waffling about for then?"

Gantry gave her a sheepish look. "It's not even fifth bell, I figured you'd want three hours of sleep."

"Auron's blue balls, Willow. This city doesn't sleep and neither can we. How many times do I have to tell you that?" She brushed past him to the foyer and hooked her weapon belt in one deft movement. He followed her with a sigh; his peaceful morning slammed shut like a window.

Outside traffic picked up. Minor nobles zipped to and fro at their master's whim. A chainwagon trundled through the intersection of Helinger and Tonscato stuffed to capacity with cut purses and punks. A Tuurakhan mottled in brown fur gave a particularly driving stare through Gantry with his grey tunic and silver buttons. Sariah's stride taxed him, she almost kept pace with the chainwagon.

"What has the Watch done so far?" she asked.

"The usual. Dropped the portcullis along the Promenade, same with the trade gates." The gates to the Palace District were kept closed except during parades, festivals, or the muster for war. "A couple peace squads were dispatched to the East End, mostly in the Mule. Traffic in and out of the city is monitored."

"Worthless. They know our methods; they'll stay in the city. Only a professional could kill a High-Father. Did they determine time of death?" she said.

"Not when I was summoned."

They waited at Tonscato Bridge as a massive six-horse carriage gilt in black and gold thundered past. Tonscato Bridge was ironworks laced like ivy suspended a hundred feet over the Emperor's Road. Traffic ran heavy down there and the grey cloaks of Citywatch were everywhere checking permits, inspecting carts, knocking down citizens that gave them too much lip.

The gilt carriage passed, and they walked over Tonscato Bridge, onto the Gods' Way. Four massive temples faced each other at the crossroads of Tonscato and Melara Lane, each as different as the gods they represented. The temple complex of Auron, Brother Summer and Father of Life, stood tallest and stern in its stained wood. The temple of Mortia, Sister Winter and Lord of Death, shot black iron spindling up like a spider web of wire. Juno, Brother Autumn and Sentinel of Decay, was baked clay; simple, round, and falling apart. Finally, there was Veridaan's, gleaming marble stooped in columns as befit Sister Spring, Guardian of Birth.

These temples had been here since the city was born, long before the Cruxian Empire sacked and renamed it. Before humans even walked Galea's surface according to the fen. Dozens of lesser temples and churches sprang up between the four great ones, even more in the past decade since the Emperor legalized open worship. The first gods, the old gods, and the new gods, all squabbling over four tiny blocks with the mortals of Cruxia their voice in the debate. Usually bustling, the traffic was kept in neat lines by four squads of Citywatch as Sariah and Gantry ascended the steps to Veridaan's temple.

Inside the great nave was empty save six constables standing guard and the Medicer Inspector Vincezzo bent over a crumpled form on the dais. Blood streaked the stained glass around the pulpit. The main doors opened on the chapel, pews split by a red carpet that ran ninety feet to the pulpit. Circular steps led up to the dais and podium where the walls bent in shaping the room like an enormous stone ship. Doors ran off the east and west walls.

"First read?" asked Sariah as they stood in the doorway.

Gantry breathed out through his nose and in through his mouth, pushing out the physical and fishing for the ethereal. His eyes milked over with steamy cataracts, his hair stood up from head to toe.

Stinging light all around. The pulse and pound of Veridaan's truth seeped into the building. Millennia of devotion. Tracks of life. Laughter of children. Weeping for the lost.

Gantry floundered in a sea of raw emotion and magic far above his pay grade. His sense of self split and frayed, bouncing from wall to wall. He smashed to the ceiling and reformed on the floor. He was on the edge of losing the connection when he felt the iron consciousness of Sariah next to his physical shell.

He would not disappoint her. Not again.

He focused, his spirit crawled along the floor. He passed the dull grey auras of the constables, the grimy yellow aura of the Medicer Inspector, dragging his soul towards the crumpled form of the High-Father. It still gleamed in golden light long after his death, still burned with holy energy. Gantry's spirit was wracked by the radiance of it, dissipated by the devotional essence. But he pulled his spirit right up to it and stared hard.

The ball of golden energy that had been Alonso was cracked with four distinct lines like mold. Gantry slammed back into his body, his ears popped as if he changed elevations. Three seconds had passed.

"There were four of them," he said. Sweat gushed from his pores. He tripped and caught himself as his body remembered his soul.

Sariah nodded once, "Good work."

The two started towards the dais but Sariah stopped just before the pews began.

"What is it?" Gantry asked, still catching his breath.

She pulled on a mule-skin glove and bent down. "A candle, smashed here on the floor." She held a shard of wax for inspection. She looked up. "The chandeliers are still lit."

"Aye," said Gantry, "no one has been permitted to put them out."

"Inspector General," called Vincezzo from the dais, "quite the crime scene we have today."

Sariah scooped up the shattered bits of wax and put them in a pouch before they walked down the carpet towards him. The front pews on the east side were bent and smashed together like some giant had given them a flick. Around the dais itself, scorch marks radiated.

"Heavy sorcery," said Gantry, not needing to sense it. "Look at the carpet leading up to him." Footprints had burned into the red velvet, one set that bee-lined to the corpse. They danced around the High-Father, then faded suddenly. "Someone juiced themselves up quite a bit to kill an old man."

The Medicer Inspector took off a pair of fine leather gloves and stowed them in a black bag as he walked up the pulpit steps. Vincezzo was sixty with long, white hair and liver spots on his face and hands. His crooked nose and long-tailed coat lent him the semblance of a vulture.

"It would appear the victim put up quite a fight. Blood spatter here and here break the laws of physics, spraying out then crawling back in. I believe he magically healed himself as they attacked him. I assess that there were three assailants for I found three individual knife patterns on him. I place time of death between the hours of eighth and tenth bell of the evening," said Vincezzo. He stretched the "i" syllables with a Monticellan accent.

Sariah and Gantry walked around the corpse. A poor and splayed-out old man with a ruddy face and kind, dead eyes. Blood was everywhere, slashed across the pulpit like some child's first attempt with a paintbrush. Sariah and Vincezzo continued on clinically but Gantry couldn't take his eyes off the dead priest.

Gantry hated violence, especially the blood. Gantry always hated blood. When he was a wee little one, he witnessed his uncle and cousin killed beneath a horse cart. His whole family lugged corn husks to the trade post when a wealthy carriage thundered up the road reckless of the serfs coming to market. His young cousin Trun, just six years old, slipped into its path. Harven, the father, screamed and tried to tackle Trun out of the way. Too late, the horses crushed the boy, splashed him and his cornhusks across the dirt. The carriage wheels caught the screaming Harven seconds later while Gantry and his mother stood frozen. But the scream didn't stop for Gantry. Long after they pulled the dead man out of the spokes, he heard the painful wail. That night it still rang in his head until he finally told his papa. That was how Gantry discovered his talent with empathetic magic.

This poor old priest hadn't screamed, thought Gantry looking at the corpse. Not once. The only psychic imprint was a deep hum. The room still thrummed with his power. Here was a soul saved from Mortia, a true believer heading back to Veridaan. They were all but food for the gods.

"Isn't that right, Willow?" said Sariah from next to him.

"Huh?" said Gantry Willow.

Vincezzo rolled his eyes. "Try to stay with us, assistant

inspector. I claim there were three blades and thus three assailants. You disagree?"

"Right, of course. My initial read of the auras in the room shows four interlopers."

"Ha! All this magic in police work nowadays," said Vincezzo. "Why not fire the lot of us Medicers? What need for science with sorcery solving all the world's problems? Bring in a damn necromancer and raise the High-Father back up. There's your witness, eh?"

"High command wouldn't approve necromancy out of respect for the High-Father and the temple," said Gantry.

Vincezzo slammed his medical bag shut. "I was being facetious, you jumped-up farm hand."

"Enough." She used the word like a hammer. "Both of you have your evidence. Put it in a report and high command will reach their conclusions."

"Yes, ma'am," said Vincezzo. "Oh, and the knives caught my eye. The first was a straight blade, seven inches long; military issue. The other two were quite distinct, curved blades five inches long. If you're itching to get started while high command pens reports, I suggest you start with Little Hanrabi." He looked up with sudden trepidation, his eyes danced over the color of her skin. "No offense."

Sariah's face remained unaffected. "None taken. We will await high command's report. Absent of bias."

"Yes, ma'am," said Vincezzo. He stalked away past the Constables, out the massive doors with a flash of his tailcoat.

Gantry shuffled his feet while Sariah continued walking around the dead man. "Who benefits from the death of a High-Father?

Gantry shrugged. "Cultists? Fanatics?"

"They would burn the whole place down. This was surgical, specific."

A man entered the cathedral clad in black leather, polished

boots cracked on the marble. Both Sariah and Gantry stood to attention. Coming closer, he wore a wide-brimmed black hat and small reflective spectacles.

"Lord Inquisitor," said Sariah with a bow, "we did not know you were coming."

He took off his jacket, a red circle marking his office on its lapel. He was a lean man of fifty with a silver crew cut and a hard jaw, Inquisitor Dietrich. "The Parliamentary Council has deemed this murder a matter of imperial security. We will assist you in the investigation, Inspector General."

"Yes, my lord," said Sariah.

Shit, thought Gantry. The Inspector's Precinct was run by Citywatch with authority over all crime in the city of Cruxia. But Parliament ran the Inquisition and oversaw the entire Empire. There was a good chance they just lost jurisdiction.

Shit, thought Gantry, and he sighed.

3

Nito smoked a tailor of tobacco in an alley off the God's Way watching the Citywatch grey head-breakers shake down the denizens of Cruxia as they headed to worship. Something was up. Something not rex at all.

Veridaan's marble majesty was cordoned off with chains and more Greys, fucking Citywatch. Two inspectors and, Auron's musky balls, an Inquisitor walked out its massive oak doors as Nito flicked his tobacco and crushed it with a heel.

Something big, alright. Something not his problem.

He shuffled into a crowd of worshippers headed for Auron's temple. Weekly devotionals, even for a washed-up old pirate like Nito. The crowd ran the gamut from destitute to hoity-toity, all crammed shoulder to shoulder by a couple squads of Greys. A linen-clad monk stood to the side passing out parchment.

"A moment to talk about our savior, Garland Cruxis?" he said to Nito. "Cruxis gone these past five hundred years but portends say his return is soon."

Nito hit him with his shoulder probably harder than he had

to. "You let me know when those portends say he's here and we'll talk."

The man balked. "The new gods are no joking matter." But Nito was past him in the throng heading to the wooden arch and Auron's complex.

Inside was a courtyard of trimmed trees and wooden sculptures of the Siblings. White-hooded nuns and blue-robed priests hurried to and fro around the bulge of people flowing in. Security was tight. The Auric Guard stood at attention everywhere you looked, temple guards in blue-steel plate and gold cloaks. To the east and west were two oak hospitals, Auron's Grace and Auron's Mercy respectively. The temple to the north dwarfed everything. Auron took up most of the real estate on the Gods' Way.

The Cruxians were utilitarian people. All the Siblings' temples worked as municipal buildings as well as places of worship. Veridaan, Goddess of birth, ran a midwifery and orphanage. Juno's temple doubled as a library. Auron boasted two hospitals, His Grace to the east was the main one doling out care to the citizens of Cruxia. His Mercy to the West took in the terminal patients of the city and the only way out was through a tunnel to Mortia's sepulchral temple and the catacombs where citizens were laid to rest.

A weathered old walnut of a nun greeted the throng with a warm smile. It wilted when she laid eyes on Nito.

"Alistair Nito, Auron's blessing on all of His children. Even those that don't deserve it."

Nito winked. "Sister Mabel, always a pleasure."

"Sister Liana is busy at her post and will not see you today. Just like always," she said.

"Maybe I'm not here to see her, rex? Maybe I'm just here to honor her mother," said Nito.

"Perhaps if you honored her mother more when she was alive your daughter would make time for you."

That one hurt but he grinned and swallowed the insult in his mouth so they couldn't ban him. "Auron's blessing to you, Sister." He pushed past, cutting out of the crowd towards Auron's Mercy and Cruxia's terminally ill. The Auric Guard watched him close through their face grills. Two broke off to casually follow him.

A steepled, oak hospital the size of a galleon with a towering mahogany statue of Auron by its doors. Weathered and stained by some nine hundred years, the statue still held some majesty; Auron in platemail, one hand on his sheathed sword, the other blowing into a warhorn.

Auron, Brother Summer, guardian of life. A right cock-swabber if you actually did your studies. No other god sired as many children, a throng of demigods from countless women, both mortal and immortal. Auron's favorite gaff was to breach the moral realm as a bull and rut with as many wives as he could before the other Siblings dragged his sorry ass back to the spirit realm. If you really went digging, legend was he raped his sister Veridaan and sired a horrific spider-thing, Ana'sia, goddess of secrets. Real class act, Auron.

But that was the way of time, wasn't it? Give a thousand years or so and people only remember the good stories. Nito waxed theological and lit a tailor outside the gates to the hospital in front of his Auric Guard escort. Some said Auron was long dead, along with Veridaan and Juno, and that Cruxia worshiped a bunch of corpses. But the seasons still came about, didn't they? More often than not people just needed the ideal to worship and were happy to throw whatever face on it that fit their views.

No, Nito wasn't here to toss any worship at the feet of Auron. He wanted to check in on his only daughter and try his damndest to respect her dead mother. He snubbed his tailor on the toe of Auron. "Just keep your blessings away from my kid, eh?" He entered the temple before the Guard could snatch him for littering.

The front hall was far more somber than the rest of Auron's complex. Nuns walked this way and that with the silence of librarians, entering rooms along with carts of alchemicals and bandage wrappings. Everywhere was the stink of vinegar and incense, which was better than the stink of piss and death, but not by much. An orderly looked up from her ledger as Nito approached.

"Morning Adara, wanted to take a swing by the leper wing. That is if you'll let me," he knocked a quick tattoo on her desk.

Sister Adara, a middle-aged woman the color of stained wood, looked up and smiled. "Morning yourself there, sailor. You can go on down, but you gotta stay above C block. You know how it goes."

"Only too well. Thanks, sugar."

He walked down the main hall to a split staircase and descended snagging a torch as he went. The leper colony felt more like a dungeon than a hospital, winding down into deeper and deeper gloom. On B block the hall stretched out with curtained wards on each side. Nuns in cloth masks pushed carts into these, the whole hall deathly silent.

Nito walked to the end and knocked on the wall next to a ward. There came a grunt. He pushed past the curtain and stowed his torch on a ring. A simple room; bed in the corner, two stone shelves built into the wall, a bedpan on the floor. Laid in the bed was the wreckage of a human man. Just a torso with an iron mask, they'd long ago amputated all of his limbs. He rolled towards Nito.

"Hey Munson, everything rex?"

Munson shrugged, a slight rise to the iron mask. He couldn't speak, they'd also taken his tongue.

"Yeah, same here." Nito sat next to an iron grate on the floor.

A similar one was built into the ceiling, an attempt to bring some fresh air to the wards. He looked through the floor and watched a nun bathe a patient even worse off than Munson. She sang a lilting tune while she sponged the open lesions and rotted flesh. Liana looked more like her mother as she got older. He watched her with a sad smile as Munson wheezed on the bed, snot leaked from his iron mask.

"Hey, Munson, what's the difference between sensual and kinky?"

Munson shrugged.

"Sensual you use a feather, kinky you bring the whole fucking chicken."

Munson hissed laughter; more fluid spewed from his mask.

"What sign do you hang on a brothel when they shut down?"

Munson shrugged, leaning on one side now to listen.

"Beat it. We're closed."

Snot flew as Munson guffawed, a sound like leather rubbed on wood.

"One more, one more. What did the elephant say to the naked man? How do you breathe through that thing?"

Fluid and rasps poured from Munson. Nito lost it too, shaking and wiping tears from his eyes. When they cleared, he saw Liana packing her things to leave the ward below.

"Look at her down there. Twenty-four years old, just about my age when she was born," Nito said. "Her mother was a right cannon of a woman. None of the gods would help if you spurned her. She was alright with me, though. Didn't mind me sailing and raiding, didn't mind the booze or the sopa neither. So long as I brought the gold home."

Munson wiggled to a sitting position to listen. He'd heard it all before. But there was no one else to tell him stories.

"That changed when Liana was born. Oh, did it change. We

fought. Constantly. Suddenly the booze and raids were not rex. Not rex at all. I couldn't give it up, fuck. Mind if I smoke?"

Munson shook his head. Nito sat on the edge of his bed, lit a tobacco on the torch as he did. "I lied to her. Herta, that is, my wife. Told her I gave it all up and went legit. Set sail like I was going to buy spice and spent three years raiding sopa lanes from Hanrabi. Snorted that sopa all the way home."

He took a deep drag, then set the tailor to Munson's mouth hole. Smoke poured from the iron mask. "Herta was dead when I made landfall. Cholera got her two months into my voyage. Little Liana was packed up and sent to Veridaan's temple. Had been the whole three years I was gone. She didn't even remember me."

He walked back over to the grate, leaned and blew smoke. "I told her, but she didn't care. Her mom said I was dead, and so I was. Shit."

Munson leaned back and enjoyed the tingle of tobacco in his lungs. He knew all about tragedy. Five years in the palace dungeons for stealing eggs. He and his sister starving, their mother not ten days in the ground. Five years in the dungeon, stinking in a hole, soaking in the fetid water on the floor. Leprosy for life after that, gods only know what happened to his sister on the streets. They rolled his gurney from the palace dungeons to the hospital dungeon. Two months later he lost his limbs.

But he liked Nito and his jokes and his sad story. Liked to be reminded he was still a human being.

Clanking footsteps echoed down the hall, thunder in the silent leper block. Nito looked at Munson and snubbed his tobacco.

"Expecting company?" Nito asked.

Munson shook his head, no.

A gauntlet thrust the curtain aside, an Auric Guard clattered in. His cuirass and gauntlets were blued steel, gold chain-mail hung around the neck of his helmet. His facegrill was closed, threatening.

"Alistair Nito, you are to come with me," said the knight.

"What's this all about?" said Nito, flicking the tobacco butt at the knight's boot.

"I don't have to answer that."

"That means he doesn't know," Nito said to Munson. One last little laugh from Munson but it was tinged with panic. "Alright, soldier, let's go."

The knight swept his gold cloak to let Nito pass, his longsword clanged against the doorway. They exited the leper ward, the knight leading Nito with a hand on his shoulder. Sister Adara gave them a worried look as they passed her desk. Nito gave her a shrug and a wink.

But fear skittered on him like lice. What was this all about? They left the hospital and cut across the complex, passing the temple-goers who lined up at Auron's great cathedral to the north. Nito took a look south to the complex entrance where two squads of Grey Citywatch congregated. Did this have to do with the hubbub at Veridaan's temple?

The knight led him north, away from the Greys. Nito's sphincter uncoiled. They headed towards the cathedral, a vast oak structure with leaves carved all over its walls. Auron's Worship boasted vast gardens of flowers tended in neat rows all leading to the temple. The knight led Nito outside the gardens on the east side to the rickety staircase the servants used.

"We going to see the big guy himself, soldier?"

"Quiet."

The High-Father of Auron was an old acquaintance of Nito's, he even used to be a friend. Mofass Salavar was the pirate king when Nito raided coasts for sopa and brandy. At the tail end of the Vohlkhan War, Mofass took a contract priva-teering for the Cruxian Empire: rushing blockades, messing with Vohlkhan supply lines. The hoary old pirate was welcomed as a war hero and lo and behold, he found the gods through Auron. Post-war the priest positions were political tickets for popular devotees. Mofass had charisma and the love of the whole Empire, plus he sired more children than Nito could count. Truly a man in Auron's image.

Nito came to the temple once a week to see his daughter, but he never saw Mofass anymore. After hanging up the booze and sopa Nito cauterized his old life. Nito grew up, Mofass never would.

The knight led Nito up a staircase on the side of the rectory, creepers tangled up the railing and along the wall. At the top, the blue knight opened a door with an iron key and pushed Nito in. "End of the hall. He expects you."

Nito walked along a blue and gold carpet to an oak door carved with Auron's face. He knocked once then entered.

The room was blue panels cut with gold inlay. A window to the south showed the whole complex of Auron, people buzzing below and filtering into the church. The opposite window sat above the cathedral itself, curtained off with a door leading to Mofass's balcony pulpit. The furniture cost more than Nito would make in his lifetime.

Mofass sat in blue robes on a gilt couch next to two teenage girls in their nightclothes. The table in front of them had a mirror stacked with piles of orange powder. One girl's eyes were red-rimmed, the other spun a coin between her fingers with complete focus. Mofass rested a hand on his big gut and belched.

"Nito, my old friend. Good to see you."

"Wish I could say the same. You could've sent a bird. Didn't have to deploy a stormtrooper."

"You wouldn't come if I just asked." Mofass stabbed a pinky into the orange powder and rubbed it on his lips. He snapped his fingers in quick succession.

Nito took a seat in a plush chair and rubbed his temples. "What's the point of all this, Mofass?"

Mofass smacked one of the girls on her butt. "Scram. I'm done with you."

"But you said—"

"I didn't say shit. Scram on out before I tell your papa just what his little girls are up to before prayer."

The red-eyed girl ran stifling a sob. The coin spinner stared at Mofass with pure hatred, then dunked her own finger in the orange pile. She snorted it as she ran after her sister. Real class act, Mofass Salazar.

"Still laying seeds in farmer's daughters, ey?" Nito said.

"And lo, all children of Galea must procreate unto eternity to keep Auron's blessing shining on the land. And so it is written," said Salavar with his deepest bass. The guy was a right bastard, but he had the voice for the job.

"How did you become the priest after we were all said and done?"

"I'm a better liar. Everyone knows that."

Nito walked over to the south window. Past Auron's complex, there were still Greys everywhere on the Gods' Way. Three more squads gathered around the temple of Veridaan.

"You know anything about the squeeze going on down there?"

Mofass grabbed a razor and cut lines from the powder. "Old Alonso bit it last night." He snorted, snapping his fingers when finished.

"Alonso? Shit. He was one of the good ones."

"What's that supposed to mean?" Mofass snorted another line.

"What got him?"

"More like who. Word is he didn't pay the syndicates. That's not rex with them, let me tell you."

"What syndicate are we talking about? You paid up, Salazar?"

His eyes got sly. "I'm doing fine, Nito. I don't like to rock the boat these days, rex?"

"I didn't come here to play sweeper, Salavar. I didn't want to come here at all. Just visiting Liana."

"You're a real sad bastard, Nito. Sad as they come. Just come by to mope each week like it was some kind of penance. You want one." Mofass cut two more lines.

"I quit all that shit. What do you want?" Nito gritted his teeth. Twenty years sober and he still wanted one.

Mofass looked up at him. "Well, this is the end of my kax..." Kax, a stimulant derived from Krodan glands. Krodan are bipedal lizards hailing from Gaiathor, a proud warrior race. It's rare, and expensive.

"Mortia's twat, I don't deal. I haven't in decades."

"You did after the war."

"Yeah, when I got to shore and they'd taken my kid. I just run the inn these days."

Mofass stood up and paced, snapped his fingers as he walked. "Come on, Nito. Help out an old friend, would ya'?"

Nito sat up. "It was the Cazaratti that hit Alonso, huh?"

Mofass spun on him. "How would you know something like that?"

"Alonso didn't pay up, but you did, and now he's dead. Cazaratti lost their kax connection to the Siegewards. You're out of kax, so the easiest answer is you're paid up through the Cazaratti."

Mofass sat down, his bulk made the couch squeal. "Juno's bowels, Nito, you still got that edge. See why I come to you? I got this measly little pile left, and then I'm out. I can't run out Nito. I fucking can't." He snorted one of his two lines.

"I don't want any part of this."

"Think about your daughter," said Mofass.

"What the fuck does that mean?"

Mofass put up his hands in defense. "Nothing untowards, man. She's about due for a promotion, get me? You got your joint down on the street, you hear things I can't from up here. Just do me this one solid. Find me a kax connect and I'll bump Liana up the roster. Get her sitting pretty like she deserves. Rex?"

Nito crumpled his hands together and squeezed until they turned white. Real rex, alright. Honor Liana's mother or run a drug deal so his daughter could rise up in the world? Same old Nito.

"This is where we're at, Salazar? You gotta blackmail me to help my kid? You could've promoted her anytime."

"Look, I'll do it whether you help me or not. Nito, please. Please. I need it."

Nito sighed like a pierced balloon. "Fine. No promises."

Mofass eyes gleamed. "Oh, fuck yeah, Nito. Fuck yeah. I'll get the permits going for Liana." He snorted his other line then cut a long monster. "This is so rex." His speech sped up, his pupils ballooned up to cosmic saucers. "Just like old times, Nito and Salazar shipping lanes and smashing dames. Fuck yeah."

Nito regretted the decision immediately.

A bell gonged from the cathedral. Mofass snorted his monster, sprang to his feet, and flung the curtain aside. Four stories below the whole congregation packed into the pews, waiting. Altar boys walked down the aisles swinging braziers of incense.

Mofass, eyes a red mess, strode out his curtain to the pulpit. He towered over the congregation fifty feet below. Nito watched through the big north window. "Citizens! Worshippers! Auron blesses you with your life, will you bless him the same?"

Cheers echoed back, people applauded, babies were raised in deference. Nito watched in disgust, out of view. He paced around Mofass's chamber, thinking. His eyes lingered too long on the dwindling pile of kax. Temptation and Nito went all the way back. He looked out the south window to where the Grey Citywatch constables milled around Veridaan's temple like ants.

Cazzaratti hitting a High-Father. That's bold.

But it really wasn't Nito's problem.

Not his problem at all.

4

Roisin huddled in an alley beside a slaughterhouse and an apartment deep in the Mule quarter. The early sun was orange choked smoke through the pollution haze. Sticky blood matted her hair. She gripped a shard of masonry like a knife while the rough texture burst blisters on her palm. She shook and wanted to weep.

But she would not. Not here. Not now. She was not some little Mule wench.

Something splashed behind her, and she spun, brick dagger ready. But it was just the contents of someone's morning bed pan sloshed into the street. The stench was imperceptible over the slaughterhouse's. She settled and tried to control her breathing. Tried to calm her panic as Father Alonso taught her years ago.

In through her nose, out through her mouth. Control your breath. Control your reality. Control within begets control without. Siblings bless, amen.

But the thought of Father Alonso spilled out across the pulpit returned in harsh color. The blood spray, the three clad in black slashing him all over while the Mole just watched. She shivered again and bit back a sob.

She took stock of herself. A gash ran above her eye to her ear. Her hair bandaged it for now, but it needed stitches. Her arms and legs were a treasure map of cuts but nothing as serious as her head. There were two great bruises on her shoulder and ribs where that girl hit her. Her knapsack was gone, along with her sewing kit and keys.

The nagging part was her job. No way Jorey would keep her on after botching first week as Candlelighter. This was asinine compared to the violence last night, but the pragmatist in her couldn't drop it. Her ticket out of the Mule, gone. Poof. Like magic.

She rationalized the night before, tried to run through the sequence of events past the panic. It made no sense. Who would kill Father Alonso? Who would want to paint him across his pulpit like a cow at slaughter?

Wrong tact, the tears welled. Don't think about why, just think about what.

Back in the temple of Veridaan, up in the rafters. She kicked a candle to the floor and hurried down to recover it. She wanted to apologize to the High-Father; honestly she just wanted to say hello. She took the position to see him again.

Down the stairs to the floor of the cathedral, a great flash of white shot her shadow to the ceiling. Worried, she snuck to the pews. There were four killers. Two Hanrabs with curved daggers, a middle-aged white man moving with liquid speed, and the most hideous Mole she'd ever seen.

It froze her. She grew up in the Mule, turned out of the orphanage at eleven. The first lesson, keep moving. React. Don't lock up. Garvis taught her that. Garvis was a brothel slopper, he used to hit six or seven of them at dawn to mop. Garvis showed her how to survive outside Veridaan's temple and didn't ask for anything in return like most boys did. "Maybe if you were a man, we could do business," he'd say with a wink. "But your first lesson is don't freeze."

But she froze as the four killers fell on Alonso, powerless as her adopted father died. Stuck until the middle-aged man pointed at her, "There's a girl over there watching us," and the two Hanrabs broke at her in a run. Her instincts fired, she spun and raced down the long carpet. She smashed out the double doors and shrieked. "Help, please help. Murder, there's been—"

She tripped over some bulk and caught the ground with her elbows. Two crumpled City Watchmen, dead she thought. But there was no blood. The man's chest rose in rhythm. They slept. She shrieked in their ears and scanned the Gods' Way. Half a dozen guards sleeping in the street.

She kicked back to her feet and ran blind, unable to remember the routes she took every day of her life. Not able to process what happened. The doors of Veridaan's temple crashed open again, the Hanrabs in pursuit. She noticed the girl limped, that was good. Father Alonso hurt her before he died.

She raced past a statue of Garland, first emperor of Cruxia, and vaulted a hedge to land on the Tonscato Lane of the Gods' Way heading south. She chanced a look behind her. The male Hanrab bent low and ran like a zephyr. The girl struggled; each step slowed her more.

She slowed her breath to focus. This was not the first time a man chased her at night.

In front of her were the closed gates to Tonscato Bridge suspended high over the Empire Road. The three guards slumped together in a pile in front of it, snoring. She vaulted off the man-pile over the gate, the cobblestones caught her with a rough slap. She glanced back at her pursuer. A Hanrab teenager with a lean face and two scars across the bridge of his nose. But she also saw fear and confusion in his eyes. He hesitated.

Roisin unslung her knapsack and took out a length of hemp rope. The girl caught up and nagged the boy in quick Hanrab. Roisin lived in Little Hanrabi for three years, she understood the gist of it.

"Get her. Move."

Roisin dropped beneath the bridge with her rope.

He pointed. "She's not any older than us. This is different."

"This is our job." She smacked him and started climbing.

Rosin hung from the side of the bridge and swung forward to catch the ironlace suspension with her feet. This was like the cathedral catwalks only three times the height. Breathe girl, don't forget to breathe.

Two bumps as the killers landed on the bridge. A network of ironworks ran like ivy under the concrete road. She looked down and her vertigo ran the spiraling metal down, down, down to Empire Road. At least sixty yards. Cold wind whipped and the iron froze her hands, this was not like the catwalks.

A black slipper appeared above her. She swallowed her fear and flung down. She dropped from level to level too fast, improvising toeholds as they came. She remembered her father. "Careful, little Rose. Careful. You climb high enough on that bookshelf and it will fall down on you." She scraped her teeth against each other and kept on.

The two scrabbled after her but she wouldn't look up. Consciousness was just the next iron bar, the next loop of metal. She held a strut above her and hunted for a foothold and there was the slipper. It crushed her fingers. She let go.

The wind screamed. Iron flew past. She had one clear thought of release.

At least it was over.

Then hard brick punched her breath out. She gasped and rolled, stopped right at the edge. She sprawled on a great column, iron supports bolted to its top. Behind her was brick, in front more twisted iron, below another fifty feet to the ground. She was most of the way there crammed right against the back wall of the bridge.

Above her the pair peeked over the struts. The girl cursed when she caught sight of Roisin, battered and alive. The boy took out a silk rope and the girl tied it over a beam. Roisin struggled to breathe; panic returned in harsh white. The concrete around the iron support was eroded. She dug in and broke out a shard, her fingernails cracked and bled.

She stood up to fight as the girl swung in and smashed her. A punch to the ribs, a kick to the hip. Roisin's head caught the iron with a wet slap. The Hanrab girl ripped out a chunk of Roisin's hair before momentum carried her away. A pendulum beneath the bridge.

Rose was back at the temple running around a pole holding streamers with all the other laughing children, she took a dreamy step off the column edge. Her foot hung over nothing. Then cohesion came back livid in tones of red. The Hanrab girl tilted back towards Roisin backwards. She waited, then slashed out with her granite dagger.

It bit hair and flesh, spun the killer. Rose speared a kick right at the girl's liver. Garvis taught her that. The Hanrab girl gasped and let go of the rope. Above, the boy cried, "Sister," in Hanrab.

The teenage girl fell, and Rose's instincts shut off. There it was. She killed someone. What would father say about that if he was still around?

But the killer only fell ten feet to catch an iron support in the stomach. She vomited white sick to the road below and scrambled for purchase. Rose thanked Veridaan and Mortia for sparing her the title of murderer at final judgement. A quick prayer then she tied her rope to the support column. Keep moving. Don't freeze. Garvis and Da' in her ear tonight.

She walked down the column with her hands wound in the rope. Ten feet down and fifteen feet out the Hanrab girl worked her legs into the ironworks. Roisin's hair was tangled in the girl's grip. She met Roisin's eyes with thunderstorms and spit a bloody wad into her face. "Donkey," she hissed.

Another soft bump above. The brother was close. Roisin dropped as fast as she could, let out the rope and kicked off the column. Down and down, the rope slashed like a white snake in her palms. She wanted to scream, she wanted to cry. But she wouldn't. She was not some worthless Mule wench. Her teeth scraped.

The boy sawed at her anchored rope with a curved knife. Rose was thirty feet to the ground. She begged Veridaan for protection. The Hanrab sister screamed obscenities from above. The brother sawed faster.

Fifteen feet to the ground, the taut rope went limp. Rose grabbed at the brick and mortar of the wall. She lost a cracked fingernail looking for purchase where there was none. She kicked off the column and hit the ground in a roll, her shoulder dragged blood across the road.

She lay there as her vision spun, the ironworks above a kaleidoscope. She was alive, maybe. Not some Mule wench gods be damned. A curse was rare for Roisin, even in her mind. Blood ran in her vision, bringing her back to reality. Her body screeched in pain, her forehead bled unabated. Perhaps not alive for long.

Again, the bump of slippers. She glanced up. The Hanrab brother tied his own rope to the column and came at her still. The girl had not moved, curled around the iron supports forty feet up. Rose drew her dagger and started to run.

Garland Cruxis built the Empire Road when he conquered Cruxia, so Rosin's father taught her. Wide enough for eight carriages, it split the city in half. The Promenade sat on rocky cliffs above it to the west and the rest of the city spread out low to the east. A giant gate closed off the Palace Road behind her. At tenth bell the road was normally packed with night traffic, coated in constables. The gate alone had six patrols day and night. But it was empty, desolate but for an abandoned wagon and feral cats. Citywatch asleep on the Gods' Way, the Empire Road empty. Rose entered some nightmare realm.

She staggered away. Her breath came in rasps, adrenaline abated and the pain flowed. Alleys yawned; apartments and municipal buildings flashed past with their lamps lit. She was the only lamplighter who didn't make curfew, a thought like insanity.

Behind her the Hanrab brother appeared, fast and uninjured. She beelined into an alley stacked with rotting food and stinking grease buckets. An alley cat tore at a dead dog, it stared at Rosin and hissed through the viscera. She kicked it and slipped on the wet cobblestones.

This was it. There was nothing left. The alley dead-ended at a warehouse wall. She turned towards her pursuer and set her knife like Garvis taught her. "Keep your elbows cocked out, set the knife in your center. Better to take one on the forearm, than in the heart, you get me?" She waited. She sweat.

Darkness, the road flickered dull lamp light. A silhouette, harsh shadows drew themselves along the walls. This was it.

He walked toward her, slow, his stance solid as steel. Behind her was the wall. The mortar dagger roared against her chapped hands. Blood leaked, her grip slippery.

She thought about the trepidation she'd seen in his eyes at the Tonscato Gate.

He came closer, slinking and capable.

She threw the knife down between them. "Please," she said in Hanrab, "please."

He froze. His eyes widened, a spark of humanity.

She flared a pitch-stick across her sandpaper bracelet. Alchemicals burst in his eyes, a miniature sun. He staggered back blinking. Rose kicked him in his fruit cart as hard as she could. And down he went.

She flung past him and snatched her granite knife. Out the alley, back onto Empire Road. She ran and ran, raw panic an animal at her side. Past the municipal buildings, downslope to the East Side with its merchant shops and stalls. Twisting through the Merchant Quarter.

She kept checking for killers. Every window, every alley, every sewer grate, she looked for them. She tripped and sprawled into a storefront. A Citywatchmen stepped out of a nearby alley. "Hey, what do you think you're—" But Roisin was away. "Hey!" he yelled after her. She shot down an alley with a low wall at the end. Over she went, crashing through a laundry wire on the other side. She zigged left, she zagged right.

Her night devolved. Her breath ran ragged, her body screamed in pain. She ran the longest circuit to the Mule. Tanneries and slaughterhouses packed the narrow roads of dirt. The smell brought her to reality in full. She collapsed into a hay pile between an apartment and a slaughterhouse. Her legs couldn't move anymore. She passed out thinking how she broke Garvis' cardinal rule of survival. Never fall asleep exposed.

There were no dreams for her journal that night. Golden motes of light shimmered out of the chimney smog and floated around Roisin like fireflies until the morning sun banished them.

5

Maharez felt a gulf of fear like none other before. His sister hung suspended on the catwalks of the Tonscato Bridge, white vomit spattered on the beams below.

She was dead. Maharez was alone in this foreign land now. The only anchor to his home and heritage hung up there like laundry.

Despite this, no tears came as he climbed the ironworks to recover her corpse. It was as if some great part of him broke in that moment and he would never quite be human again. Never be Hanrab, again. Now just another grain of sand down the hourglass.

Then she coughed white-tinged blood and cursed at him in three languages. "Maruth' kaba. Doth hrester. Cockswabber," she groaned out in Hanrab, Vohlkahn learned from Hook, then Cruxian. Same word in three languages. She was alive though.

"Shh, shh, don't try and talk Fati, let me help you," he said.

"I don't need your help, donkey. I can do this my—" she screeched in pain as he shifted her weight.

Maharez knew not to talk to her in a mood like this. He just softly got her over his shoulder. She whimpered and cried out as he worked. He could feel at least three broken ribs. To carry her this way would be agony, but he had no choice. Krentor's Bell struck eleventh toll and the Citywatch would be out soon. Polo's bribes would only protect them for the hours of the job, after that they were just a couple black youths in the Municipal Quarter at night. A different kind of crime in Cruxia.

Maharez balanced across the beam with Fatimah on his shoulder, then climbed turtle slow to the street below. It was two long miles to their apartment at Ganon Hall. Maharez started a mental route that would avoid public spaces and patrols when the clip-clop of a cart pattered up the street.

Someone was coming.

Maharez looked left and right, they were stuck against the Palace Gate and the locked city works buildings that surrounded it. He realized how much worse he looked with a half-dead girl on his shoulder. Murderer, they'd call him, or worse, rapist. But he couldn't drop her, couldn't ever leave her.

He spun to flee when Hook's sardonic voice whipped down the road. "Hey there, brother. Looked like you could use a lift." Hook rode up the Empire Road on a mule-drawn cart, street lamps flickered behind him. "Better get in quick, that sleep whammy up there on the Greys has only got a few more snores in it, get me? We gotta dust."

Maharez softly slumped Fatimah in the bed of the cart, she had passed out from the pain. "Again tonight, I thank you," he said to Hook as he vaulted in next to his sister.

"Ah, horse swallow, Mortia knows you'd've done the same for me." Fatimah made a soft whimper as the cart bumped into motion. "Did you kill that girl?" he asked, glancing back at Maharez.

He still couldn't get used to how casual Hook asked things like that. They dead? How much blood? Will the bodies be an issue? Maharez missed Hanrabi, he missed shaking rice into canoes in the lowlands, he missed who his sister was before the galley slave ship and the horror.

"Hey." Hook clapped three times. "Did you kill that girl?"

Maharez sighed and lowered his head between his knees. "No. No, I did not."

Hook turned back to the reigns and shook the mules moving. "Ah well, tough shit. Let's get your sister looked after, eh? Tomorrow is another day, ain't it just?"

Ganon Hall was a hack of grey limestone slumped on the pylons of the Commons. Bilge green algae stained a splash up its west side where the boats pushed the breakers against the shore. The crayers, cogs, and tug boats paid extra coin to stay off the rosters. Ganon Hall hosted all of them with no questions asked.

A mile and a half down the broken-toothed smile of sloughs and slips the Crimson Moor jutted out, furthest south you could go in Cruxia. Even the crooks and sweepers of the commons gave the place a wide berth. And it wasn't just the reek: sulphur, vinegar, and cinnabar mercury.

The criminals of Cruxia hung down by Commons. The necromancers, soul-eaters, and warlocks sludged further south to the Crimson Moor where the Red Market festered. Need to sell a kidney or get rid of a load of corpses, you slunk down to the Crimson Moor, and you didn't look no one in the eye down there, neither.

Hook shook his collar as they turned down Melchior Way towards Ganon Hall out of sight of the Crimson Moor. The place gave him the willies and he'd been slinging magic going on three decades. It had a metaphysical stink to it, worse than the actual stink for sure. Hook was shit at reading auras, but he guessed that place was just a big black stain.

Fatimah coughed in the bed of the cart behind him.

Maharez, diligent brother, sat up front trying to act tough, but Hook could see the pain flicker across his face whenever she groaned. Poor kid was too good at the work to not be built for it. Maharez, that was. Fatimah was a manipulative animal born for this trade. Hook had to admit in his heart of hearts the bitch needed a couple knocks down the ladder. But he felt bad for her brother. The poor kid didn't belong in this line of work. But that's life, ain't it just?

Hook pulled the horse cart into the shit stables attached to Ganon Hall. A pock-faced youth took the reins, and Hook tipped him too much before scooping the girl out of the bed and leading Maharez inside and upstairs. The staircase reeked of stale beer and spent sex, a special kind of damp known only to whore houses and dishwasher stations.

Maharez stepped behind Hook, avoiding the eyes of the sparse patrons in the mainhall. Fatimah was real hurt. A small trickle of blood continued from her mouth and a new stream ran from her nose. Internal bleeding. He slowed his breath as their grandmama showed them. Maharez let go of what he could not control and held onto the thing he could, his breath.

At the door to their room, Hook turned to Maharez. "He's gonna be pissed. Know that and deal with it."

"Yes," said Maharez.

"We got our mark, but you know Polo's only rule. His fucking platinum rule."

"No witnesses."

Hook nodded. "No witnesses. We got a loose one. Better believe that is all we will be doing until she is dead."

The last words hit Maharez like a mule cart. "...until she is dead. Until she is dead." Like some sort of mantra, or a spell, Halladar protect. Until she is dead.

The past five years of Maharez's life ran like a shadow puppet show through his mind. Shaking rice from fronds into canoes with his mother and sister smiling by his side. Then the

Turvaali. The slave galleys and their soldiers. The conquest. His dead mother drifting in the fronds. The chains, the manacles, the oars. Push, pull, push, pull, push, pulls, push, pu— Then the Cazaraati carrack and its canon and magic shredding the Turvaali slave galley. Maharez and his sister marched onto the deck in front of the new captain, the Cazaraati carrack, and its new law. Five years. They owed the Cazaraati five years' service. Indentured until their freedom.

And Hook just put it into better words than Maharez ever could. One of Hook's few virtues, his way with words. Until she is dead. They were murderers, he and his sister, at least until she was dead.

The door to their room squealed on tortured hinges. Polo paced around their small common area; his cane cracked with each step. A new sore developed on his right cheek, joining a score of others. He looked up at them over his tiny, round spectacles.

"Did these worthless oilskins kill her? Is that little bitch spy still alive?"

"Negative," said Hook. He placed Fatimah on a small couch by their single window. Her breathing came labored and blood ran from both nostrils.

Polo moved with unexpected speed, bashing his cane into Maharez's nose, a thunder of sudden pain. Polo swung the cane on Fatimah. Hook caught it with a wet thwap.

"She's taken a beating tonight. We can't afford to lose a sweeper with this shit of a mess. You need the three of us in shipshape, eh?"

Polo's murky yellow eyes stared hard into Hook's baby blues. "Fine," he said. Polo had never hit Hook, nor would he. There were few things Polo feared besides wizards.

Polo paced again. "Seventy-two hours. Once a job begins, we have seventy-two hours to complete it. We are now six hours into this one. It was clean and simple and should've been done in three, but we are at six hours with a little girl spy out there fucking up all of this." He spun, pointing his cane like it was a finger. "A simple job with simple tenets. Kill an old priest. Shouldn't be so fucking difficult, huh?"

Hook leaned in a corner while Maharez took a wet rag to Fatimah's forehead. "Think she's the Emperor's girl?" asked Hook.

"I don't fucking care who she belongs to, I want her dead and I wanted it two hours ago. Take the boy. Go kill her. Simple. Clean. Fuck's sake."

"Yes sir," said Hook. He patted Maharez on the shoulder and took some herbs from his belt pouch. "Crush these up and get her to eat it or breathe in the vapors. Hethbara, it speeds up healing and kills the pain."

Maharez took the leaves and shredded them in his hands. He tried to pry her mouth open to no avail. Hook took out more Hethbara, ground it up, and rubbed it under her nostrils.

"This should do her just— hold on a tit," said Hook. He took her hand and rotated it. She still clutched a clump of the spy's hair and scalp. "Hey there, Fatimah, you just cracked the case."

"What are you droning on about?" Polo asked.

He looked over and held up the clump of hair. "I can track her with this. Call your bagman, get us a couple of Citywatch uniforms. Maharez, we're gonna try our hands at being Greys."

"What?"

"Citywatch, my brother. Let's go on patrol."

6

W hen Rosin awoke, she still clutched the granite dagger, blood-slick and chafed. Her eyes darted at shadows, but the panic faded. The animal slumbered. She thought back through a dizzy haze. Last night was no nightmare. It was an actual thing. She thought of her lost job and Garvis the brothel slopper.

Garvis was a brother to her, showed her how to exist in the Mule as another discarded soul in the city. When to run and when to fight. How to look tough and how to be tough when there was no other option. "We're all animals, deep down Rose. Some wear nicer clothes than others, but at the end of the day all we wanna do is fuck and eat and sleep. Down here closer to the bone we pretend less than those up on the Promenade."

Garvis left though, three years back. Four dock workers caught him outside the Gilded Hen and worked him over as hard as you can without killing them. "Fag," they yelled as they stomped, Garvis curled up in fetal position and shuddering. He lost his job after that. Couldn't go to work pissing blood and barely breathing for eight nights. Rose took care of him between her Lamplighter shifts, just like she took care of her da' in the end.

He awoke one night, his fever finally broken. "I'm out," he said, "not a gods damned thing for me here anymore." Rose begged him not to, but his mind was set. He took his five silver and bought passage on a logging vessel, headed to some village called Gred. All the way north against the mountain ranges of Vohlkhan. As far from the capital as he could muster. It broke Rose's heart, but she was happy for him.

You had to be happy for someone who got out of the Mule. Most don't.

That was it then. She'd hit her own breaking point. She didn't want to leave the birthplace of her parents, but Garvis was right. There was nothing here for her anymore. The decision freed her. Her job no longer mattered, only escape. She started to look at everything with the prudence she got from her ma'.

She was witness to a murder. Worse, it was on record that she had been there. The Lamplighter's Guild kept good records. She might have Citywatch hunting her along with the killers. Nowhere was safe for her. She needed to get to her room and get her silver, but she had to be as discreet as possible.

She wiped garbage off and stretched in the alley. She was between Durkot Way and Farceberger Road. Her own apartment was about nine blocks east and north. She ducked out onto the street, keeping her head low and her pace quick. That's how women traveled in the Mule.

Her paranoia thrummed. Her eyes darted searching for killers. But a touch of logic creeped in. She was miles from the Gods' Way and the Tonscato Bridge. Cruxia was a big place, she had that to her advantage. Citywatch were another matter, but the two she passed paid her no mind, buying their breakfast from a goat monger at the markets.

Nine blocks took about forty minutes. Her building loomed on Merkle Street, towering over the two blocks of stables it sat on. A sad structure of granite with no glass on the windows, just heavy strips of canvas. The door was solid oak and iron. She considered the front door, then thought of Citywatch. The smaller a footprint she left, the better.

It was midday, the stables a raucous market. Horses sold and bought, rented to the poor, big merchants with big rings shaking fists at disheveled grooms. Coppers counted, deals shouted; an easy street to avoid notice. Roisin snuck past a fat Hanrab man in blue silks purchasing eight bulls. "For my daughter's wedding, yes?" he said to the head groom, counting silver coins from a heavy purse.

She made her way to the back of the stables where a stack of hay sat against the wall of her apartment building. One quick glance around, then up she went. Her room was on the second floor, she had to make a small leap to catch the windowsill. She pulled herself up, her aches from the night before relighting. She felt fresh blood squeeze out of her forehead, but then she was past the canvas, rolling awkward to the floor.

Oh, it felt good to be home. Her room was a desk with a candle, a bed with a wool blanket, a chest with clothes. A sewing kit was on the desk and her silver and journal were below a floorboard. She changed and splashed some water on her wounds from a bowl the innkeeper laid out each morning. She grabbed her sewing kit and shifted the floorboard.

Heavy boots stomped in the hall. Voices.

She froze.

"—glad to help in any way I can, sir. Nasty bit of business, that. A young girl out helping murderers. What's this city coming to, I ask ya's? Just what is it coming to?"

She recognized the voice, her innkeeper. Panic roared back to life, it slashed at her and took her breath away.

A new voice, "It's the way of things. The Citywatch appreciates your help in our investigation." New, but familiar.

A key slipped into the door. Click. Roisin fought back her panic and leaped for the window, smacked a knee on the edge as she rolled out. A five-foot drop into hay then a ten-foot roll to the ground. She stumbled away, trying not to run, her heart beating like war drums.

The fat Hanrab merchant finished his business as she turned the corner. He rode a carriage with eight bulls in tow down the narrow road, his valet ringing a bell and shouting to clear a path. Roisin used it as cover and stayed with them for six blocks until she could breathe again.

She wandered after that, but not at random. She worked her way farther south, out of the Mule and towards the Crimson Moor. The worst part of Cruxia. A place to disappear one way or another. She had no money, no way of chartering a ship besides stowing away or selling herself. Her pride allowed neither. She needed more options.

The Red Market tapped itself at the Crimson Moor, a sinking marina of necromancers and warlocks running a ragged half-mile of swamp. As far south as you could get on the East End. Rosin would never sell her chastity, nor her soul, but there were lesser things in demand. Three copper for her fingernails, sixteen silver for a pinkie, seventy for a thumb. Should she muster the courage it was ten thousand for her eye. If she survived surgery.

In an alley she found a window to see her own reflection. Her sandy brown hair was filthy, blood stamped and ragged with garbage. Her face was bruised, eyes puffy and red from exhaustion. She took out her needle and thread and started to work on her torn forehead. She flinched with each pierce of the needle, groaned with each pull of the string.

Back in her room, that had not been a new voice. "It's the way of things," he said. Same voice she heard in the temple.

"There's a girl over there watching us." That middle-aged man clad in black with the Mole and the two Hanrabs.

Her killers worked for the Citywatch.

7

Hook and Maharez cut through the throng of Market Boulevard between midday shoppers, a berth provided around them due to their Citywatch disguises. Market Boulevard thrived, one half of it a roiling food market touting cuisine from every corner of the world. Plainslizard on long kabobs, Cruxian roast beef in piled slabs, a whole cornucopia of produce from the Krodan jungle preserved magically on the long voyage. The people were just as international, crushed together, shouting and haggling in seventeen different languages. The boulevard wound downhill as all of the East End did; the city Cruxia sauntered slowly down to the sea.

Maharez pulled at the starched collar of his stolen City Watch uniform. He assumed it was stolen. Hook walked with a lazy strut in front of him, enjoying the power the uniform lent. The wizard chomped on an apple donated to City Watch. He'd also picked up three bribes from corner stalls along the way. "Might as well enjoy it while it lasts, eh?" he said to Maharez with a wink.

This was why Maharez did not and could not like this white

man. Not his practice of magic, though Hanrabs were generally superstitious of wizards. Nor was it the man's ruthlessness on a job, he was in fact kind and gentle outside of the work. No, it was his inability to take anything serious that irked Maharez.

"Is this all a big joke to you?" asked Maharez.

"Eh?" said Hook, pulling his eyes from a particularly juicy rump in a red dress.

"You're strutting around town eating lunch while we're supposed to be hunting the girl. You don't seem bothered at all. Is this all a joke to you?"

"Kid, everything on this planet is tragedy unless you were born rich or a god. All you can do is laugh and not give those upstairs the satisfaction of your tears. Mark that one down."

Hook always told Maharez to mark something down, but Maharez never did. He steamed at Hook. Fatimah was laid low with Polo, Halladar only knew if the herbs Hook gave her would do anything. Following Hook's jaunty path through the East End, Maharez wondered if the wizard really was just a big charlatan taking them on a goose chase so he could eat lunch and leer at women with large butts. It was not the first time he'd wondered if half the shit Hook claimed was magic turned out to be a con.

Hook stopped at a stall, talking with the clerk in Vohlkhan before getting a smile from the woman, he turned back to Maharez with two cigars. "Perks of the job."

"Enough," Maharez said, flinging the cigars into the gutter. Hook raised an eyebrow and walked them away from the stall. "Two hours we've walked this city and we aren't any closer to the girl than when we started."

Hook shook his head. "That's where you're wrong, mate. Every place we've been so far she's spent a good chunk of her life. This market in particular. I keep finding her trace auras up on these lantern posts, girl probably used the Lamplighter's Guild as a cover. Trust me, we're getting close. The further we head south, the stronger the trace gets. Magic takes time if you want to get it right."

Maharez blinked. "How...how does this magic work?"

Hook overacted a gasp. "Are you asking me about magic? The stalwart Hanrab assassin asks the lowly wizard about magic?" He turned to the crowd and grabbed a woman by the shoulder. "This motherfucker is asking me about magic, can you—" But Maharez snatched his collar and dragged him away from the bewildered woman.

"This is what I mean about it all being a big joke," Maharez snapped.

"Easy, easy, just having a walkabout with you. C'mon, we'll work while we talk." Hook couldn't help ribbing Maharez, the poor kid just took everything so damn seriously. It physically hurt. When you were a Cazzaraati sweeper, you had to find a way to cope. Taking it all at face value would hollow you out.

Hook took in a deep breath of the mixed market; warm basil, fresh citrus, roasted lamb; before turning them down Junger towards the Mule Quarter. In his pocket, he rubbed the clump of hair lightly, kept it warm to ease the magic. He was shit at reading auras, but the girl's hair strengthened her signal. He saw ghost tracks of her, followed them for two hours. A light blue specter that bounced from store to store, lamppost to lamppost. Whomever she was, she was poor as fuck. Or she pretended to be. Everywhere she frequented was dingy, in disarray, in the worst parts of town. All the ghost tracks led to the Mule, a place poor girls went to die. He had a droning headache from the constant use of magic.

Maharez walked behind him in the pregnant silence, waiting for Hook to say something. "Well?"

"Right, magic," said Hook. "Vorcan below, where to begin? Magic is like... a fire."

Maharez snorted. "A fire? If you are just going to treat me like a fool then—"

"Hey, easy. It's like a fire, bear with me. What does a fire need?"

Maharez shook his head. They walked along a small bridge that led Junger Street over the drainage canals that ran the city's sewage past the poor districts and down to the sea. "A fire needs fuel, air, and...uh, a spark?"

Hook snapped his fingers. "Exactly, those three ingredients start a fire, and a fire is what?"

Maharez scrunched up his face, then shook his head negative.

Hook went on, "Fire is energy. Magic is an energy that requires the same three things in a different kind of way. See, there is another realm right on top of ours. If we are in the Mortal Realm, consider the other one the Immortal Realm. It's a place of gods, demons, and everything in between. It's like our world but has its own rules, its own laws of physics and such. Some call it the Spirit Realm, the Glass Mirror, the—"

"The Loom."

"Exactly. The Loom in Hanrabi. Every culture has a name for it. You've heard the old cuss, 'all the gods above and below,' everyone has. The secret is this realm is on top of our own, just vibrating at a different frequency. Magic is the drawing of power from that realm and converting it into this one. Take from the Immortal Realm to cast in the Mortal Realm. You with me so far?"

"I think so. The land of the gods is all around us, but it is, how did you say? Vibrating differently?"

"It mirrors our realm," Hook said.

"So how is it a fire?" said Maharez.

"Right. Fire needs fuel, air, and a spark. Think of the air as our realm, for whatever reason, it conducts the shit out of magic. Soon as something from the otherside crosses over, it flourishes. That's your air right there, magic burns bright over here. The spark is the connection to the Immortal Realm. That tiny portal I open to siphon off some power. Nothing could happen without that."

"What is the fuel?" They turned off of Junger onto Mutton Way, Hook still leading. The stench of the Mule Quarter caught them both. A two-mile stretch of cattle farms, tanneries, and slaughterhouses. Maharez didn't know what was worse, the stench or the constant keening of dying livestock. "What is the fuel for this fire?"

Hook tapped his own temple. "That would be the wizard. See, the power that channels from the other side is virulent. It burns while it conducts through us."

"Sounds dangerous."

"Ho boy, you have no idea. Most wizards spend decades learning rituals. Shortcuts. Some have hand motions worked out; others chant in dead languages. The lucky ones aspect to gods. You become their conduit, and they'll protect you from the harmful energies flowing through you. Trouble is half the time the god turns out to be a demon. Honestly, most of the gods are worse than all the demons, and if you aspect they have your soul forever. Do not return to Halldar, do not get reincarnated on the Great Wheel of Life, ya dig?"

"What about you? Were you aspected to a god?"

"Fuck no, mate. I was Mage Corp. Cruxian Army, fifth regiment, the ninety-sixth. They don't let you in if you aspect to a god, too much loyalty claimed elsewhere. No, we had other tricks. Mostly it was diet, eat five times the normal person because the Immortal Realm was burning calories in us at an exponential rate." He patted his growing gut. "I watched guys develop tumors the size of bread loaves running too much power. Remember you are the fuel in this. It's a careful balance, you can't run a god's power through your mortal frame, you just can't. I'm a bit of a jack of all trades, never focused on a specific type of magic. Found little connections between them, my own shortcuts."

"Where were you stationed with the army?"

A shiver went through Hook. "Hanrabi."

Maharez waited for more, but that was it. Hook's back was straight as an arrow. They walked the last three blocks in silence, passing a busy stables and a slew of leather workers. Hook stopped them at a two-story stone and mortar inn with a thatched hay roof. Hook looked back at him and any trace of a change was gone, he gave Maharez his old easy grin.

"C'mon mate, she stinks on that second floor. And I'm shit at reading auras, mind. Remember you're a constable. Try and keep a look of casual disdain on your face."

Maharez glared at Hook.

"Yeah, just like that. C'mon."

Krentor's Tower struck second bell of the afternoon. You knew you were in the Mule when the cheap tin bell tinged at Victory Tower. Maharez and Hook swept into the inn with the bull confidence of City Watch. Hook was impressed at how Maharez carried himself, the boy didn't have much to act proud about these days.

The inn's mainroom was a sawdust floor and the bitter reek of discount spirits. Hook was not a proud man, but he couldn't abide a cheap liquor. There were three things in this world you paid top coin for: booze, tattoos, and prostitutes. Ain't no one proud of a cheap tattoo.

The few patrons looked up with criminal daring as the pair walked in, then tried to look at every corner that wasn't the constables. Maharez did a great saunter to the center of the room, then panned a wilting scan of every afternoon drinker. Kid missed his calling, would've been a great authority figure. Hook hitched his belt, let his shortsword hang out of his longcoat and tap against chairs while he crossed to the bar.

The bartender was a bald man the width and weight of a bull. His brow set a heavy canyon over his eyes. He cleaned a glass with a filthy rag and tried to look tough. "What ya'want with my joint?"

Hook flashed a seal of the City Watch, three years out of date, but the bartender didn't know that. "We're here under order of Citywatch, praise Cruxia." Hook saluted, a fist to his left shoulder.

"Praise be," said the bartender with little conviction.

Maharez walked up behind Hook and kept his casual disdain trained on the bartender. "Reports have that a suspect lives here under your roof. No crime in that for you, an independent landlord. That is, as long as you cooperate in the investigation and allow us to search your premises for any evidence of her," said Hook.

The bartender nodded along, straining at the larger words. "Oh yuh, oh yuh, you can look around where'e'er you be needing. No problems here with the Watch, just can you do's it upstair? My guests be a bit nervous with constables crowding. And a Hanrab one at that. They letting jus' anyone in the ranks these days, I swear. My pa's day wouldn't seen a black man in the finery of the Empire."

Maharez hissed in rage, Hook raised a hand. "Ain't up to the lowly ranks of us to guess at the great minds of Parliament or the Emperor, we just do as we're told. You have a young woman here renting a room, mid-teens, red hair."

"Oh yuh, oh yuh. Room four, last one at the end of the hall upstairs. Here," he grunted as he stood up, "come wi' me. Sorely, get your ass out here an' watch the taps, eh?"

Sorely popped out of a burlap curtain, a man the same shape and demeanor as the potato he shaved. He rubbed a snotty nose. "You say so, boss."

The innkeep walked them up straining cedar steps to a hallway of doors.

"We appreciate the help in our investigation," said Hook.

"Oh yuh, jus' what's the investigation about?"

"Murder," said Maharez.

"Well, I'm glad to help any way I can. Nasty bit of business, that. A young girl under suspicion of murders? What's this city come to, I ask ya's? Just what is it coming to?"

"It's the way of things. The Citywatch appreciates your help in our investigation," said Hook.

The innkeep shrugged and fumbled a key into the lock, turned it with a clank. "Jus' keep a mess out," and the man walked back downstairs.

Hook looked at Maharez. "This door is blazing with her mate, get ready for anything." They moved in quick. Hook went low and right, Maharez blocked the door. The room was empty but for a burlap curtain blowing in the breeze. Hook took out the clump of the girl's hair he used as a focus. It blazed and ignited, burned up in blue embers.

"Well, this is definitely where she lives," said Hook.

"Was that supposed to happen?"

Hook clucked his tongue. "No. It was not. That spell is preschool. Tear this place apart."

The room was sparse; a bed, a desk with a candle, one bookshelf over-stuffed. Maharez tore out the books and ripped them apart looking for hidden notes, weapons, anything. Hook flipped her bed and slit it with his longknife, naught but feathers. Maharez knocked on the walls with an ear.

Hook kicked some of the books around on the floor. "Kid's gotta be working for someone with pull. Look at these; *Algorithms, Meditations on Humanity, Krentor's Ruminations: War and Civilization*. What would some Mule kid do with all this shit?"

Maharez shook his head. "Who can afford books?"

"That's what I'm saying. Hold on." Hook tapped his foot twice. A hollow thunk both times. "Here we go." He bent down and wrenched a floorboard out. A hollowed little cabinet was built beneath it. Maharez crowded over while Hook sifted through it. "Mortia touched, never mind. There's not even a dozen silver down here..." He pulled out a weathered journal with the mark of Veridaan on its cover. Maharez bent over the hole and tried to pry up more hidden panels, counting the meager silver as he did.

"What if she's just some girl?" The thought froze him to his core.

Hook flipped through the journal, "Ain't up to us lowly sweepers to guess at the great minds of Baron Cazaraati, just to do as we're told."

"Doth h'rester," said Maharez under his breath. But Hook ignored him, his face lit up.

"Juno's asshole, Maha, this is better than we could've hoped." He looked up. "This is hers."

"Who cares?"

"You should. This is a window to her soul. Fuck auras, this translates her spirit. Keep lookout while I start a ritual."

"How long?"

"Two...maybe three hours."

Maharez scanned the streets from the window. A large commercial stable took up most of the block, hay piles dotted the alley. The crowd below milled at afternoon sales but there was no sign of the girl.

Hook sat in the middle of the floor amidst the torn books with the journal out in front of him. He took a dripping, rotten onion from his pack and carved it right below his nose. He leaked mucus, his eyes watered. Hook read the journal, his face dripping onto the pages and soaking it. The ink spread.

Maharez wrinkled his nose. "That smells awful."

"Old babba swamp magic. Dirty stuff. Personal." Hook sneezed, his eyes a red mess of tears. "I'm getting a sense of her soul and mixing mine with it. After this, I can trace her through her fucking dreams, mate. We'll find her while she sleeps."

8

"Veridaan's steamy cooch, Nito. You ever fucked with a sperm whale?" He didn't wait for an answer. "Out there we were, the sea the loudest bitch you ever heard." Bert took a double-shot of cheap Fontaigne whisky while Nito wiped a black spot on the marble bartop. Nito didn't like to keep Fontaigne, but it's all Bert ever ordered. Nito's joint was the dive of dives, but he kept good liquor, a mark of pride.

The early afternoon dragged towards the evening rush, hot and soggy and not nearly as busy as Nito hoped. He wiped the spot harder, a black spot burned there five years past. When there was nothing left to do, Nito wiped the black spot. He didn't mean to ignore Bert. Where in the name of Juno's balls could Nito find kax?

Bert went on. "We were out on this pearl of a whaler, hundred ten foot, Nito. Hundred fuckin' ten. Not forty of us, out in the fierce cold of the Steel Sea. Up north near Vohlkhan ice out she came." Bert leaned forward to see if his shot glass was empty. It was. He tapped two fingers next to it and lit a handroll. Bert hated tailors, little tobacco-rolled jobbies they sold in packs of twenty at the market stalls these days. "White nonsense," Bert called them even though he was as white as Nito.

"Out she fucking came, man, like a virgin wife gettin' that first good toot. Auron would've nutted over the size of this fucking whale, Nito, let me tell you." Nito poured another double, leaning toward a triple, and Bert slammed it back. "We sent out four fifteen-foot cutters, strangled with guys. Nito, nine of us crammed on these things, brimmed to burst with harpoons."

Bert was somewhere between forty and seventy, Nito really couldn't tell. He was a stocky white man coated in black hair and tattoos, bald with a full spider web inked around his ears and pate. Eyebrows thick as caterpillars.

"This whale, she fucking wanted it, Nito, fuck, did she want it. First thing she does is blast up out of the sea beneath O'Henry's rig. Pop!" He made the sound with a hooked finger to his mouth. "Like a keg tapping. But it sent O'Henry and his nine smashed to the sea. Like fuckin' ants when you dump a pint on them. Just washed out." Nito poured another triple, and Bert raised it to the meek light of the lanterns. "Fuck, Nito. All of 'em gone in a heartbeat." He popped his finger on his gum again and drained the drink. "All of them men," he stared deep into his empty glass. "Like a drink, Nito. Gone." Nito poured another. Bert stared at it making a pop noise under his breath.

Nito's joint sunk half a story below Skelton Boulevard, a marina adjacent road split by a flower bed. He was lucky to have the cheapest spot on the nicest block of the Docks. Three steps down from the road took you to his dirt floor taproom. Four giant kegs commanded the north wall, his marble-top bar curved around them. The liquor collection bragged bottles from every corner of the world. Two rooms to rent and his apartment hung by balcony over the taps. His kitchen was a converted washroom where he boiled potatoes, chickens, and nothing else. What was cooking besides chopping things into smaller things? He'd never figure it out. He also kept bread and cheese. You get more fights in your joint if you don't have food. Out back you had to take three steps down to the road as the city sloped to the sea.

Nito leaned on his counter, rubbing the same black spot, sort of hoping Bert would keep going about the whale. But Bert just stared at the Fontaigne whisky, quiet and drifting. Around his sparse tables, a few session drinkers stood talking politics with no actual sense of reference. Nito took a long, deep sigh. You only missed the drink when you were bored.

"Say, Bert. You know where I could find some kax? I got a friend in need."

Bert looked up from his triple, all bloodshot eyes. "Kax? Lizard dust? Did I fuckin hear you right? Thought you were clean as a priestess these days, brother."

"It's not for me, and I hate to ask." Nito also hated saying that. It made him feel like a junkie.

Bert waved a hand. "I don't give a fuck. You own a bar and don't drink? What, you buy a whore and just make her dinner? Fuck man, not for me to tell you how to live your life. But I can't fuck with the kax too hard. Half the whalers anymore are Krodan. You know that shit is made from their guts, right?"

"Adrenal gland, yeah, I know."

", you need a dead Krodan to make the stuff. Dunno if you've met many Krodan, but it's pretty fucking hard to make one dead. Seven feet and three hundred pounds of leathery muscle and shit can they heal? Watched one lose an arm to a beluga out on the big blue. Fucker grew a fresh one by the time we hit land. Fuck. Not to mention I like the boys too much. No bullshit with the Krodan."

Nito's head throbbed. "I know it's not the most moral substance out there. Just forget the whole thing."

Bert lifted a hand. "Always gotta help a friend in need. A

pal's a pal. Just a tough number for me since I'm a bit close to the equation, rex?"

"Rex, Bert. Real rex."

"Most kids off the vessel, not the Krodan ones now, but most of these kids hit the Crimson Moore right off the boat. Get goofed up on sopa or some magic mushrooms. The Siegwards cornered your kax market a while ago, so they say, hard to pick it up off the street."

"I don't have enough pull to mess with the Siegwards," said Nito.

"Fuck, who does besides the Baron fucking Caz? Outside of catching a rigger with me all the way to Gaiathor and dealing with the ancestral Krodan, you're shit out of luck. The same ancestral Krodan who produce k'axalcaldous to induce visions of their past lives so they can read the constellations and divine the wheel of stars. I don't think I can help you, brother."

Nito rolled his eyes, his headache cooked. "Don't worry about it, Bert."

"I bunk with these Krodan, Nito. Just want you to know what it's really about. If the old continent is out and the Siegwards are out. Fuck, brother, you might wanna go see Mama Roeneck. What she ain't got she knows where to find, rex?"

"Not rex, Bert. I was afraid of that."

Bert, whale forgotten, tipped his drink back with a shit-eating grin. He hadn't bathed since landfall, grime coated his face. His teeth were white as albinos against it. "Eh, she ain't so bad once you get over the smell."

"I never did." He tapped himself a shot of fizz water he made by keeping a small water barrel suspended in his largest beer keg. The main tap poured beer, but a small one up top poured water that fizzed like the beer. Nito didn't drink, but he could pretend. He missed the bubbles on his tongue.

An old woman the shape of a dumpling swung open the door. She walked up to the bar and bought a wedge of cheese and a pint. She found a small corner booth, one of three in the joint, and opened her cheese. Out of her pocket came a family of rats, a recent mother with seventeen pink pups. They scattered on the table like confetti until she whistled a lilting tune. The rat pups all lined up in neat rows and she broke crumbs off to feed them.

"What the fuck is that?" asked Bert.

"Ah, that's just Minerva. She's alright."

"Your fucking joint, brother."

An early rush hit Nito's as a hulk fresh off the Claret Sea spilled out its crew. Sailors packed in boasting and drinking and smacking the low-hanging beams of the balcony. He broke up two fights, cut off seven people in forty minutes, and threw out a mammoth of a man for scaring Minerva's rats. It was a good day, coinwise.

Around sundown the rush dissipated. Bert snored over the marble, bubbles of snot popping with each breath. Two bells earlier his scullery girl showed up to sweep out the ash droppings and drunks. Maria was a tough number from the Mule. Nito helped her father kill himself with cheap Fontaigne whisky over a decade. When the man's liver finally popped, Nito invited her in for a full-time gig. She was short and full of vinegar. Curly red hair and an explosion of freckles. Nito rarely needed a bouncer.

Krentor's Tower struck eight dull notes, echoed even in Nito's joint. Minerva whistled a quick tattoo, and the rats scurried back into her pockets. She left with a respectable tip in her wake, few taverns let her bring out the rats. Nito's was a repository for the freaks, the losers, and the lost.

At the bar, Nito wiped the black spot again. He didn't realize they had slowed down again until then, such was the life of a tavern. Maria put her broom down to poke the comatose Bert. "Oi, fuck off. If you wanna sleep, it's a half silver, five for the fortnight."

Nito raised a hand. "It's okay, he's rex tonight."

Maria signed the star of Veridaan over her chest. "Well, bless him then. Bless him for bringing the rent down on this place and scaring away the paying customers who are still awake. You know, when you hit the floorboards in the end and this place is willed to me, I'd still like a small clientele base. Maybe don't run it into the ground, oi?"

Nito threw his washrag at her. "I'm out for the evening. Think you can manage the floor until close?"

Her fake indignation immediately became real indignation. "The fuck you are. We have six more bells until close and this place is trashed." She swept an arm across the joint. It was indeed trashed. Empty glasses clung to half the tables, three spills pooled into one massive wet spot on the floor. There was a puke pile that had been sawdusted but not mopped.

Nito smirked at her. The smirk had lost some traction in his forty-eight years, but it still made him a handsome devil, by the gods. Receding hairline be damned. "See what you can't do about improving that clientele base. Consider it training for your future."

He winked and grabbed his cloak, a subtle thing of black wool. He gave it a whirl as he left, theater laced in vanity. Almost five decades in and Nito still wanted to be slick, to be stylish. To be relevant.

"Fuck you, old man," Maria cursed as he hit the door.

He spun. "You have to buy me dinner first."

Her eyes rolled hard enough Nito thought they might fall out. He grinned and burst out onto Skelton Boulevard. Cruxia punched him in the face with her mugginess, sweaty and oppressive. The buildings on the wharf were short so the massive cogs and riggers dwarfed over them, tilting beasts in the night. Nito did miss a life at sea.

He walked up Skelton, drifting a hand through the flower beds. Mama Roeneck. That was a name he did not want to hear again. Nito spent his early adult years raiding the coasts and merchant rigs that frequented them. He could always count Mama as a fence. The Crimson Moor changed every few years as the crime syndicates and low-level pushers molted, but Mama Roeneck was a constant. Like how all of evolution returned to the crab.

Nito, fresh-faced and seventeen years on Galea's surface, frequented her quite often. When you came home off the big blue with cargo you found a buyer that asked no questions and paid good coin. Mama Roeneck, every stinking bit of her, always smiled with a two-tooth grin and told you, "Coin ain't got no providence in the Crimson." Then she'd cackle and young Nito would almost shit himself. You couldn't tell her skin color, or even her race, she was so filthy. Human, Fen, Tuurakhan, perhaps even Krodan? Nito didn't want to ask. And now it was his only connection to kax. Kax so his daughter could get a promotion in Auron's Temple. A drug deal to help his kid. Hopefully the last drug deal. How many times does a junkie say that? Once a junkie, always a junkie.

Deep down Nito craved the excitement. He knew this was morally reprehensible even if it helped his daughter. Nito wanted the old juice, hiding in an alley waiting to strike or be struck. Nito was so desperate to remain relevant.

He had a mile-plus change of downhill rambling through Cruxia. The entirety of the Market district. South he'd cut through the Mule, lots of connections in the Mule. The Mule slouched down to Wharf and finally the Crimson Moore. Nito was in the mood for a good walk; it was hot as the three Hells.

Mama Roeneck and the Crimson Moore? Nito felt like a teenager again. He felt relevant.

9

Gantry Willow stepped to the right, and then the left but it didn't matter. His undergarments were stuck in the crack of his ass and there was no hope of dislodging them without use of a hand and that would draw unwanted attention. Worse, he was sweating. Badly. These state gatherings demanded the finest clothing, layers upon layers of them. All this wool and over forty people stuffed into a room not built for twelve. Gantry sweat profusely. Worse, he was three glasses of lemon wine in, two past his usual.

The funeral for High-Father Alonso finished three bells earlier. Gantry sat in awe that the massive bureaucratic edifice of the Cruxian Empire could arrange an event so magnificent so quickly. Every member of Parliament attended, lining the walls of the Palace district with the Imperial Guard. Four hundred people all said and told. Gantry wondered who could design a seating chart in such little time. The Inspector General and Willow left the man's body at sixth bell that morning. The funeral was seven hours later.

The Citywatch cordoned off the temples of the Gods' Way but let the citizens of Cruxia flood its streets. They shouted their benedictions and prayers to the High-Father's body. His casket hung suspended from the walls in front of Veridaan's stained glass temple. High-Father Alonso's congregation had a place of honor on the Palace wall, right in the middle of the politicians and royal soldiers. They sang all five Fates of Veridaan, their voices magically carried across the whole city, her story told in perfect meter and every stanza of it pure beauty. Gantry Willow did love a good opera.

Willow stood with the Inspector's Precinct, somewhere above the crying masses but quite a bit below Parliament and the Guard. The Citywatch spread out twenty feet below the Precinct on a hastily erected amphitheatre of cheap wood. It was a place of mediocre acclaim, something Willow had sparred with his entire life. But he didn't mind so much while the opera sang.

Sariah Sternwood was six seats above him, standing with the Lord Inspectors of the high council. He noted the bulge of her flask by her breast, but she wasn't wiping her lips compulsively so she hadn't started drinking. Yet. That was good, the funeral was just the beginning. These affairs of state always ran into the long hours of the night as every official within forty miles paid their formal respects. Gantry flourished in a bureaucracy, but the forced esteem felt cheap to him. Gantry never knew the High-Father and he assumed none of these stuffed tunics did either.

The funeral finished with Emperor Sentelpedeo Cruxis himself addressing the crowd. He wore the basic finery, a purple vestment down to his knees filigreed with silver. A deep blue cloak chased in bear fur was the only ostentation. His speech was curt, powerful and magnanimous. Gantry bet the Emperor wrote it himself.

And now, the funeral three bells past, Gantry stepped awkwardly into the Lord Inspector's council with forty other heads of state as Krentor's Bell struck seventh bell. Drunk and trying to pretend he was not.

The room belonged to the High-Lord Inspector Margaeaux, the top of high command in the Inspector's Precinct. It was an office packed tight with shelves; the moldy, lovely smell of books packed in as well. Histories, laws of the past, religious texts, all perfectly organized on the High-Lord's shelves. Gantry was in awe of a nice library.

The High-Lord's desk was half the size of Gantry's apartment, empty but for an ink well, ledger, and ashtray. It screamed of importance, though it lost some luster as the ashtray overflowed with forty-some official's pipe droppings. Some ash even made it to the table, the High-Lord grimaced with each wandering tap of a pipe or cigar.

Gantry was the worst person to talk to when it came to the "who's-who" of the upper echelon. He had a nice spot in the shadow of Sariah Sternwood and was happy to stay there. She had broken every convention on her ascent to Inspector General. First Hanrab in the City Watch, first woman to join the Precinct. She was a local hero, but here in this room of old white men, she looked more awkward than Willow felt. She was in desperate need of a drink.

A mutton-chopped old Earl, four glasses of wine past parliament-drunk, said, "I think this business is just what you would expect. Let any old foreigner into the infantry, the City-Watch, the Inspector's Precinct, and watch as High-Father's start getting murdered. Especially these dark Hanrabs. That's a fact by Juno's cock." It was that perfect indelicacy in a state affair where every other voice dropped at the exact second. And, of course, everyone looked at Sariah Sternwood. She didn't blush, or even acknowledge the rush of faces, she just lit a tailor cigar and finished her conversation about goose tax levies on the fourth district with the Earl of Valais.

The High-Inspector Margeaux, a bald, grave man of sixty-four with a severe goatee, laughed at the perceived joke and then raised a hand. "Earls, Inspectors, Principal Officers of Parliament, your honors are but too much for an old functionary as myself. The esteem you bring to my office, and the respect afforded our Holy High-Father, is consummate in its elegance. But now I must ask you to allow me my grief in these times of conflict." His face had a measured half-smile that both disarmed and gave confidence to the room. A perfect politician, thought Willow.

The forty-some officials left in a flurry of tailcoats, powdered wigs, and expensive perfumes. Gantry gathered himself to leave with Sternwood, but Margeaux gave him a burning look that said don't. After, there were only five people left in the room. High-Lord Inspector Margeaux, Inspector General Sariah Sternwood, Inquisitor Dietrich, Gantry Willow himself, and High-Mage Louise Sternwood of the Mage Corp.

The same High-Mage Sternwood who declined Gantry Willow's acceptance into the Mage Corp three times running. Also Sariah Sternwood's adopted father. Just great thought Gantry, just fucking great. And he was standing right next to Willow.

The High-Mage wore a crimson cloak over a starched white and red parade uniform. His badges and medals of office took up his entire left breast. He had a handlebar mustache more clean cut than his uniform and, somehow, at seventh bell in the evening there was no stubble on his neck.

High-Mage Louise Sternwood looked at Sariah Sternwood with a mix of pride and awkward unease. Louise commanded the Mage Corps forces in Hanrabi during the Turvaali Sia'sah. He came home with Sariah Sternwood, a twelve-year-old refugee. It was no question he propelled her through the bigotry of parliament to a place of honor in the City Watch. Her own aptitude and drive brought her promotions and eventually to the Inspector's Precinct. It was also no question that in doing so, the High-Earl scuttled any chance of joining Parliament. Sariah was both his greatest pride and lowest embarrassment.

"So," the man said to Gantry, "trying for the Mage Corps again this year."

It was all the more awkward coming from one of the most powerful wizards in the Empire. He didn't want to be there in that room any more than Willow did.

Willow sighed. "No, I think that's all behind me." And he finally pulled the underwear from his crack. What could they do, demote him?

Inquisitor Dietrich, the same man that Willow and Sternwood met at the High-Father's corpse, wore his black cloak and wide-brimmed black hat. He sat to the right of the High-Lord's desk, smoking a cigar while his reflective spectacles flickered across the room like mirrors. His voice slid like a lizard on sand. "The death of a High-Father is not only grave sin, but also a threat to national security. The High-Lord Inspector and I brought you here to discuss the case our two offices share."

Willow wanted to roll his eyes at the way the man said "share".

High-Lord Margueax cleared his throat. "Indeed. The Inquisitor's office has worked diligently and surgically during the time of our mourning."

Sariah Sternwood stepped forward. "That is quite irregular. Mourning a High-Father of the Empire takes precedence over—"

"Sariah," said her father. The statement was a blade, she closed her mouth.

The Inquisitor's spectacles beamed into Sariah Sternwood. "Irregular, yes. But efficient. We've apprehended three suspects and have drawn confessions plus undeniable evidence from a scientific origin. These three are our murderers and the proper procedures will be observed."

High-Lord Inspector Margueax drove his stare into Sariah

as well. "An accolade we thank you for from one office to another. Three murderers taken off the street. High treason dealt with succinctly. The Precinct and the Watch are lucky to have your assistance, Inquisitor."

It was High-Mage Sternwood's turn to look at his daughter. A sad, watery look quite uncharacteristic on his face. Please, it said, please just go along with them. Everyone in the room was part of a detective office of the Empire, all except the High-Mage. Gantry Willow was no politician, but he could see that the man was only there to twist Sternwood's core of honor.

Willow spoke up, "Three confessed killers, no fourth?"

Dietrich and Margueax shifted their gaze to Gantry as if they forgot he was even in the room. "No," said Dietrich. "Three Hanrab youths who swore their souls to Turvaal. An unfortunate reality, especially with so many Hanrabs in the city these days."

Bile crawled up Willow's throat. How terribly convenient, three Hanrab Turvaali. Three youths sworn to the god of chains, an easy villain for the city. But there had been four killers. Willow knew it. He had seen the aura of the High-Father still burning incandescent after his death. He had seen the four cracks on his soul. Four murderers.

He was outraged, he wanted to rail against these old men. Yell in their faces with his spittle raining upon them. But he would not. He was Gantry Willow. He was weak-willed and a shit wizard and he would be nothing without Sariah Sternwood. The massive shadow she cast. He once again had a wedgie.

Sariah's throat bobbed once. Her jaw bunched on muscles of steel wire. "If this is the order of the Inspector's Precinct, I will honor it," she said to Margueax. She turned her dead stare to Inquisitor Dietrich. "We, of course, thank the Inquisitor's office for the assistance."

Last came the High-Mage. "Father," she said. His face all but collapsed. Sad to see a man of honor hung by politics.

"If there is nothing else, my assistant and I will take our leave," she said, turning.

Dietrich leaned forward, his broad mouth split in a grin, gleaming pearl. "Oh, but please join us for a drink. I have a Valais vintage we were to open. I've heard you are fond of spirits, are you not?"

Sariah wiped her lips, the only break in her demeanor. "Thank you but I must decline. My duty remains. This funeral prevented me from my paperwork."

Margueax raised a hand, "Habberdash. The case is closed, assign a clerk to it and enjoy yourself. This is a closed meeting, quite good for your career, no?"

Dietrich pulled a bottle from his satchel and cut the seal with the tiniest knife Gantry had ever seen. The blade was no longer than two knuckles of the pinkie. "Surely one of your station can appreciate the position you now have, can appreciate the opportunities presented in meetings such as this. Wouldn't you say?"

Gantry's blood blossomed. How dare he? Sariah had the most arrests and cases closed across five districts. She worked three times as hard as any other officer to attain half as much prestige. And she was still the youngest Inspector General at thirty-four. Her stepfather broke her into the Watch, but she clawed her way to the top. And Gantry was just a tad bit drunk.

"I don't think you have any right to speak suchly, Inquisitor," Gantry said way too loud. Was suchly a word? Shit.

Everyone looked at Gantry Willow, every one of them graced with enormous responsibility. Literally his greatest nightmare. Sariah's eyes said stop, now. High-Mage Louise rubbed his septum. High-Lord Margueax bit his knuckle to keep from laughing.

Dietrich drove his rimless spectacles into Gantry like a

canon. "Oh. Gantry Willow is it? Do you know of any other woman with the rank of Inspector General? No?" Now his gaze swiveled to Sariah. "How many Hanrab nationals were in our ranks before Sariah Sternwood? Well, Mr. Willow?"

"None, sir." Gantry could've died. One of the five most powerful men in the Empire was rolling him over the coals in front of two others. Worse, he had embarrassed Sariah. He snuck a glance her way and saw the stoicism creaking under Dietrich's tirade.

The Inquisitor went on, boring into Sariah with his stare but still speaking to Gantry, "She is a black woman in the Inspector's Precinct. You are a fool if you don't see her station as a barrier."

The High-Mage, Sariah's stepfather, stood up like a bolt. He couldn't meet her eyes. "If you will excuse me, I have much to—"

Inquisitor Dietrich cut him off with a wave. "Sit." He sank like lead in water. "I wonder, Mr. Willow. Has Ms. Sternwood ever thanked her father for the position she is granted? Do you think it is possible for a black woman to waltz into our ranks?"

Sariah Sternwood stepped forward in parade stance, full military precision. "I appreciate the offer provided here, Inquisitor, but my assistant and I have much to do. If this case is closed, there are forty more cases my precinct must attend to. You have my honor. Please, High-Mage," her stare swept over her father, "stay in my place and enjoy the fruits of your position."

The High-Mage wilted. Dietrich poured wine in glasses set by Margueax. "So be it," said Dietrich, and somehow his grin widened.

Gantry's heart hammered, his blossomed blood floundered. He felt like a man beat up in the gutter. He couldn't move, anxiety a thousand spiders in his veins. Sairah took his hand and dragged him from the room.

Down gilt hallways of chased gold, across carpets so thick you sank into them, Sariah dragged him. It was only the fourth time in Willow's life he had been in the Palace District, and he was now too drunk and anxious to catch any details. His wedgie was terrible, it chafed red scabs between his thighs.

Suddenly they were outside in brilliant fresh air. A sidewalk ran next to fine gardens, fifteen feet away the battlements of the district towered over the Promenade and the rest of the city. Gantry walked over to them and leaned.

All of Cruxia spread out below him. A beautiful, complicated, mess of a city. Gleaming marble domes and statues taller than the temples designated the Gods' Way. Tonscato Bridge stretched like a wire splitting the Promenade in half. The East End dumped out farther below, a spread of merchants, apartments, slums, alleys, mongers, stables: the heartblood of the city.

"I'm so sorry, Sariah. I should not have said any of that."

She walked up next to him at the palace wall and gripped the stonework. "Fuck that. I'm glad you did."

"What?" He had never heard her swear.

"Fuck what they said in there. Three Turvaali youths? Hanrabs like the racist old Vincenzzo first predicted? Fuck all of that. This is the fourth time the Inquisitor's office removed my case and pinned it on some Hanrab kids. All under the guise of homeland security."

She took her flask and tipped it, her perfect brown neck bobbed five times. She wiped her lips with a savage brush and spit. "You said there were four killers in there and I believe you more than that Inquisitor. They're dirty, I know it. Parliament buys the offices it can't control anymore. I don't know who, Willow, but one of the syndicates is behind this. The Siegewards, maybe? The Marlowes?"

"The Siegewards? Shit," said Gantry. He took Sariah's flask

and tried to drain it. But it was strong Steel Coast whiskey. He coughed and sputtered. "Shit, where does that leave us?"

She pulled a shard of wax from her belt. "We solve the case. You say it was four killers, I say we use the only bit of evidence we have. Someone from the Lamplighter's Guild is involved. The candles were lit the night before, but not put out. And someone knocked this to the floor from a chandelier." She turned to Gantry, her face lit with furious intent. "Take a leave of absence with me. No more than two weeks. We will solve this, fuck what all those old men had to say. Fuck them."

Gantry Willow vomited over the palace battlements. He vomited until he was dry-heaving spittle. He puked all over three Hanrab youths hung from the palace wall. Turvaali insurgents, caught for high treason and murder of a High-Father, swinging for all the citizens to see.

They swung wide, the wind heavy this high up the walls.

10

Nito swept his cloak and took a right on Jalisceer Way, the night market. Nocturnal flora and fauna were delicacies in the city where they couldn't be found. Jalisceer Way ran from tenth bell to just before dawn and they were provided extra Citywatch plus an enforcer on horseback in full plate mail. This week it was McEntyre. He was a good sort; no bribes, no favorites. A rare type of constable.

A tiny shop painted indigo opened only for two bells as the Wisp-o-wills and Nightingale Roses bloomed for just one hour at night. Three hundred silver a pop. Nito stopped by the bat monger and looked at the alien sky rodents from up north, some the size of a labrador. Finally he found Shep setting up his stall. Three poles and a canvas roll for the roof plus a roll for his knees.

Shep was a wrinkled old raisin of a Hanrab. His fingers were all lost to leprosy, so he used the stumps to carve. Better than the Tuurakhan petrified wood carvings across the world in Gaiathor. More beautiful even than the Has'hanasa, a Hanrabi temple devoted to Veridaan carved from one giant tree. Shep sliced a log held by his knees with a curved knife between his hand-stumps. He moved so quick Nito couldn't follow, his eyes unfocused and he could only see the figures emerge. Twice Shep switched to a hatchet, spun the log with his shoulder, and chopped four quick strikes to remove chaff, then the knife was back. Nito sat down, he waited. Nito had little time for religious mumbo jumbo, he cursed most gods. But here? This was divine.

Shep finished; three great figures on the log's wide base. Halladar, Hanrab god of the sun and life, stood next to Veridaan, Sibling of spring and birth. They faced Auron, Sibling of summer and life. Halladar screaming in meshed-steel armor, a short sword and shield etched with a shining sun. Veridaan bald and armored in vines, wings like a dragonfly that rained little wooden roses. Auron towered in plate armor with pauldrons like greatshields, his features Cruxian and noble.

Eleventh bell of the night clanged Nito back to reality just as Shep turned and smiled, a grin with one brown tooth. "Do you know of the Great Schizma? When Veridaan and her lover Halladar fought Auron for his sins? Did you know Hanrabi was once a verdant jungle full of life? The battle of three gods laid it low. Their blows cracked mountains, extinguished forests; their ire decimated cities. Glittering cities of marble and gemstones, can you imagine? The pinnacle of civilization. All gone but for the jealousy of Auron. All because he would not let his sister love a new god. Both Siblings died in that conflagration, only Halladar walked away. A broken god, a broken man, a broken continent of endless desert. But *darasanasa*, do I go on, no? What brings a man such as Alistair Nito to my stall?"

Shep reached behind his tools and pulled out a whalebone pipe scrimshawed with Hosiris. The bird-headed Hanrab god of the hunt twisted along the pipe. "More puzzles today?"

Nito couldn't tear his gaze from the three wooden figures, carved in an hour, each almost a foot tall. "Actually, I need a favor and it's a tough one."

Shep's thrush white eyebrow flicked, "Eh?"

Nito swallowed some spit laced in bile. Almost five decades walking the planet and the shame of this question remained. "I'm looking to score some kax. Can you help a brother out?"

Shep shook his head. "No, no, no, I'm afraid. Forces larger than Shep move the lizard dust. I hope you understand the importance of the substance. It is holy. It allows the Krodan to see their gods, to experience the past of their ancestors. You are a good man, Nito, rare in this time and place. I only hope you wish to procure this for its actual use and not the mundane waste of this modern era."

Shep took out a black ball of sopa from his pouch, rolled it between his stumps until the tar was soft and sticky, then dropped it into the scrimshaw pipe he held with his knees. From a breast pocket he pulled a pitch-stick with his teeth and scratched it on the scrimshawed surface of the pipe. A special divet was carved into the pipe which he fit the burning stick into, then took the pipe with his stumps and drew deep. The carved Hosiris glowed with the embers of the opiate.

"Now if you need sopa, I can help you. Hanrabi's blessing. My curse." He chortled and coughed on the harsh smoke, his pupils dilated to the size of coins. "Puzzles I can sell you though, puzzles for a puzzle, no? Nito, you are the greatest of puzzles. A man who leaves the life of the street," Shep pulled an absolute monstrous hit, the coals brimmed dark red, "but drags himself back monthly. Why? Reliving the past? I think not. You may have quit the junk, but you are still a junkie, no?"

Nito waved the thick, white smoke away. Shep blew rings inside of rings. "Just the puzzles then, Shep. Give me three."

Shep's eyes were bleary and bloodshot, he smoked and smoked. "Hahaha, three wood block puzzles then. I am sorry I could not help you, but I am happy to share my work." He turned and stared at his three carved gods on one base. "If only the world knew what Hanrabi once was. What it could be again. If only I could share that work with the world. But then again, I can always share it with the sopa," he laughed.

Nito bought three wooden puzzles, complex things that fit together but only in one specific configuration. Shep made his sopa money with them. His works of art rarely sold. People wanted entertainment anymore, never history. Shep would smoke all night and carve until dawn. He averaged three sculptures, each more prolific as the sopa took hold. Most he donated to the temples in Little Hanrabi. Others would be kicked to kindling by hoods or malicious constables.

Nito pocketed his puzzles, Shep already turning to his next log with sopa-fueled eyes. He fiddled with the things in his cloak's pocket, but they weren't for him. He walked from the night market and steered himself deeper through the city toward the sea. The brick roads became concrete, jagged and cheap. Passing between two apartments he entered the Mule. Even at night the braying of cattle and smell of slaughter continued. A red channel of blood, wastewater, and offal squished under his boots.

Half a mile in he cut north to Dunwich Park. Decrepit during the day, it was a horror show at night. Constables didn't patrol this deep in the Mule past sundown. A broken, bronze-now-green statue of Garland Cruxis marked its center. Around it grew a sprawling junkie camp. Pushers, wheelers, sopa-heads, kax-hounds, ether-fiends, all staggering and snorting and tying one off in between ragged lean-to tents. Thieves steered clear of Dunwich, the junkies shambled into a horde when threatened.

Nito let his cloak billow and walked with purpose from the safer fringes to junktown. The secret to traveling in dangerous parts of a city, act the part. Don't look like you're scared and you won't get jumped. Don't break eye contact if it's made, don't slouch. If you drop your tobacco, act like you meant to. An old game, Nito's favorite.

Business near the center was booming, or stumbling in this case. Two dozen degens sat around the statue. A girl no older than fourteen clapped at the air chasing fireflies only she could see. Nito did a double take, it was one of the girls from Montka's office. The coin spinner. An old Tuurakhan man with skin like an elephant grabbed Nito's leg, "Nice coat, white boy. I buy? Three silver? Sixteen hits, howabout?"

Nito smiled. "Six hits of kax, and I got you Tuura." Tuurakhan hailed from Gaiathor, across the world. They had varying types of fur or tough skin, and each tribe was delineated by their horns or tusks. Tuura was a respectful title, what they called themselves. Cruxia had many nicknames for them that weren't so respectful. Nito spent four years shipwrecked on Gaiathor in his wild days. He broke bread with the Tuura, listened to their stories, and finally joined them in war. But that was a couple lives ago.

"Kax? No say, no say. So sorry. Too dangerous." He let go of Nito's leg and sat back on his wicker mat. He had cut off his tusks, probably to buy sopa.

Nito lit a tailor tobacco and moved through the throng. A boy of seven stepped carefully between comatose drug addicts until he found a dead one. He managed to clear its pockets and disappear before anyone else took notice. Dunwich Park was not known for happy endings.

Towards the south side of the sprawl, a human man sat with a burlap cloak tied with dock rope. Long dreadlocks clumped around his neck, and he wore dark spectacles in the middle of the night. As Nito got closer he spoke, "Got smoke. Got dust. Got most. What you need, Crusa? We all rex here tonight." He let out a peal of laughter, extra loud after the silence of Junktown. His accent was sonorous, hailing from the western islands of Hanrabi. Crusa was Hanrab slang for Cruxian.

"Hey, Jamir, need some help." Nito offered him a tailor.

"Ah, *bunyoon si basa*, sweeper."

Nito put his hands up. "I don't sweep no more."

"That's where you wrong, Crusa. Once a chimney, always a chimney. *Si basa*, no?"

"If you say so. I got you something." Nito took out the three wooden puzzles. Jamir pulled his glasses down to look. One eye was a brilliant green like lit jade; the other was milky white with a ragged scar down to his cheek.

"These are marvelous, Crusa. Absolutely marvelous," he looked up at Nito, "from Shep?"

Nito nodded.

"Ah, *bunyoon siakasa racha*. Thank you, Nito. Thank you." He set the puzzles aside, put his glasses back, then crossed his arms. He returned flawlessly to drug dealer, mild contempt in his sneer with a threatening slug to his shoulders. No one did it like Jamir. "Now what you need, white boy?"

"Kax."

He sucked a tooth. "No *guinee* Crusa, no *guinee*. Only crabs with their claws in that mess are the Siegewards and ol' Mama herself. Jamir don't fuck with that, rex?"

"I really don't want to see Mama."

"Oi, white boy, no one wants to see Mama, doubt she even wanna see herself in the mirror." He ripped laughter at his own joke. "But we tight, okay, Crusa? We tight. Three puzzles buys you info at least." Jamir lit his tailor and blew the smoke out through his nose.

"Alright," Nito sat down next to him, "hit me. What's three puzzles buy?" Jamir wasn't allowed at the night market after his alchemy shop was busted three times in one month. He was a predatory drug dealer, but the man loved puzzles and only Nito brought them anymore. In return, Nito got the straight shit on what happened in his city. Nito had to keep his edge, had to stay relevant even pushing fifty.

"Oi, Crusa. Lotsa' go around. The Greys are shaking deep, deep scared. They put a crunch on us but it was a fade. A thing of smoke, a thing of mirrors, you get me? Big trouble up on the Gods' Way, dead priest brought some headbreakers downtown our side. Buncha' armor came in all clubs first and no questions later. They pull three Hanrabs from here. *Sasa biyadoo*, Junktown boy be up killin' priests? *No guinee*, fuck that, Crusa. But they got their goats and the headbreakers went back behind their high gates."

"You talking about High-Father Alonso? I saw the Greys staking out his temple."

"Oh ya. They see a priest murdered all the way up there and figure it for three black boys all the way down here. Typical Crusa logic. Shit, we only kill white boys when they as deep as we. Who wan' the heat of a dead white boy, eh, white boy?" He cackled.

Nito's headache came back flanking. A lot cooking up and he was a little too close to it. Finding Kax in Junktown was about as deep in the game as he wanted to get. Dead high-priests? No, thank you. Twice today he was in spitting distance.

"Alright, what's the word on the syndicates? Three puzzles buys me more than gossip."

"Gossip? *Si basa no guinee*, Crusa. Jamir only give you the straight shit. Syndicates are moving, Crusa. Rumbling and tumbling. Siegewards have taken over a lot of the city. They runnin' the kax, the hethbara, only thing they ain't runnin' main is the sopa. Marlowes are almost done for, Crusa. Siegewards dropped a hard crunch on 'em. Not much left to clean up the pieces," said Jamir.

"What about the Cazaraati?"

Jamir leaned back, his tailor burning so low it singed his knuckles. He tossed it and reached out for another. Nito gave him the remnants of his pack and lit a pitch-stick for him. He leaned in, the flame caught the jade of his eye.

"Baron Caz been quiet these days. He has his sopa connects from all over Hanrabi, he let the Siegewards take ground. Not like him at all, *guinee guinee*. What's his game, they wonder? Dukes, Earls, even High-Priests be droppin' these days. Third dead white man of power in a season. Maybe he playin' a long game, *no basa* Crusa?"

Nito sat down and took back a tailor from his pack. Jamir offered his burning tobacco as a light. "*No basa bunyoon,* Hanrab, *no basa*. Ah, fuck."

They sat and smoked their tailors in silence for a bit.

Nito watched Junktown from a ways, watched the degenerates stumble and dance and live a life he missed. Silhouettes around the statue of Garland Cruxis.

Deep in the city and no closer to finding kax, Nito rocked to his feet and offered a hand to Jamir. "Always appreciate the dialogue, brother."

"Just keep bringin' the puzzles, white boy. Much love." He gave his fist to Nito for a bump, then pulled out the first puzzle and disappeared into it. His hands buzzed left and right over the complex grooves. A girl approached from the gloom, the finger-sucker from Montka's office.

"Hey, sexy—" she started.

Jamir raised a hand. "Not yet, little kitty. *Suyasa si basa*, you gon' wait."

She stomped a foot and Jamir ignored her, wound up in his puzzles. Nito walked away with more problems than answers.

Out of Dunwich Park, the roads sloped as they ran to the dock districts. The Claret Sea surrounded Cruxia from the west and south, the city built on the crags of a great peninsula. Shipping lanes from all over the world could find purchase near the city. The Fen built it two thousand years past, marble and limestone architecture long lost to the sands of time. Modern humans couldn't produce an aqueduct drainage system so intricate, but they could maintain it. The city Cruxia had always been of strategic import, had traded sovereigns a hundred times since it was created. Cruxia ruled it for a five-hundred-year stretch, the record. Nito figured it was why the empire thrived as much as it had. Control the economy, control the world.

His great-grandfather fought Cruxia in the Monticellon Revolution. Their ragtag rebels pierced through the empire, right up to the gates of Cruxia about ninety years prior. The walls of Cruxia broke them in three bloody days and great-grandpa's head was spiked to the gates with three thousand others. He who controls the city controls the economy. Control the economy, control the world. His grandmother taught him that wrapped up with her tales of rebellion.

But none of that history got him any closer to kax. Nito went for a tailor and remembered he gave them to Jamir. Not rex at all. On Melchior Way in Commons, he found a street vendor to buy a fresh pack of tailor tobacco. Ganon Hall loomed like a beached whale, green-stained with algae. Nito spent years of his youth at Ganon: dealing, wheeling, sweeping. Just the sight of it made him feel young, though the slop looked older than the aqueducts anymore.

Nito picked up his pace. Too much history kicking around tonight. Off the harsh concrete of Melchior, onto the driftwood berth of the Crimson Moor. A staggering shantytown of shacks on poles, Cruxia developed a stinking mire of sewage and refuse. Right at sea level a quagmire gushed, the city spread out like a cut vein. The Crimson Moor sat on raised pylons above the man-made swamp. Citywatch Greys, Inspectors, even the Inquisition; none had jurisdiction on the Moore.

The planks squelched beneath his boots with each step, sewage soaking through the cracks. At two in the morning, the place crawled with dark figures. Warlocks, soul-eaters from the western continent, wizards coated in tumors looking for an easy way out. A yellow-toothed warlock, bald but for a spiral tattoo, smiled at Nito. He returned it with a sneer. Nito preferred Junktown. A junkie was predictable, a wizard was unknowable. Fucking magic.

Each creaky step scared Nito, below him a green and red river of waste and blood coagulating from the Mule. Bones rose to the top of the refuse soup, no trawlers came this far to clean it up.

And all the way at the end of the road, as far as you could go south in Cruxia, sat Mama Roeneck's shack. A tar paper roof and balsa wood walls, three cheesecloth windows with potions and vials lurking in silhouette. There was a great wooden dumpster across the street brimming with garbage.

Nito pushed into the shack. An explosion of shelves and dressers, none matching, all cantilevered this way and that stuffed with jars of herbs, liquids, and swimming creatures. Two great potbelly ovens dominated the far wall and their heat made the stench all the much worse.

And then there was Mama. Humpbacked and swaddled under three patchwork quilts, her bulk shifted this way and that between the tight lodgings. Her face was covered by a Hanrab burqa, but it was torn, and snatches came through: grey wrinkled skin, bulbous pustules, one eye a beautiful emerald green. The eye swiveled on Nito, it had been brown when he came here decades past. Whose eye did she have now? He shivered.

Mama Roeneck cackled at him. No one cackled like Mama, she probably invented the practice back when humans struggled with stone tools. "Alistair Nito, hehe, has your little ship of legitimacy sunk? Have you dragged yourself back to be top sweeper once again?" She turned to stir a cauldron. It was full of skinned rabbits.

He put up his hands. "Nothing so dire as that. I'm just dredging the grounds for a friend. Looking for an open market, get me? Mind if I smoke?"

She clucked her tongue. "Not at all, pretty man, just stay on the east side." She pointed to the west wall. "I keep the combustibles over there." She said 'pretty man' like Nito would say 'pretty bird.'

He lit his tailor and leaned on the east wall keeping a wary eye on the explosive gels and spirits decorating the west. "I'll cut to the—"

Mama Roeneck smacked her wooden spoon on the cauldron. "No cutting in line, hehe. No cutting the cheese." She cackled again and broke wind. It stank. "It has been some time since I've seen you, pretty man, you will indulge Mama. Try this." She took the wooden spoon from the second cauldron and closed to Nito in a terrifying lurch. It was brown and thick on the spoon, whatever it was.

Nito's sweat prickled his armpits and ran in tickling streams down his side. But he kept the terror out of his stance. Keep eye contact, don't flinch, same old game. "I'd rather not, Mama."

"Oh, but you will, hehe. How are your bowels, pretty man? You keeping regular?"

"What?" said Nito.

"Are you pooping at the same time each day? It was the bowels that killed Juno, Brother Autumn."

"What?' said Nito again, off-kilter and feeling a fool.

Mama thrust the wooden spoon into Nito's surprised mouth. He gagged. It was thick and hot...and sweet?

Mama cackled again. "Corn syrup. Three times as sweet as sugar and twice as cheap. I sell it to candy makers. Makes the kids fat so they're easier to cook."

Nito really wanted to be anywhere else on the planet right then. He swallowed the syrup with a gulp and dragged on his tailor, sickly sweet. Mama reached into an overflowing shelf and pulled out a cigar, a nice one too. She put her leg up on a stool, a morass of oozing blisters and varicose veins that coated her grey-pink ankle. She pulled a pitch-stick from a garter belt.

Mama lit her cigar, and the smoke filled the small shack,

clogged on the cauldron steam and apothecary stench. "It's good to keep regular, especially a man. It's the guts that kill a man most of the time. That or the lungs or the heart. But here in Cruxia, it's always the guts. No one eats their vegetables, hehe. Brother Juno, wisest of the Siblings, first out of Galea's cunt and eldest of the seasons. But did he eat his vegetables? No, no, no, hehehe. God of wisdom? Folly of the gods not to adhere to their own, hehehe."

As she smoked, she blew great shapes into the shack. Brother Juno, wise and old and grandfatherly in perfect detail for three seconds before a draft whisked him away. Then all four Siblings, Auron, Veridaan, Juno, and Mortia. Nito stared transfixed at the sorcery.

Mama continued. "Brother Juno, counsel to the other three, always there with sage advice. But they didn't listen. As Juno's bowels stopped up and a cancer grew, Auron grew jealous of Veridaan for she had found herself a sweet young thing like all us women want, eh, pretty man?" She licked her lips with a white tongue through the screen of her burqa. "Veridaan took her sweet young thing, a human god mind you, she took that young god to bed and Auron could not take this. They were the first gods after their mother Galea, the planet itself. How could a pure god fuck a demi-god, thought Auron? So, the great Brother Summer, god of life, he raped Veridaan."

She blew that action into the room with her smoke, but Nito looked away. He knew the legend. He did not need to see it.

"Veridaan gave birth to Ana'sia, deformed and spider-like. She was hidden away with Mortia, Sister Winter of death, a neutral Sibling in the war. The young godling became the goddess of secrets for she was the first one."

Nito's headache picked up to ramming speed. Every one of Mama's story beats were told in the smoke, beautifully etched like Shep's wooden sculptures. But the smoke cloyed, he could barely breathe.

"Juno was complacent in everything, god of wisdom but never action, hehehe. He watched his brother rape his sister and did nothing. He saw the spider godling born and did nothing. And so the cancer in his guts grew and grew and grew, and since he was a god born with the will of creation, his cancer gained sentience. It was alive, but is cancer not already a living thing? An anathema of our own?"

Nito was bleary-eyed and foggy. What was in her cigar besides tobacco? He blinked awkwardly; the last question was not rhetorical. "Uh, what?" Ever the fucking font of wisdom, eh, Nito?

She smacked him with the wooden spoon. "Pay attention. You want something from Mama, you listen to her stories.

"Juno's cancer," Nito spouted.

"Yes, yes, Juno's cancer. So, Brother Autumn watched the desolation of his original pantheon and did nothing as cancer boiled in his bowels. Well, it finally burst, tearing him open and the cancer emerged as a new god. Queklain it named itself, god of rot and decay. A farce of Autumn and wisdom, a mockery, for Queklain was born in the bile of stomach acid. Juno died and the new god raged across creation. It took Garland Cruxis and all his new gods to ensnare Queklain and Turvaal and Meazakala and trap them in the triumvirate of Hell, deep, deep in the Immortal Realm."

Her final smoke image was a work of beauty. All the new gods under the banner of Garland Cruxis lined up against the three gods destined to Hell. But Nito was too high to catch any of the deep details and he only could name one out of five of the gods arrayed. All that religious hoodoo was never his strong suit. Mama Roeneck farted and the smoke blew out of the shack. Nito's mind came back sharp and ready.

"Now, pretty man, what did you come all the way down to

old Mama for? You must need something, folks don't come see Mama because they want to."

Nito shook his head, free of the last wisps of Mama's sorcery. He swore the gods fought at the corner of his eye. "Kax, Mama. I'm looking for Kax. The Siegewards cornered the market and I'm almost out of options."

Her emerald eye swiveled on Nito, something crawled in the iris like a maggot. "K'axalcaldous? The lizard dust, eh? You must've fallen further than I thought."

Nito rubbed his eyes, still he saw the clash of the gods against his eyelids. Each meteoric smash or sorcerous blast shocked his headache into white flashes. When you quit the junk getting drugged is a nightmare. "It's not for me. I need it for a friend."

"Do not feed me the bullshit. A friend would not send you to the dankest corners of town to see me. Not a friend at all to risk your life." She chomped her teeth, three uneven rows of sharp razors like a shark's, then her white tongue came out again to lick them.

"It's for my daughter," Nito said.

"Tsk, tsk, even worse, pretty man. Finding junk for your kid."

"It's for her priest. Salavar, you know him. I find Salavar some kax, he moves her up the roster. Maybe enough of a raise to move out of the Mule."

"I don't see the difference, pretty man. Junk is junk no matter the reason you need it. But here." She lurched across the hut and snatched a jar from the east wall. It was the size of a loaf of bread, packed full with the foul orange powder. A million gold's worth of kax. Enough to flood the market.

"Mortia's tits, that's too much, Mama."

She cackled, "You want the juice but just a tad of it? No, pretty man." She tossed him the jar.

It weighed over three pounds. There was enough money

after a flip to buy half the Mule, enough to buy a bar in the Promenade right up against the Palace district, maybe the whole block. But it was also the Siegewards' connection and enough to bring their syndicate down on Nito. Fuck. That was Mama Roeneck, always a price.

"It's all or nothing, pretty man."

"Let me smoke on it." He lit a tailor and held the jar like a baby. The shack was clogged with cauldron steam, so he went to the window and held up the cheesecloth for air. More kax than the city saw in a while, what was he to do with that? Help out Salavar and propel his daughter through the ranks, yes, but also bring the second most powerful family in the city knocking at his door. His judgement stumbled akilter. Every time he closed his eyes to blink, he saw the war of gods. Fucking sorcery.

Out on the rickety docks, his smoke waltzed with the sewer fog. A silhouette staggered in the mist. Nito blinked twice, making sure it was real. It got closer, stumbling left almost off the moor into the sludge. Closer, Nito could see it was a girl, no older than sixteen. Her clothes were torn and dirty, her forehead bled. She collapsed into the dumpster across the dock.

"Oh fuck," Nito said.

"What?" asked Mama.

Nito pointed. "Some girl just died across the street."

Mama careened over, thrusting Nito aside with her bulk. "Does she look like a virgin? I could use a dead virgin."

11

Fatimah roiled under a heavy wool blanket, her mind foggy and turbulent. Her body jolted and thrummed out of control, healing too fast. Hook's herbs, the heth-bara, dulled nerves and increased cellular regeneration, but the mind remembered trauma. Three months healing would be finished by morn, but her brain felt the initial pain over and over until it was done, the shock of the fall.

In half-consciousness, she saw Polo stalk their tiny apartment. His cane tapped with each step. He muttered and murmured to himself, but she was too far gone to hear any of it. Probably just the usual hatred and bile Polo spit. She was coming back to reality in fragments. The chase on the bridge, that stupid spy girl, the witness. That cunt of a girl out there fucking up everything Fatimah had built these past four years. If Fatimah was here and Maharez wasn't, it meant she got away. The cunt.

Maharez, the stupid donkey, she loved him still at least as much as Fatimah's twisted moral compass could. She thought she loved him; he was her brother after all.

She was supposed to love him.

It was what was expected. But he was just a dense block of iron. He still thought they could escape the Cazaraati, a lie she fed him nightly. "Only another year, brother. Just one or two more cities, maybe five jobs and then we're out." He was unaware she had manipulated them into this prestigious position. Polo was top sweeper in the capitol, this was a place of honor by his side. Yes, Polo was a sadistic sociopath and scary at the best of times, but he didn't touch her. Not like the Turvaali slavers...

Stop, she told herself. That is weakness.

There is no fear, no hate, no love.

There is only power.

She repeated that until she calmed herself and pulled away from the slave galley. That part of her life was over. Now there was the Cazaraati and the opportunities it offered.

Five years. Five years' service they owed the Cazaraati crime syndicate after Maharez and Fatimah were rescued from the Turvaali slave galley. Once five years were up, Maharez thought they were out. But really they could start making money for their work. Hook pulled three thousand gold each job; gods above and below knew how much Polo took. Fatimah became a master manipulator on the slave galleys, once they'd broken her body and she realized it was a commodity. She used the same vagaries to pull through the Cazaraati ranks and now she was on the cusp of realizing her dream.

She would be top sweeper in Cruxia.

"Mortia's tits!" Polo shouted startling Fatimah. She cracked an eye and watched him through stripes of eyelashes. He gripped their dining table, white knuckles on his liver-spotted hands. "Nothing to be done about it, nothing at all. Shower of cunts. Everywhere I go, a shower of cunts." He took out a black candle at the table and lit it with a pitch-stick. Polo steepled his fingers and waited.

Cold. Absolute cold filled the tiny apartment. Fatimah's

lungs quivered with her first breath. The black candle burned harder, taking the light from the room the more it burned. It sent darkness into the corners, cold air following. Panic seized her, like drowning.

There was a presence in the room with her and Polo. Cold and bitter. She clenched her eyes shut. She had to physically think to stop her rectum from sputtering.

She half opened an eye, her long eyelashes a black curtain. Polo was but eight feet away at the table. The darkness in the room made him look hazy and small. Every breath she took froze the mucus in her nose.

"Hernsau Amadeus Polo. Your contact means failure," a voice shook out of the darkness. Fatimah clenched her eyes shut. The voice took her to the darkest recesses of the slave galley. Fatimah hated weakness, years ago had sworn it off, but here she was weak again.

Brought to her knees again.

The voice continued. "Your task draws unwanted attention. Even now your agents hunt in this city. Failure is unacceptable. This you know."

Polo wheezed. Through her curtain of eyelashes, Fatimah watched a small drop of blood coalesce from his left eye and drip down his pale cheek to the floor. "Yes."

"The Emperor is weakened. His agents lose ground in my war of words. Absolute control is almost in my hands."

Polo shook like a seizure. "Yes, Baron."

"Do not squander the trust I have placed in you."

Polo sneezed red mucus across the table. Twin tracks of bloody tears ran down his face. "Yes, Baron."

"You have one day. Twenty-four bells as of now."

Panic stole Polo's face. "But sixty-two hours still remain on the contract and—"

The darkness swelled; the cold took Fatimah's lungs to the

point of suffocation. "TWENTY-FOUR HOURS." The words were a cannon blast in their tiny apartment.

Polo screeched, black blood blasted from his nose, ears, his mouth. He collapsed to the ground, shaking.

"Twenty-four hours, Hernsau. Do not fail."

And the darkness was gone. Air returned warm and sweet to Fatimah's lungs. She gasped in breaths as Polo seizured on the floor.

He shook bad; his head cracked against the floorboards, his neck muscles scrunched in scary knots. Brown blood spattered from him in sneezes. Fatimah suddenly smelled the harsh reek of shit in the room. She clenched her eyes closed, wished it all away. For once she didn't want any part of the Cazaratti syndicate.

Slowly, with effort, Polo brought himself back from the seizure, crawled over the floor in small shudders. He pulled his half-mutated body across the room in bursts, bloody mucus dripped from his face and smeared on the floorboards.

He leaned up against Fatimah's couch. She could smell the shit from his trousers and her face scrunched.

"Eh?" he said in a bloody, snotty mess not two feet from her. "You're awake. I hope you heard all that. I hope you are not half the cunt your brother is. I hope you now understand the import of what we do. The cost."

Fatimah wanted to cry. She wanted to be back in Hanrabi with her mother. She wanted to brush the rice fronds with their oars and bring back enough food for the whole village.

But she was here in Cruxia. She was here with the Cazararatti, indentured to their work. Enslaved to murder. She was here in this small apartment that reeked of mold and pain, and now it reeked of shit because this Mole in front of her shit his pants.

And her mother was long dead.

She would never. Ever. Get what she had wanted.

She would never find peace. Not peace like her mother found. Drifting in the fronds.

Polo feebly smacked his cane against the floor, a farce of his normal tap-tap. "Do you understand it? The import of what we do?" Blood pooled at his chin and drip-dripped on the floor.

Fatimah started to cry.

There came two raps at the door. Hook and Maharez were back.

12

Roisin faltered as the waking world drifted loose around her. The gash over her eye stung and she felt dizzy, maybe a concussion and definitely an infection. She could get medicine if she had any money, maybe she could steal some. Her morality collapsed in the bewildered haze. The Crimson Moor loomed around her, usually terrifying, now just foggy.

Rickety cedar between nail-studded pylons, shacks on raised poles that swung in the light wind, toxic steam rising from the flotsam waste under the dock boards. Years ago, she and Garvis would play chicken, see how deep into the Moor they could manage before dashing back scared to the relative safety of the Mule. All sorts of wizards and Moles frequented the place, dark figures with furtive faces or drawn hoods.

The docks were crowded tonight as she limped to and fro, punch drunk and unsure what to do next. Pain radiated in rhythmic waves off her forehead, it kept her awake but made it impossible to reason. The pain in her forehead, the wet piercing in her foot where a piece of glass found itself, this impossible task of finding coin to buy voyage. This rat's nest her life gnawed to. Like in her free fall off the bridge, she just wanted it to end.

Out of the green-tinged steam, a figure formed. A man of fifty, his neck taken up by a slug-like growth the size of a pear. His teeth were yellow and his eyes a milky brown. Roisin called to him, "Oi, thousand gold for an eye, five hundo' for an ear. What'ya got, sir?"

Compassion flooded his miserable face. "Oh, you poor child."

Roisin laughed at him and danced away. She closed her eyes, for one moment she was back at the temple of Veridaan, dancing around a pole while her fellow orphans held white twine attached to its top. Father Alonso called to them in his comforting baritone and they all tried to sit at the same time but there not enough seats and it was so much fun and-

She stopped herself just one step from walking into the green sludge that radiated beneath the Moore. Her stitches screamed and screamed. Maybe a bit of rest would do her some good. She was in control of her dreams after all. If she was to sleep, she could control reality, take herself from this terrible place, if but for a moment. She was utterly in control of her dreams. Roisin needed control.

A nagging piece of her mind, that pragmatism she got from her mum, bit at her. Sleep now would be death. She had to stay awake if it was a concussion. Think of what the Mole's would do to her?

Sleep now and it can all be over. The thought was a blade, precise. There was a dumpster not ten feet away. *Throw yourself away with the rest of the garbage, Rose.*

Odd, only her dad called her Rose. She did in her journal too, but that was beside the point.

Sleep now, Rose.

The voice was hers – it was in her head after all – but it was also commanding like a father. It just made sense. Sure, sleep it

off. Rest would help, wouldn't it? She collapsed into the dump-ster; a sharp, wet, and stinking kind of sleep.

But to Roisin it felt like Veridaan's kiss. Praise be to the Siblings.

Amen.

———

Packed into the Gannon Hall, all four of them a sweaty mess, Hook looked up from where he'd sat for the past two hours. Fatimah slept on the couch, almost up to full strength. Polo stomped around, his cane smacking enough to bring three complaints from the innkeeper. Maharez sat in the corner feeling useless, like usual.

Finally, Hook sat up, his eyes opened. "I found her. Gave her a little push to sleep it off even. And get this, she's not a mile away."

Polo's knobby knuckles turned white as he strangled his cane. "Kill her. Take the boy."

"What if she's the Siegeward's girl? This could be a trap to draw us out," said Hook.

Polo sucked his tooth. Self-preservation was his only trait besides cruelty. If Hook was right there could be agents ready to strike feeble old Polo once he was alone with the disabled girl. That's how Polo would run the job, devour the weak first. "Fine, go alone. You should be more than capable of killing a teenager."

Hook geared up and went out softly into the night. It still amazed Polo a man that big could move that quietly. Polo watched Hook slip out the back door and stalk down the docks towards the Crimson. Worst case scenario he sent the man to his death and there was one less wizard to deal with in this fucking city full of them.

Rose's dream world was tarry and somehow wet. Once asleep, her spirit usually left her body, and she manifested an environment to her will. The control Father Alonso taught her all those years ago. *Control within begets control without,* his favorite of Veridaan's lessons. There is no better sense of self than the dream world, he told her. Everything in your dreams is a translation of your mind, a rendition of your soul.

But here there was darkness. All around. Her body shifted in the dumpster. Her soul screamed. She tried to fly, tried to gust off on the winds of her imagination. No avail. Something held her. She tried to walk instead, bleary and slow. With effort she put one foot in front of her, then dragged another, then another. Ever try to run in a dream? Up was left and down was right, a mess of broken rules.

Still, she trudged. Her father did not raise some weak little Mule wench. Her father...

No, no reason to broach that. No reason to feel more pain. But just the thought of her father brought the door.

She hated the door. Before her therapy with Father Alonso, before her dream control, there was always the same dream and the door. Darkness like the one around her, but the frame was visible in the gloom. She didn't know where she was, there was only the rectangle of grey light. The door. Something rustling too, in the dark. When she closed off all her other senses to focus on the door, she heard it. A light swishing noise. Almost imperceptible at first, but once realized it deafened her in the silence. It grew and grew until she could bear it no longer, she would go to the door and almost open it. But then came the knock.

Booming, terrifying. She wilted, assaulted by the two sounds. The rising swish-swish and the stentorian knock. Finally, the door would fly open and light would burn her eyes and skin and she would awaken screaming. Always the same dream as a child.

The door. The Door.

And here was the Door again. At the worst possible time. There was nowhere left for her; nowhere to run, nowhere to hide. So, of course, the Door would return. She heard the rustling.

No, please, no. Not now.

Swish-swish, swish-swish.

She turned to run, and it grew exponentially.

SWISH-SWISH. SWISH-SWISH-SWISH-SWISH!

She went to scream and something filled her mouth, as if the rustling noise could somehow have form, and she tried to spit but she gagged and gagged and started to vomit no food just bile and the rustling exited her and entered her and filled every orifice she had mouth eyes ears no no no no. She could not scream assaulted by the *swish-swish* crawling and she stumble-ran up right down left nightmare twisted she rolled on the ground. Never this bad, never never never never. In dream-soaked panic, she rolled up to the Door. It boomed, someone knocking. No no no no no, she did not want to die like this, she did not want to die, did not want to die—

Then arms around her. Someone pulled her out of the dark, out of the rustling, away from the Door. It shrunk in her vision, miles in seconds. It was just a pinprick in the dark. *KNOCK KNOCK* it boomed below.

And then she was in a dumpster. Coated in wet garbage, her physical form soaked in sweat. Some man dragged her from the dumpster. A broken bottle caught her calf and tore it as she went. She screamed.

"HELP. FIRE, FIRE. HELP."

"Fuck's sake," he said. He dropped her hard.

The grimy dock punched her face, she rolled away from the stranger. The stench returned her to reality. Wooden shanty shacks on poles, algae-coated pylons looming, toxic steam rising. The new pain in her nose and calf met the drudging pain of her forehead, her mind sharpened all the dreams gone.

"Who the fuck are you, then?" She slashed her stone dagger at him.

The man backed up and raised his hands. He was old but not ancient, black hair flecked in grey receded up his skull. He was a gaunt and tall white man with sharp cheekbones and nice clothes; handsome. The handsome ones were usually dangerous.

"I'm not trying to hurt you."

She leapt back a foot, swiping between them. "That's what any pervert would say."

"Ah, fuck," he rubbed his eyes. "Look, I'm a father."

"That's the next thing they would say."

He threw his arms up. "You aren't dead. Confirmed. I need this like a boat in the desert." He walked towards the last shack on the pier then turned back. "Just get out of here, you want to die or something? There's nicer dumpsters to sleep in, all I'm saying." He gave her a bow and turned away.

Rose's teeth scraped. Her jaw clenched. "Who are you?"

"Alistair Nito."

"Who?" She leaned against the dumpster. White spots danced in her vision. She didn't have much left.

"Nito." He raised his hands. "I saw you in that dumpster and wanted to make sure you're okay. You're okay so I'm going to leave. Rex?"

Rex. Her dad used to say that. "You better. I could mess you up." She swung her dagger and almost fell.

Nito swept in then stopped. "I don't need this, good luck. Try not to die. Whoever you are." He turned to enter a creepy shack.

"Whomever."

"Ah, fuck's sake. Really? Grammar?" Nito said and turned.

Then his shoulders straightened, his jaw bunched. His eyes shifted past her. He called down the docks. "Long time no see, Hook."

Another man came out of the gloom, bulky like a boxer. His steps made no noise, squelched nothing from the plankboards. Roisin's leg gushed fresh blood, stark red against the grey-green of the Moor. Hook stopped about forty paces from her facing Nito. The green steam stuck to him like a cloak.

"Didn't expect to meet a pro tonight," he said.

Nito didn't move, didn't blink. He kept his gaze level with Hook's. "Let's cut the shit, rex? You here on business? How's Baron Caz these days?"

Hook spit over the railing. "You know your shit."

"It pays to. I got no beef with the Cazaraati. I'm just out for a walk tonight. This is just a chance encounter. I be on my way, you be on yours."

Hook nodded. Roisin stumbled, pain screaming at her shoulder. Nito took a step towards her. Hook stepped forward and grinned. "We're at more of an impasse than that, soldier."

"How do you figure?" said Nito.

Hook pointed at Roisin, his face caught the toxic light. "She means nothing, rex? Nothing at all."

The voice gonged in her head. That man at the temple and her apartment room. Her vision righted itself for one clear moment and she saw him. The bulky killer who moved like mercury. Father Alonso's murder last night. Reality in a wave, she almost vomited.

Hook was what this stranger called him. Hook killed Father Alonso last night.

She wanted Hook to die. Her certainty silenced the Door.

Nito took three steps forward. "That's a problem, buddy."

"My job is to take care of problems. You told me that a long time ago."

"Too long ago."

Hook gave a sad smile. "Walk away, man, please."

"You can walk away, too. Not with the girl."

Twenty paces from both, Roisin watched them like a cobra. She bled freely from her leg, that was a problem. The murderer was here for her, but the stranger protected her. Why? He scared her more than Hook. Who the fuck was Nito? Did he want her? Always an angle in Cruxia.

Hook laughed, boomed his confidence across the Moor. "Ok, tough guy. Let's play tough then."

He twisted his fingers like the deaf did. A blue ball of energy appeared. Roisin squinted, it burned so bright.

Nito broke into a run. Roisin staggered towards the killer. Electric blue light lit Hook's grin, it shot tall shadows into the night sky. The ball rolled like a coin around his knuckles, it burned brighter, now the size of a fist.

Nito tried to grab Roisin, but she was too far ahead, rushing Hook with her stone knife. Hook aimed the spell at Roisin's face ten paces away.

A wet croak erupted from behind them, "Chock-taw hashimpa!"

Hook's ball of energy burst into a cloud of flies. Sudden buzzing around him, a million bites. "Ah, fuck, fuck." He swatted. Rose stopped at the guttural voice and Nito tackled her to what he thought was safety. They rolled in a heap across the coarse dockboards, away from Hook.

"Get off me," Roisin shouted. She twisted away and to her feet, fresh pain everywhere.

Hook stood still as the flies buzzed. Facing him was a nightmare creature, some bent-backed hag witch like in one of Roisin's fairy tales. Her face was covered by a burqa but a bright green eye stared out. "You trespass on my dock and attempt to steal my property."

The color drained from Hook's face. "No intention on

either, Mama. I'm here on the Baron's orders. I need that girl dead. Business, right?"

The flies buzzing were joined by scores more from the toxic bog. They didn't attack Hook, just hovered around him like an aura. "The girl is mine by scavenger rights, she decided to die in my dumpster," said Mama.

"I'm not dead," yelled Roisin.

Mama raised her hand. "Irrelevant."

Something slithered by Roisin's hand. She flinched from a centipede the same girth as her thumb. Nito shifted uncomfortably next to her as a train of insects ran around him. Dozens, hundreds, no, thousands. Creeping and crawling from under the dock, up the pylons, a flood of cockroaches out of the dumpster. For one nightmare moment, Roisin remembered the Door.

The pestilence surrounded Hook in the middle of the dock. His eyes played over them and Mama. "I'm not looking to start trouble here, Mama. Just doing my job."

The insect mass grew into one chittering carpet, a roiling nightmare tensing closer and closer around Hook's feet. He stepped back but it was all around him. "Leave this place, dabbler. What you do in the rest of the city concerns me not. But here, Mama Roeneck is law." The swarm surged, congealing into one giant insect shape that snapped at Hook. Then they crashed back into the chitinous horde circling his feet. One gap opened in the circle – north, out of the Crimson Moor.

Hook sighed and backed up through the gap. "Ok, Mama, territory claimed. Heard and received. The Baron won't be happy, you've made a powerful enemy tonight."

"Tell your Baron I'll bite his cock off after the best head he's ever had," Mama said. Rosin laughed.

Hook backed up, never breaking eye contact. About sixty

paces away he turned to Nito. "You're dead, soldier. No hard feelings."

They all watched him walk off, boots clacking. He raised his hand in a lazy wave just as the mists enveloped him. Mama Roeneck farted, and the insects broke apart in mindless normalcy. Nito scrambled to his feet, suddenly in their way.

"Mortia's twat. I fucking hate bugs, Mama."

She glared at him with her twisted eye. "Lucky for you so did that wizard." She reached behind her and a jar full of orange powder flew out of the shack at the end of the dock. She caught it and thrust it into Nito's arms. "Now, fuck off with your drugs and your dead girl and get off my dock. Fight your own battles, Nito. Away, shoo."

Roisin stamped her foot. "Sweet Veridaan, what is going on? Who are either of you? I'm not going home with a dealer."

Mama swiveled and lurched over to Roisin, her gait was spider-like and too fast for her size. "You are more than welcome to stay with me, dead girl. Are you a virgin?" Roisin wilted.

Nito stepped in between them. "I'm no dealer, just an innkeeper. You don't have to come with me, but I have supper and clean rooms. You could use both."

Roisin, still holding her dagger in defense, looked from the rakish Nito to the amorphous Mama Roeneck. "I'll take my chances alone."

"You will die then, dead girl."

"Stop calling me that."

"That wizard is no slouch. Just what did you do to pull the ire of the Corpse Baron, I wonder?"

"Who?" said Roisin.

"Do you like your dreams, dead girl? Because that wizard does." Then she cackled so loud it scared away some seagulls.

Hook bashed the door open to the room in Ganon Hall. Maharez shot up with his curved blade then sat down again. Fatimah sipped black tea at the table, venom in her eyes like usual. Polo's pockmarked face grinned.

"Did you kill the cunt?" he asked.

"No dice," said Hook.

Polo screeched. He took up his cane and smashed the candleholders on the wall, then he spent his rage on the couch. The three watched as the little man-thing broke the frame and beat the stuffing out of the cushions. He turned to Hook with bloodshot eyes.

"And just why the fuck not? Eh?"

Hook hung his cape on the wall and sagged his bulk onto a chair. From a pouch at his belt, he took a little vial of powder and three glass flasks of orange gel. "Mama Roeneck happened."

Polo took a step back. The Mole feared magic more than anything in the world. Mama's was ancient and terrible. "What does that mean?"

Hook looked up. "It means you gotta tell Baron Caz the Crimson is off limits. Her territory. Official."

"And?" He smacked his cane on the floor. "The girl?"

"Heh, we're lucky there. She got herself a white knight. You remember Alistair Nito?"

Polo's eyes danced, he most certainly did.

"Well, he owns an inn down near the Mule. Right at the end of Wharf." Hook kept unpacking: a pitch-stick, three black masks. "How you feeling, Fatimah?"

"Fuck you."

"Good enough. Get your stuff. We're gonna pull a burn."

13

Gantry Willow could not find a clean place to sit. Inspector General Sternwood tapped her foot and glanced at the lowering sun through the filthy window. The office of the Lamplighter's Guild was crammed full of scrolls and ledgers, splayed out everywhere like some crook cut the building's throat and it bled only paper. Normally his favorite smell, Willow's nose wrinkled at the moldy, mistreated books. Dozens of hourglasses ran around the room on a shelf, none of them recording the same time. Pitch-sticks and sandpaper bracelets sat in a lockbox on the main counter. Willow and Sternwood had been waiting the better part of an hour.

A dirty child no older than ten zoomed in, removed their bracelet and slipped it through a slot on the lockbox. He monkeyed up a stool to reach the top shelves and flipped a rosewood hourglass just as the last sands dropped. He finally saw the two City Watch standing in the middle of the room and almost fell off the stool out of shock.

He pointed to the hourglass, "All on the up and up, no trouble. I work here. Honest."

Gantry wanted to give the kid a silver piece, or even just a loaf of bread. But he was also on the verge of panic at the thought of touching something so filthy. "What's the hourglass for?" he asked, stalling.

"That's my shift, I run the butcher block in the Mule. Start at fifth bell and need to get all my lamps lit before them sands drop. Once it runs all the way down again the douser will go out next morn to cover them. We're called oilers, us who work the lamps. They don't trust us with the candles. Look, am I in some sort of trouble?"

The kid was talking faster and faster, a common effect of the badge. Sternwood raised her hand. "We have some questions for your supervisor, no one is in trouble."

"Ok, well, glad I could help." The kid shot out of the cramped office in a flopping run.

Sternwood watched him run past the front window. "Did you have any trouble getting the time off?" she asked. It was offhand but also the first either made mention of their clandestine operation. Technically they hadn't done anything wrong. Yet. But if the Inquisitor's office heard they were investigating a closed case it would start a political landslide that would see them out of a job.

Probably in irons. Willow shivered.

"Not really. I've accrued time off since my assignment to you, we don't ever take a break."

"That's because—"

"—this city doesn't sleep and neither can we."

She turned to him, "I know you are taking on more than is expected. One bad solve by the Inquisitors is a fluke, two could be a problem in the chain of command. Three though, that's conspiracy." Her cold stare warmed, a sad smile that didn't fit her face. "But you're risking your career for me. That means more than I can say."

Willow dreamed of this moment, imagined dreary paperwork away playing scenes like this in his head. Her sad smile, her cold eyes melting, a sheen of sweat across her perfect brown brow. He would lean in and press the small of her back, just so, and she would melt in his arms and...

But he was Gantry Willow; weak and nervous, and scenes like that were for his cock at night and no one else. He sighed and took a half step back, rubbing his hands too hard. "It was nothing, Sariah, nothing at all." He changed subjects before heating up too much. In truth, time spent with Sariah Stern-wood was torture, but what was a life without her? "You're saying Father Alonso is a cover-up? What about the other two?"

"First was Jorgen Halfstaat, a bookkeeper for the docks district. Well-known philanthropist, loved by the community, father of eleven. Inspector Vargus called me in to consult. No suspects, no evidence, no reason why anyone would want him dead."

"What about sorcerous evidence?"

She took out a notebook from her belt pouch. "Murder took place at Brimly and Keppler."

"Oh, sweet Veridaan. The orphanage arson," he said.

"Exactly. The wizard on duty couldn't pull emotions from his read. Too much interference from all the dead children." Gantry Willow shivered. It could drive an empath insane, the cries of the dead. "Halfstaat's neck was slit with a standard knife, but his defensive wounds came from a curved blade. That was the first raid of Little Hanrabi looking for Turvaali."

"Turvaali, what would chain cultists be doing this side of the sea?"

"Precisely. Here, more recent." She flipped through her notebook. "Two months ago, Earl Gunther's assistant died in similar circumstances. Neck slit with a straight blade, curved blade marks all over. Curiously, Earl Gunther was to vote for a Citywatch levy but ended up voting it down in Parliament."

Things clicked in Willow's brain. "Gods above and below,

the man died to put pressure on the Earl. Bookkeeping at the docks, blackmail in Parliament..."

"And now a High-Father dead," she finished. "Someone is escalating their agenda. This is not mere Turvaali terrorism. It's far too specific. What slave to the Chain God knows the inner workings of our government? This must be a syndicate. I know it."

Willow wanted to vomit again. Everywhere. Investigating a botched case was one thing. Uncovering an imperial conspiracy was three hells of another. He started breathing too fast.

And then the door flew open banging a shelf of scrolls so hard they spilled across the floor. "Ah, Mortia's left tit, who the fuck left my office in such a way? I swear to the god of all fucks, if it was you Homer, I'll plant my boot so far up your ass, you'll be—" The man twisted and saw Willow and Sternwood, off duty but still in uniform. "Well, to what do I owe the pleasure this evening, ya' fine sirs and madams?" He reached out with a filthy hand the size of a ham sandwich. "Name's Yorrick, at your service."

The Lamplighter Guildmaster was a heavy white man of forty. Bald but for the long hair around the back of his head, his nose sat like a squashed turnip. Yet he smelled like cinnamon toast. He took their hands in a meaty squash then pushed behind his desk with a grunt.

"I ain't got no chairs, not even for myself, so sorry. Spend most time standing, or walking lanes to make sure my wards are sticking to their schedules."

"Your wards?" asked Sariah. She moved up to the desk and leaned.

"Ah," he raised a hand, "my employees, what have you. You get a little sentimental in this gig if you do it long as I have. Start seeing these whelps like they were your own, ayuh." He leaned past his desk, looking out his front window. "Oi, Homer! Yeah, I'm talking to you."

Outside, a filthy kid froze in the street where he was talking to a blushing flower girl. Yorrick roared, "I pay you to light lamps, not some flop's cooter. Get your ass to it, huh?" He turned back to the inspectors, all smiles. "Now what is it I can be helping you with?"

"We are part of an ongoing investigation, we would ask your cooperation as is stated in the Imperial Guild Act, part 5, section—"

The Guildmaster nodded his head. "I know the procedures, ayuh. Lay it on me then."

Gantry stepped up, perhaps if he was to ask the off-the-record questions, he could protect Sternwood from the inevitable backdraft. "We need information from your guild. Specifically, the employee rosters assigned to the Gods' Way last night."

Realization dawned on the man, his brow smoothed. "Ayuh, ayuh. Nasty times seeing the High-Father murdered and all that." He walked over to a shelf bursting in scrolls and pulled out a leather ledger. "You guys back for the official records or something? I already told the first crew this stuff before the evening came about."

Sariah's body straightened as if shocked. "Excuse me?"

Gantry grabbed her arm and squeezed. "Exactly, sir, hence the formality. We ensure the chain of evidence is accounted for." He was amazed at how easy it was to lie. Gantry Willow had never tried it before. "The first crew filed no report, didn't come back to headquarters. You can imagine the mess it left for us." Willow tried on a grin his father would've called shit-eating.

Yorrick laughed, a throaty one that rumbled his belly. "Gods above and below, sir, that's the story of my life." He swept an arm around his office. "Paperwork and paperwork, enough to bury me, but do any of these little shits listen? No, sir, not at all. They scurry around like there ain't a care in the world; meanwhile, we have to fuckin' account for everything, don't we just? Pardon my language, madame."

"Not at all, I'm sure," said Sternwood. She looked uncomfortable. Gantry marked this as the only time in his entire life he felt relaxed and natural, and she stepped the foot awkwardly.

"So," said Gantry leaning in himself, "what of this work ledger?"

"Right," said Yorrick, "we have six candlelighters on the Gods' Way each night, but only one assigned to Her Sacrament of Veridaan. She's a little fairyfire too, I tell you. Shame about all this business. Here," he tore a page from the ledger, "her name's Roisin." He passed them the paper. "She can even write her own name, Siblings bless her."

Sariah took the page and read; the information was basic. Name: Roisin. Origin: Cruxia, East End, Mule Quarter. And so on. "What's her surname?" she asked.

"Uh, all my apologies, madame, but you don't get a lot of surnames down here in the Mule."

Gantry's head gonged. Roisin. Where had he heard that name before? It was common enough out near the Horn Forest, but you didn't meet a lot of Roisins in the capitol.

Sariah folded up the paper and stored it. "Now, about the first officers to come in. Anything you can tell us about them? HQ will want to know for reprimands."

"Ayuh, I got you. Fine the bastards their bonus pay you ask me. Gods, there are reasons for all this paperwork, ain't there?"

"Cornerstone of civilization," chimed in Gantry.

"Right?" said Yorrick. "It was two of 'em. The one in charge was big, square jaw and buzzcut like a solider. Other one was Hanrab, like you madame. Nice to see you all in the outfit. My second wife hailed from Hanrabi, and she was the best woman I've ever known, Siblings watch over her. Amen."

Sairiah wrote it down in a small notebook and thanked the

man, Gantry was still thinking. Roisin, Roisin, where did he know that name?

"Thank you, Guildmaster, your service is noted by the Citywatch and the Empire," she saluted, one closed fist to the left shoulder.

He returned it with a sense of civic pride, "Ayuh, madame. Good luck to both of you. I sure hope Roisin is ok in all this. I was heated when she didn't show for check-in, but now with all this nastiness I just hope she's ok. She's not in trouble, is she?"

"Her safety is our greatest concern," lied Gantry. And they left into the bustling heat of the East End.

"How many constables on the East End are Hanrab?" asked Sternwood. She took a silver flask from her instrument pouch and sipped.

"None," said Willow. She offered the flask, but he shook his head. Willow felt alive, he finally felt like an inspector in truth, not just some failed wizard and pencil pusher. No need to cloud his judgement.

"My thoughts exactly. A conspiracy is afoot."

"Oh, fuck me sideways," snapped Gantry. Sariah shot him a look. Gantry thought 'shit' was the most a man could cuss.

"What?"

"Roisin. I knew that name from a long while back. Roisin the Beau they used to say."

"What are you talking about?"

"It's a Citywatch myth, Roisin the Beau. It was a story our drill instructor scared us with. I can't even remember the gist of it."

She shook her head. "We aren't investigating hoodoo and hocum."

"I know, I know. Roisin the Beau's an old story, but it's a case on file."

"That won't help. We can't go to headquarters without showing our hand."

"We won't have to. My drill instructor was Harven. He told the story so often because it happened to his partner. An old dog, Henry Gilliam."

"I know the name. The man's been retired for most of the decade."

"He's a regular at the Red Crow off the market district. Come one, Sternwood, we might have a lead."

———

The Red Crow: an old Citywatch bar on the clean side of the Merchant District, close enough to the docks that you'd get the occasional sailor. Sina O'Henry's great-grandfather was City Watch and he built the pub after retiring. Four generations of City Watchmen and innkeeper women after that. Sina was a tough old nut, and she never needed a bouncer with a bar full of constables.

The place was made of granite bricks with a thatched roof; in other words, it was too pricey for Gantry Willow most nights. Plus, it was a good three-mile walk from his Mule adjacent apartment. Inside was lit for early evening, a half dozen constables and retired veterans clumped in corner booths.

Gantry never felt this way, in control. For once he caged his anxiety. Insecurities blown to the wind, replaced by white-hot confidence. He chased a conspiracy that could run all the way up to the Inquisition, plus he had the world's most beautiful woman at his side. Gantry finally felt like the man his parents thought him to be, a hero of the Inspector's Office. No, hero of the Empire. "There. Gillam." He pointed to the shadowed side of the bar and a doughy old drinker.

Next to him, Sternwood felt as uncomfortable as she had in the Lord Inspector's office. This was an old City Watch pub, quite a few miles from Little Hanrabi and worlds away. She was used to this feeling from her teenage years; enter an establishment, everyone looks, everyone scowls, everyone goes back to their business with a little bit of hate behind their eyes. She crossed to the bar and ordered a double Steel Coast and a black porter. Sina gave her a neutral smile, but Sternwood could tell the woman didn't want her there agitating the regulars.

Gantry joined her. "Oh, no thanks. I don't need a drink."

She gave him a look, then tipped her whole double and took a slug from the porter. "I wasn't offering. But if you're looking for information from an old dog, you better buy him a couple and keep up with him."

"What about you?"

"I'm going to sit here and try not to drink too much. You're running this lead."

Willow started to turn red. Anxiety rattled its cage. "But... but what do I do?"

"Do what you're best at, what I'm shit at. Be nice. People like you."

"Right, strike up a conversation. Sure."

"And buy him a drink."

"Of course, of course. Barmaid? Two pints of the Janoe lager, please. Thank you so much."

Sariah watched Willow tip too much, then carry his sloshing glasses over to the end of the bar where the old constable sat flipping peanut shells. The man looked like every retired constable in the city; still kept the crew cut, thick in the middle, and a bad drinking problem. Sternwood looked at her porter, almost gone in less than three minutes. Then she looked up at her haircut in the mirror over the taps.

Fuck if she wasn't two-thirds there already.

Things must be in flux, she was introspective. She never had time to think about herself in regular times. Her whole life had been a drive forward. More, keep going, do better, do better than that. No, better than that. She didn't remember much of Hanrabi, just endless brown deserts and the smell of spice. Her stepfather took her to Cruxia when she was six and she recalled the ship more than the province. Sternwood treated her as his daughter, but the city didn't share the sentiment. He acknowledged it only once when she came back from primary school bloodied and beaten. She sobbed to him the terrible names they called her, the awful things they said. He sat down on his knee, looked her in the eye, and said, "Things will never be easy for you here. You will have to work ten times harder than any of those fools and they'll still only credit you for half of what some stupid Crusa kid can do. Always be better, always strive harder. They can hate you but they can't stop you. Only you can do that."

Sternwood's reminiscing took up another Steel Coast double and two more porters. They were heavy and boozy, and she drank them fast enough to have a stomach ache. She failed her only mission here, don't get drunk. At the end of the bar, Willow bent over in deep conversation with Henry Gilliam, the retired constable. Willow came into his own once the yoke of bureaucracy lifted. Ironic for a man who dated his shirts after laundry.

Ten minutes later and another porter, Willow returned. He looked as if he'd just drowned a hamster. Sternwood realized he also looked a little like a hamster. She stifled a laugh. Too many drinks, her great weakness.

"What did you get from him? Was this a waste of time?"

Willow shook his head, then ordered a double Steel Coast from Sina.

"I'm good, Gantry, I don—" She stopped as Willow tipped the whole shot back and swallowed with a grunt.

"I found out more about this Roisin. Shit, I can't tell what it means. She might be the killer; I wouldn't discount it."

"Fuck's sake." She smacked the bar a touch too hard. "Out with it, man."

"Roisin was orphaned at age seven. Her mother died in

childbirth, her father was a schoolteacher who died of the wasting seven years later. She was taken to the Sacrament of Veridaan and raised there until age fourteen when she was legally released. High-Father Alonso was her guardian."

"There's our fucking connection then. Though it's a leap to say she killed Alonso."

"Yeah," said Gantry, "but it's the circumstances of her dad's death that earned her the name Roisin the Beau. Henry Gilliam, that poor old dog. He was the officer that found her."

"What are you getting at?"

Gantry Willow told her the story straight from the dog's mouth, not the report. Sariah Sternwood ordered them both another drink.

———

Time passed as Sternwood drank and Willow questioned. The night dragged itself to Citywatch shift change and the lamp-lighters flocked to the posts. The pub saw a surge. Medicer Inspector Vincezzo stalked in like a vulture, his standard stop three nights out of the week. A university man, he didn't find many kindred spirits in Citywatch, but Sina O'Henry was an old family friend and he could get away with a free glass of Valais wine or two. Vincezzo was a miser first, everything else second.

It was an interesting day, starting out with his report on the dead High-Father, a report he falsified, and ending with his signature for the death warrant of three Hanrabi youths accused of murder and high treason. A farce, of course, but what were three more black kids off the street? Gods knew there were more where they came from. Yes, his purse jangled pleasantly, filled to bursting by the Cazzaratti syndicate. Accounts paid for his work in the cover-up. His fifth payment and by far the largest. Vincezzo felt, how would his grandson say it? Ah, yes, electric.

That is until he saw Sternwood and Willow at the bar, drunk and speaking too loud. He snuck into a side table and listened. His ulcer flared so hard he bit his tongue.

They were talking about exactly what they shouldn't be talking about.

14

Nito's hands sweat, the jar of orange powder slipped this way and that. That would be rex, huh? Let's just drop a million gold worth of kax, flood the market. Literally. He chuckled as they passed through the Merchant District and into Docks. He kept his collar up and his eyes out for patrols. His heartbeat picked up. Same old game.

"What could be so funny?" Roisin asked from behind him.

He almost jumped. Fuck, he forgot she was there. "Nothing, it's nothing." He held the entire city's kax supply and his head was still foggy from Mama Roeneck's harsh smoke. If a constable saw him now, he would be crucified. That was the punishment for drug traffic in the city. Plus, he had a teenage girl with him. Why had he stepped up to help her like an idiot?

Because it was the right thing to do.

Where did that fucking come from? Alistair Nito never did the right thing. He made a living out of the wrong thing back in the long ago and these days he sold drinks and rooms to people just like him. He was nobody's knight. Just ask his daughter.

They turned onto Skelton Boulevard.

"Once we get past Docks, I can make my way down to the Mule. You don't need to take me all the way," said Roisin.

"Do you know who that was back there?"

"Murderers," she said, "common enough in Cruxia. And he knew you, so I'd rather not follow you home." She was tough, or she talked tough at least.

He whirled on her, but the momentum carried the jar almost out of his hands. The intimidation lost its oomph as he juggled it on slick fingers. "That was Hook, one of the most ruthless sweepers for the Cazzaraati."

"What's the Cazzaraati?"

"Auron's blue balls."

"Watch your language." She made a sign of Veridaan over her chest.

"He was trying to kill you, who cares about language? Gah." Nito rubbed his headache. "The Cazzaraati are the third richest House in parliament, they control the trade lanes to Hanrabi as well as the Steel Coast contracts with Vohlkhan. They're the largest criminal syndicate in the world."

Roisin paled a touch, but her jaw didn't waver. "That doesn't mean anything to me."

"It means there is nowhere in the world you can hide. Juno's sake girl, what did you do?"

"Why couldn't I stay with Mama?"

"Because she would fucking eat you."

"What's your name?"

"Alistair Nito." They were walking fast past the flower beds. Citywatch two blocks away were visible by their torches. Nito kept a circuit that would avoid them but the road was empty. They were exposed.

"Why are we going to your bar if they know who you are?" she said.

"I need to gather some things and let my staff know, I can't just disappear."

"What do you need all that kax for?" she asked, pointing.

"It's for a-wait. What the fuck? You're not interrogating me here, ok? It's the other way around."

"Are you convincing me or yourself?"

Why? Why did you save this girl, Alistair Nito? "I want to help you. Call me old fashioned but I don't think a little girl should tangle with the syndicates all by herself. There's cheaper ways to kill yourself."

"Why does it matter that I'm a girl?"

"Because you're a kid. You're just a kid."

"I saw Father Alonso die," she said abruptly. Roisin hadn't said it out loud yet. Her eyes got heavy and blurry. "They killed Father Alonso. At his own pulpit. That Hook and two teenagers stabbed him. So, so many times. All the while this Mole watched from the pews. They killed him and there was blood everywhere and then they chased me and chased me and—" Her tough act finally split. Hearing it all out loud, speaking it with her own words, made it real. She finally stopped running long enough to catch her breath.

It was better to run. You didn't have to deal with anything if you just ran.

In the back of her mind, the door reappeared. KNOCK, KNOCK, KNOCK. She fell down sobbing. Sobbing like some weakling. Just a stupid Mule wench after all.

Mortia's twat, Nito. Now what the fuck was he supposed to do? He'd missed all this with his own daughter. Kids were not in his wheelhouse. He stood there over her for a good three minutes. "Do you— do you want something to eat?"

"Do I want something to eat?" she asked between snotty sobs. "What would that solve? Why would that help?" She laughed and popped a snot bubble from her nose.

"Shit, I don't know. I don't drink anymore so food helps when I get down. You could have some of this, maybe?" He held up the jar of kax.

"Siblings, you're joking."

"Whatever helps, can we keep moving?"

"Fine," she stood up. She couldn't tell if this guy was a degenerate or a jester. But he didn't seem dangerous. Not like Hook and the others. She was empty. The pain was there, but the catharsis cored her out. She would focus the pain into action. Alonso taught her that. "Paint that pain on a canvas, jot it down on parchment, play it on a harp. It can kill you or you can use it," he would say.

They cut through some alleys and a backroad, a tight one where shops dumped their slosh buckets. Twin canals ran along the side to take the refuse to the sewers, it all reeked. But not as bad as the Mule. There weren't piles of garbage leaned a story high against the walls; this district had trawlers. Work crews of prisoners and Moles that dragged the garbage to Siblings knew where.

They popped back onto Skelton Boulevard where it bisected Lettle Avenue. Nito's tavern sat crooked, sunk half a story into the street like some drunk turtle. A creaky wooden sign claimed "SPIRITS." There was nothing else to note.

"This is it?" Rosin asked.

"This is it," said Nito with a warm smile.

He took a step towards it when the clank of boots moved in on them. Lots of heavy, metal boots coming from three directions of the crossroads. Nito set the jar down and moved in front of it, he pushed Roisin behind him close to the bar. "Careful. Stay close."

"I don't think you'll make much difference," she said, pointing. Four squads of armored men came at them.

"Thanks, kid."

Closer Nito saw the gleam of polished blue steel and gold trim. A platoon of Auric Guard, Salavar's stormtroopers. The armor was heavier than Citywatch could afford. Chainmail hung around their necks and knees. Great helms covered their faces but for six vertical slits over their eyes. The first four in each squad held a shield taller than the Roisin girl and a broadsword. The fifth in each held a wide greatsword up in attack position.

"Hey, boys, we all rex tonight?" asked Nito.

A lieutenant the size of a rhino walked up and spoke. His voice came muffled and metallic through the greathelm. "By order of the holy High-Father Salavar, chosen of Auron and protector of life, you and current company are remanded to his care."

"Whoa there, soldier, that's a lot of words." Nito craned his neck around, no Citywatch. No one else on the street, nor any for three blocks come to think of it. Fuck, did the churches like throwing their weight around. "Tell Salavar I've got his package, and I will be there in two bells' time. I just got home, I need a shit and a shave, and this girl needs dinner."

The lieutenant took a step forward and the squads closed in around them. The uniform clank of metal got Nito's heart hammering faster. He did not like knights, especially church knights. "Negative. The High-Father was clear on this matter. He was quite...distressed about it. You and your ward are to come with me. Effective immediately"

"Or what?" asked Nito.

Roisin watched from behind Nito, confused. All her life church knights were friends and protectors. The Legio Verdant, Veridaan's knights, patrolled the orphanage and watched the children as they played out in the city. They fought off kidnappers and scared off the Moles when they got too close to the students. She remembered one, Hollister, who always had an acorn for each kid every time he was on duty. She always thought about the time he must've spent collecting those acorns.

But these knights were scary, why did they need to approach with those big swords raised? She had seen the Auric

Guard before, but only in passing from the gates. They never waved.

She tugged at Nito's coat. "I don't want to go with them."

"I don't either. Look, soldier, I understand you have your orders. What else does a soldier have in this world?"

The squads stopped hemming them in. "I appreciate that," said the Lieutenant.

"So," said Nito, "I'll give you what my great-granddad gave the Empire's best." Nito forked both of his thumbs up and flicked them, the common sign for 'up your fucking bum' in Cruxia.

The Lieutenant stomped his foot; it echoed in the empty streets. "First and second squads, flash," he yelled. The east and west encroaching squads lifted their shield as one and brought them to the cobblestones with a bang. Static-charged sorcery built between the shields and exploded blue-white light. Blinded, Nito tripped over the jar as he scrambled to cover his eyes. Roisin made it three staggering steps before she ran into a trash can and hit the ground in a clatter.

"Nice move," she yelled at Nito in the cacophony of armor. Someone grabbed her rough from the collar like you would a cat.

"I'm fucking full of them!" Nito shouted back before a boot caught him in the face and knocked out his consciousness along with two teeth.

Roisin screamed. She screamed everything Gantry taught her growing up in the Mule. "Never shout rape," he'd tell her. "No one gives two fucks about it. Yell fire, yell robbery, yell property damage, Citywatch will always care about property damage."

"Fire," she shouted, "fire, fire, the blocks going to burn." Still blind, she tried to bite the hand that grabbed her. Her teeth scraped on his armor.

"Gods be fucked, this little bitch is pissing me off." The

knight shoved something in her mouth. Cotton soaked in metallic chemical. Its vinegar reek punched her mind all the way down, down, down, down into darkness.

From the deep, she heard a KNOCK. KNOCK, KNOCK and the slithering whispers.

15

Polo paced around the small apartment. He kicked aside the fluff from the couch and its splintered frame. His cane cracked the broken glass he'd smashed. "Shower of cunts," he muttered under his breath, finishing his circuit before starting it over.

In the kitchen, Fatimah and Maharez packed their belts with small capsules of combustibles. Hook held one up to the flickering candlelight, it was the size of his thumb, a wooden tube with a hinged lid. "We used to call this fairyfire back in the Mage Corp. Shit will burn anything: stone, flesh, bone, even in the rain. Don't get it on you, and don't get it any closer than this to flame until you're ready."

"What did you use it on?" said Maharez.

Hook grimaced. "Cities, when we were lucky."

The kitchen was clean, cleaner than the rest of the inn. Hook kept it that way, old army habits. Keep your kitchen clean and boil your water. Hook cooked most of their meals, the food was the only part of the job Maharez liked. But all the spices, vegetables, and meat were packed away in the cold box. The tools were out across the counters and table.

A curtain pick, rake picks, bump keys, glass cutter, piano wire, small length or rope, long loop of rope, grappling hook, black sweaters, black socks, black knit caps, and the fairyfire tucked away in six wooden tubes. Hook wore his long army knife. Fatimah sharpened her curved blade. She looked haggard but healthy. Hooks herbs worked wonders.

Hook went on, "We're going to find the entrances and start the burn there, it will keep everyone hemmed in and increase panic. Doors first, then under the windows. Pour a little but don't light it until the signal. Once lit get going fast or—" He stopped and put a hand up. "Someone is here."

There was a knock at the door. Polo looked at Hook, Hook shook his head and put his finger to his mouth. Fatimah and Maharez moved out of the kitchen and along opposite walls in silence. Hook waited until they flanked the door, then crossed over creaking every floorboard along the way. He put his left hand behind his back and weaved a tiny spell of static black energy around his index finger.

"Who is there?" asked Hook. Twenty seconds had passed.

"Inspector Vincezzo, Medicer's office first rank."

Maharez almost bit his tongue. This was it, the wheel of stars finally caught up with him. Here was Halladar's judgement in the form of the Inspectors. He would be crucified. As he should.

Polo signaled to Hook in their sign language, "Who?"

"The coroner," said Hook out loud. "Disengage," he signed to the siblings.

"Yes, the bloody coroner. Would you let me in?" Hook opened the door and Vincezzo stalked in with vim. "Neither of our employers would be happy to see this clandestine meeting. A death sentence for all of us." His beady eyes lingered on the Hanrab siblings, mouth wrinkled in contempt. "But fates worse than death await us if we don't." He turned to Hook.

The four criminals stood in the destroyed living room

forming a loose circle around the medicer inspector. "Can it with the theater, what the fuck are you talking about?" asked Hook.

"Our cover blown, that's what I'm talking about."

Polo cleared his throat and spat a grey wad of mucus at Vincezzo's feet. Hook hated when he did that, wouldn't allow it in the kitchen. "Cover? Who the fuck do you think you are? You speak of death sentences as if you will leave this place alive."

"I report to the Inquisitor directly, only in matters related to the Cazaraati family and the protection of their name and seal. I'm the silver line that shifts the ledgers away from your exploits. I'm the doddering doctor that keeps you sad excuses for men from hanging on the walls where I'm sure you belong. That cover. And it is in danger."

Polo smacked Vincezzo stumbling down with his cane.

"You would dare," said Vincezzo, pulling a rapier from under his cloak.

Hook put up his hands and stepped between them. "Ok, ok, we are all on the Baron Caz's payroll, which makes us coworkers by convenience. Let's be friends here."

Vincezzo stood up with just his legs, keeping the blade level as he did. Maharez was impressed, an old man but a great fencer. "We are most certainly not friends," he sheathed his blade, "but we are also aware of the Baron's wrath and the length of his... influence."

The criminals relaxed, backing up and giving the coroner space to walk into the small apartment. He lifted his nose and threw back his tailcoat, Vincezzo the Vulture in full. "Now, two members of the Inspector's office, including an Inspector General, are sniffing around the circumstances of the High-Father's death. Specifically following a lead on a young Candle-lighter who may or may not have been in the temple at the time of the murder."

Hook's face went grey, Fatimah spat curse words in five

languages, Maharez bit his tongue. Polo stood perfectly still while his sphincter puttered.

Vincezzo continued, "I'm assuming she was there given the gravitas I witness around me."

"Fuck you," said Polo.

"Tell me," Vincezzo steepled his long, thin fingers, "is the little bitch dead?" He enjoyed the power shift in the room.

"Not yet," said Hook.

Polo hissed at him.

"Oh, come off it, we've spent a night and a day chasing that girl to no avail. This Grey here doesn't want the heat raining any more than we do."

Vincezzo leaned forward and glanced in the kitchen and the tools assembled on the table. "Are you planning on another assassination before the loose ends are dealt with from the previous one?"

"The girl is with an old sweeper, Alistair Nito. We were gonna hit him tonight."

"I don't know the name."

Hook waved a hand. "He's a nobody, retired for years. Long out of the Baron's good graces. But Inspectors bring a lot of heat. I thought your offices dealt with the cover; no constables, no investigation, that's what the Baron pays for."

"Believe you me, the accounts are falsified and the culprits hang from the city walls. All channels are paid or duped. I'm very good at what I do. This Inspector General is a hound dog, breaking protocol and direct order. A mongrel, some upstart sand-born bitch adopted by a decorated general and raised far, far beyond her means. She has a useless little man as her assigned wizard, a practitioner of empathetic magic."

Hook snorted. "A woman's magic, he shouldn't be a problem."

Vincezzo looked around, Polo was close enough, listening and cursing under his breath. Fatimah and Maharez had moved to the kitchen and whispered to each other, looking down at the wharf below. "Well?" asked the vulture of a man.

Hook dragged his hand down his face. "Ok, ok. Fuck. Ok. Ok, ok, ok. Look, ok. What can I work on with these Inspectors?"

Vincezzo nodded and pulled an envelope from his cloak, it was stamped with red wax, the Inquisition's seal. "This is everything."

Hook nodded and stood up. He dominated the tiny living room with his bulk. "Fatimah, Maharez, take a few hours. Smoke 'em if you got 'em"

Fatimah cursed, "What about the burn, old man?"

Hook picked up the envelope, slit the wax with a fingernail. "I need to invite a couple more guests. Vincezzo, stick around a bit until I have more than a silk skin of a plan."

16

Gantry and Sternwood walked down Skelton Boulevard under the flickering lamplight. Tenth bell and two full hours of canvassing turned up nothing. Gantry was beginning to lose the gumption he'd found earlier. Here there be anxiety. Were they exposed? Sure felt like it. What if it was the two of them that ended up swinging on those walls by the neck?

"You are lost in thought," said Sternwood.

Gantry leaned against the flowerbed that bisected the road. He rubbed his eyes and cleaned his spectacles, "Just getting tired is all, a lot of walking today." Not to mention a dawn murder scene, a funeral for the High-Father, travel to the highest tower of the palace, and then hours of footwork around the city. The blisters on his feet had long popped and he had a rash on his thigh from his balls rubbing there.

"We are getting closer, I can feel it. Justice will be served." But the words were for Gantry more than herself. She was still shaken by this Roisin and how the Citywatch found her after the death of her father. Sternwood saw criminals develop from less trauma.

Justice would be served? Ha, tell that to the Hanrab teenagers hanging from the tower walls. She could see the shapes of them up there if she squinted. Justice indeed.

"Where should we go next? I don't think I can take another door slammed in my face," said Gantry.

"Yes, the Constable work isn't as easy as I remembered," she said. "But we can't stop quite yet." It was a while since she worked from the bottom up. Gantry had moved from the University to the Inspector's office directly; he never walked a beat.

A woman with vibrant red hair poked out of an alley behind them, then popped back behind it. Sternwood had seen her a block or two back and thought nothing of it. Now, she made note. Gantry and she knocked on six more doors down the boulevard. Five nothings and one sweet old lady that promised Gantry a flatbread recipe if he would only come back during the daytime. Sternwood was tired. She kept her peripheral glancing for the red hair. Twice, no three times, it flashed from behind a dumpster or alley.

Someone followed them. No doubt about it.

Gantry let out a dramatic sigh after the little old lady and her recipes. "Nowhere, this is getting us absolutely nowhere."

"Don't look now, but there is a woman following us, dammit, Gantry, I said don't look."

The woman poked out from behind a parked carriage on the side of the road. She was gorgeous and so he panicked. "Halt, in the name of our Emperor," he boomed. Not the instinct he expected.

The woman froze mid-flight, her foot caught in a puddle. Down she went in a muddy slap and roll.

"What has come over you, Gantry?" said Sternwood.

"I wish I could tell you," he said, leaping from the front porch stoop and landing right in front of the woman on the street. Up close, he floundered. Creamy white skin, no make-up but still radiant, an explosion of red and orange curls. His left leg jarred, screaming from the landing. She looked up at him like a cat caught in a candle.

"Please sir, don't kill me," she whimpered.

Gantry realized his hand was on his short sword and he had unclasped the sheath-lock. He clipped it back on and reached out a hand for her. "What has come over you? Don't you realize the fine for interfering in Citywatch business? Why, that there is an Inspector General, first rank."

She put her hands up. "I'm so sorry, sir."

Shit, thought Gantry, was he on edge or what? "It's ok, let me help you up." Her hands were smooth and lovely. He started sweating, always sweating Gantry Willow. He inadvertently took a read off her aura, he had never seen anything like it, a brilliant swirl of red and orange to match her hair. Like fire-works. She was maybe five or six years his senior, somewhere in her early thirties.

"Please sir, I have information about a Candlelighter, I work the morning dowsers and word said around the Guild was two constables were looking for her. That's what our Guildmaster was spoutin' anyways."

Sternwood marched down to them and took his shoulder. "Let's take this somewhere less exposed."

"Of course, General," he said. "Here, come along with us, and I promise you won't be hurt." It was the first time he ever exercised the power and pride of his badge. He gave her hand a firm squeeze, far from the milquetoast handshake Gantry had his whole life. She looked at him with big, soapy eyes and he felt his heart drop out from below him.

Gantry had fallen in love only three times in his whole life. Heddy Lamora in the University who had laughed and dashed his hopes like a bottle smashed. Inspector General Sariah Sternwood who would never reciprocate the feelings. And here and now, this Candlelighter woman with a nova of red hair and eyes like a deer drinking at a stream.

He stood there too long. Sternwood cleared her throat behind him.

"Shit, let's get you somewhere safe," he squeaked. They turned into an alley and found shadows behind a dumpster. Sariah stood back and blocked the entrance, making sure they weren't followed.

"Now love, how can we help you?" Why did he call her love, he'd never done that before in his life. No matter, ride the storm.

"Yes, sir, it was like I said. The Guildmaster talked of some Citywatch that came by looking for a girl, my friend Roisin. He offered a two-silver reward for information. Now, meaning no disrespect," her voice quavered at first, but she gained confidence as she spoke, "it's just the Guildmaster favors the drink, and I didn't think the information would make it too far this late."

"So, you took matters into your own hands," said Gantry.

"Ayuh, sir. My friend Dassar, she lights the Nightmarket lamps. She saw Citywatch types knocking on doors over yonder, so I took it up to see you myself. Please, sir, I meant nothing untowards." She raised her hands in defense, poor citizens were terrified of Citywatch Gantry realized with shame.

"It's ok, love, here you're safe now." He took her hand. She gasped slightly and her face flushed. Warmth crept up through him.

Sariah glanced back from the edge of the alley. Gantry questioned a witness like he asked her to the Solstice dance. Gods above, she smirked. Why did she care? Was this jealousy? Impossible.

"I feel safe," the woman said.

"Good, we'll keep you that way. What's your name?"

"Theresa," she said.

"Theresa, a lovely name. Don't worry, my partner and I are Inspector Generals."

Her eyes lit up in shock. "Oh goodness, is Roisin in trouble? She wouldn't hurt a lamb." Theresa made the mark of Veridaan over her chest.

Gantry glanced around the alley. They were alone. "No, nothing like that. But she could be caught in between some bad action, understand? We have to find her as soon as possible. If you can help us, it will keep her safe. I promise."

Theresa stared into her eyes, baby blues beneath bangs of red fire. The warmth creeped lower. "Ok, I trust you. I don't know where she is, but I know where she lives."

"Can you take us there?" Gantry asked.

She glanced to each end of the alley. "Not right now. I have to check all the lamps between Docks and the Mule. But I can when the shift ends, about two bells from now. I'll meet you at the end of Skelton Boulevard, right by the bay. Ninth bell, at the end of this block by the water. Can you do that for me?" She squeezed his hand ever so with the question.

Gantry squared his shoulders and set his jaw. He had never done either of those before. "Sure, love, I can do that for you. We'll find our answers and your friend, I promise."

"Veridaan bless you," she whispered and dashed to the alley edge opposite Sternwood. Theresa turned back to Gantry as if she was gonna blow a kiss, but instead just smiled and laughed.

"What's your surname?" Gantry called to her.

"I don't have one," and she winked.

Sternwood walked back to Gantry Willow. She was used to male Constables and female witnesses. Step aside, make yourself scarce, nobody else wants you crowding that particular dialogue. 'Wait your turn,' a common theme as a woman in the Watch. So, why did this time she feel spurned?

Gantry's face was like a stupid wide moon. "I found a

witness, I found where the Candlelighter lives. We're almost there, we're so close."

"Good work," said Sternwood. She felt a cold blade slip in her ribs, unknown to her ever before this moment. This was jealousy. She did not like it.

Did she have actual feelings for Gantry Willow?

Impossible.

Gantry floated, even here in this granite alley coated in restaurant grease sludge with the unmistakable reek of the Mule blowing on the low tide winds, Gantry floated. He opened his inner eye and could see her aura blazing fire red-orange over the shops of Skelton Boulevard.

17

Roisin sunk through a dreamless dark. From a wet distance, she heard a knock, knock, KNOCK. She thrust awake gasping but was stopped by tight binds. She choked on snot and blood that caked from her nose to her mouth. Her vision blurred, still sticky with sleep. She shifted left and right, but she was tied to a chair. A nice rosewood chair, she noted. She blinked her eyes back to focus on the most palatial room she had ever seen. There were thick carpets, furniture carved with the Siblings, a marble-topped table with ivory and ebony chess pieces. Great tapestries of blue and gold thread showing the glory that was Auron. Brother Summer and guardian of life in his resplendent blue and gold armor. He was a great warrior, so sang the hymns and operas.

But the blue and gold armor brought back the memories. She and the strange Alistair Nito with his jar of orange drugs, the churchknights of Auron surrounding them with riot response. The flash of magic and darkness. She still needed more sleep, only had three bells' worth in two days.

Behind her someone groaned. She creaked her neck

around as much as the harsh rope allowed. Nito was bound behind her, their chairs back-to-back. His lanky black hair hung over his face, stuck there with blood. He snored abruptly and grunted again.

"Hey, Nito," she said. "Hey."

His head lolled and he kept snoring.

"Hey, gods dammit!" She reached her foot back and smashed it into his calf.

"What the fuck?" He tried to stand up, and the two chairs shuddered against the bindings. "Mortia's tits, what's the safe word?" He craned his head around and saw it was Roisin. "Oi, fuck, forget I said that. This has happened to me before."

"I'm gonna forget you said that too, thank you very much."

Nito shifted as he took stock of the room. "Fucking a, Salavar, thought we were more rex than this."

"High-Father Salavar?" she asked. The four temples of the Siblings were on the same block of the Gods' Way and the students or orphans would rotate between the other temples for weekly prayers. She had seen the magnificent Salavar at his pulpit, ferocious in his sermons on the sanctity of life and the community support of each other.

"High-Father Salavar of Auron's Temple, where do you think we are?" He jumped their chairs towards the curtained balcony in a slow arc. Through a slash in the curtain, Roisin could see the great chandeliers of Auron. She didn't want to believe him but there it was. She knew those candles; she lit them for two months before her transfer to Veridaan's temple and High-Father Alonso.

High-Father Alonso, she bit back sudden tears. "No, it's not true, it can't be."

"Sorry, kid," said Nito. He was a cynical bastard, sure. Why drag her like this? Maybe so she'd understand what they were up against. "Who do you think I got all that kax for? I quit the junk a long time ago. I was picking up for the High-Father here."

She bit her molars hard and sucked the tears back in. She couldn't cloud her judgement with emotion right now. "No, you're lying. These are good men, holy men. I know them."

"Maybe some, but Salavar's a right asshole. Pirate that bought his way up to priest so he could abuse the young— uhh, city."

"You are just a drug dealer, just some pusher for the priests."

"No," he shot back, "no, I got forced into a squeeze. My daughter—"

"Are they all like this? Was—" Her jaw bunched. "Was High-Father Alonso a customer?"

Ah, shit, Nito. You stupid old git. Woke up with a hangover and decided to dash this kid's idea of decency and sanctity. Same old Nito. Worse, he had to think. Think hard and think fast. What's up Salavar? I got your Kax, you get impatient and send your joeboys and I make an asshole of myself and get kicked in the head. Cool, that's fine. Joeboys and constables kicked in his head as long as he could remember.

So, why take the girl? And why am I tied to a fucking chair?

Because she keeps talking about the dead High-Father, that's why. She saw it happen.

Oh, fuck a dozen ducks.

Nito took a deep breath. Ok, he could handle this. He never helped raise his own kid, but shitting on a teenager's hopes and ideals seemed to be too type for the genre. Now to bring it back and become the good guy, classic manipulation. Classic Nito.

Was sweeping this much like parenting? Watch yourself, asshole, don't get cocky.

"Look, there is no way your High-Father Alonso was in the same trade winds as this guy. I would know, I keep their tabs.

Alonso was the only one who refused the syndicates. It's why they murdered him. That's my working theory, anyway."

"Alonso was a good man. I know it."

"It got him killed," said Nito. The main doors burst open, and Salavar stalked in. He bumped a vase, and it smashed to the floor. He was higher than a star, his pupils deeper than the abyss.

"Hey, Nito, shit. That was three hells of a score. Shit." He picked his nose and took out an orange booger. "Didn't think you'd get me the entire continent's supply, had my chemist take a look at it. Seven pounds of the stuff and purer than a nun's twat. The Siegewards are finished, blown to pieces. Kax was the only racket they had left and now the Baron Cazz can fuck them right up the ass." His voice came rapid fire; his eyes drifted. He chomped down the bright booger. "You've made me a very happy man, Nito. Rich and content."

Nito snorted. He wasn't even facing Salavar. "You'll never be content, Salavar."

"Too true. Sorry about the girl, real sorry about that. She was in the unlucky position of seeing what she ain't supposed. You know how it goes in this business."

"You're a dirty old junkie dressed as a priest," Roisin spit at him.

"Holy shit, she's a dagger, huh? The adults are talking, little Rose." He stumbled over and casually slapped her across the face. It cracked in the room, left an orange handprint on her face. She stared at him with falcon eyes. "Yeah, little Rose. I know all about you. Alonso's pet project, his special orphan girl. The catatonic freak he rehabilitated. Cry me a river, didn't give a fuck about ya' until the whole city flipped over searching."

"Leave her alone."

"Fuck off," said Salavar with sudden ice, pacing around Roisin. "Yeah, little Rose. Besides the tiny Cazz sweeper team that couldn't kill you, the Inquisition is rooting through the Mule. Fucking Citywatch is canvassing I heard, like they could find their dicks with either hand. But you are mine little Rose, ha ha. Nito and his Kax made me cash," he leaned in so his brandy breath engulfed her, "but you're gonna make me rich." He ran a finger down her cheek, tracking more kax.

Roisin closed her eyes and tried to pull away from him, but his sweaty bulk was everywhere. The harsh rope tore at her neck. She was terrified of the orange powder on her face, tried to breathe low through her mouth to keep from inhaling.

Nito rocked up and down. "Get off her, Salavar. You ain't this much of an asshole. You gonna sell out a teenager to a syndicate?"

"You done worse, Nito. You done a whole hell of a lot worse." He leaned in close to run his face against hers, his fat fingers drifted down her bodice. "I was there when you did worse."

She spit in his face. "I'll kill you."

"Don't you know that stuff just fires up the old oven?" His hand moved lower.

"Salavar, get off her. I will make you regret it." What an impotent threat. What an impotent man. Look at what you did here, look where your actions got this poor girl. Same old Nito.

But now all your old power is gone.

Salavar chuckled.

Nito yelled his name.

Roisin closed her eyes and heard it.

Of course, it would come. Here close to this vile man and his vile intentions. KNOCK, KNOCK, KNOCK. The skittering feeling on her flesh, the scuttling darkness, and the Door. Always the Door and someone knocking on the other side.

Rosin felt the monster's hand go lower.

She opened the Door.

Salavar was doing fucking great. Honestly didn't think he could reach a higher apex of pleasure. The only thing Salavar cared for was pleasure, to be full of life's bounty. Just like Auron. Sometimes that came at the cost of other's pleasure, or even life, but Salavar put in time, didn't he just? How many years at sea, how many years starving in his youth? He deserved this, all of Auron's children deserved their bounty. Their land, their riches... their women.

This little bitch had caused a stir, hadn't she just? Can't rock the boat when you make money shipping lanes, she should know that, the dumb little bitch. The kax thrummed in his fingers, it lit auras around every living thing, it cascaded his thoughts until there was only Salavar and the piece of flesh in front of him.

A young one. She probably didn't need to shave yet. Salavar wanted to pee on her.

And then his high twisted, took his breath away and sent his consciousness sprawling through blinking strobe lights. Overdose, there Salavar. You've done this before, just breathe in and out and lie face down so you don't choke on your own puke. He definitely would vomit, collapsing to the floor with both hands but it melted.

What?

The floor melted at his touch, he sank down and down and down, the liquid floorboards moving through his hands like paint. He opened his eyes, foolish in an OD, he didn't need the spins.

He sat on the floor of a ship's cabin, not his temple office. He looked for the liquid floorboards in his hands, but they were empty. The floor below him was solid with just a bit of that moisture ships absorb. What happened to Nito and the girl? Oh, it didn't matter. Look at this cabin, would you?

Red silks hung over a circular mattress of down feathers. Hanrab gods carved from gold perched on every shelf. A great carpet of thick Pinda thread ran from the cabin door to the bed. This was his cabin, three decades prior.

He stood up and looked down. He was young again. My gods, his gut was flat and ribbed in muscle. His scimitar hung at his hip. He ran a hand through his thick, black hair and grinned. Juno's sputtering rectum, he was in his prime. To swing the blade through Cruxian sailors and raid and steal and fuck anything he wanted with no cover-ups or blackmail pay. This was freedom again.

Faintly he thought of a man and girl tied to the chair, but it flowed away like liquid floorboards. He could now feel the creak and sway of the ship, smell the brined-wood mold smell. He was alive and young and captain again and he was going to fuck this whole world in the mouth for the next thirty years.

The cabin door flung open, his cabin door. Two burly head-breakers dragged a girl in and threw her on the bed. She was gagged. Something was wrong in this reality. He remembered something like this moment, but he'd pushed it down with drugs and whores and decades.

"What is going on?" he asked. But the sailors surged past him and out. He couldn't focus on their faces, they were shrouded in black smoke. Must be an illusion, must be all that kax. He did remember fucking himself up on kax so hard he overdosed.

Ah, overdosing, that made sense. Just roll with the punch Salavar and breathe.

But why was there nothing outside his cabin door? It slammed after the sailors left, but he caught a glimpse. There was nothing outside that door, just grey.

Overdose is all. Had to be. Nothing wrong.

Now let's look at this bound girl on his bed. The faceless headbreakers knew the deal. You take the finest of the girls from the chainroom and bring them up to Captain Salavar. Thus began his devotion to pleasure.

This girl was gorgeous, even bound and gagged. That got Salavar going harder actually, his cock blossomed with blood. He took a gem-hilted knife from the table and stalked over to her. She had dusky, brown skin and green eyes. A splash of brown freckles on her face and arms. Black hair shorn short, a turnoff. Nothing to rip out at climax. He stepped closer with his knife.

"Hello kitty, this will be easier on you if you don't struggle. Better for me if you do," and he pushed the knife between her gag and skin. Her eyes widened. The knife pulled and the gag tore away.

"Brother," she cried.

Salavar staggered back. "No, no no no no." This reality, this thing he'd pushed down. His third girl delivered from the chainroom.

It was his sister.

"No," he screamed.

"Brother, thank Halladar and the great wheel of the stars. You've come to rescue me. All of us. Cazaratti slavers on the sea raided our village." She crawled towards him still bound. She bumped awkwardly on the floor. "Father and mother are gone, but little Hensa and Aditi still live, just sick. You came right in time."

No, no, no, no, no no no no no no no no. Not here. Not this moment. The room filled with details as the memory sludged to the surface. Salavar was not there to save his sisters. No, he purchased those slaves from the Cazaraati to sell to the Lestat. He was not aware his own sisters were part of the haul. No no no no no. Not this again.

In the nightmare-reality, his overdose fever dream, had to be an overdose, had to be, had to be, had to be, had to be, but whatever it was he stood shaking with his sister dragging herself at him. He could see sores around her nose and mouth from the horrible conditions downstairs in the chainroom. Three hundred slaves chained on slats, crammed in like sausages in a can. Maybe two hundred survived the voyage. But Salavar never went down there, too depressing. Never had a chance to see his sisters chained like mules. Didn't know they were here, on this voyage.

"Please, Salla, what do we do now? How will we overpower the guards? There are so many, and they are so cruel. Where will we go? Is there a ship out there waiting for us?" She crawled closer, too weak to walk. "How did you find us?" Her bleary eyes took stock of the room. "Why are you in the captain's cabin?"

Salavar's heart hammered, just like an overdose. His sweat was warm then instantly cold, and his asshole quivered.

His sister, he couldn't remember her name, put a knobby elbow on a side table to lift herself to standing, her arms so thin. So weak. But her eyes were full of storm clouds. "Why did you call me kitty?" Her mouth hooked into a snarl. "What did you mean it would be better if I struggled?"

Salavar drove the gem-crusted dagger into her eye and pushed it through the back of her skull. She shuddered as if struck by lightning and shit out a watery discharge all over his plush carpet. She fell so hard her arm snapped. Salavar wept as she died on the floor. It took four minutes. In the end, he cradled her head and apologized again and again and again. He could only apologize to her corpse. There were two more sisters downstairs.

He took up the knife to finish the work. He was incapable of processing these emotions, but he knew if they lived and found out what a monster he was, then Salavar would have to take his own life. He giggled with insanity. Two more and he would be free of all restraints forever and ever and ever and ever and ever.

He stood up dripping blood, snot, and tears. He walked to the cabin door and inhaled. He would forget this. He would kill his two younger sisters and then blackout on sopa or booze or both until he forgot or died. Yes, yes.

He walked up to the door and opened it. There was just grey.

That made no sense.

Not grey skies, not a grey deck, just a wash of grey. Pure color. He shrugged and walked through—

—and sat up on the floor of a captain's cabin. Disoriented. He was just standing, now sitting. Must be a dream. Oh, right. The overdose. Breathe in and out, roll with the punch. Not his first overdose.

But then the cabin door flung open. His cabin door. Two burly headbreakers dragged a girl in and threw her on the bed. She was gagged. Something was wrong in this reality. He remembered something from this moment, but he had pushed it down with drugs and whores and decades.

It all came back.

This moment. This was reality now. Over and over and over and over.

No no no no no overdose no no no no no no must be an overdose had to be an overdose no other explanation none other had to be an overdose roll with the punches breath in breath out breathe through me not his sister not his sister memory didn't matter memory lies memory dies memory no no no no no not again roll it again change it this time change time change change change change no not again the grey walk out back to the cabin floor stab her again and again and again

and   again   no   no   no   no
NONONONONONONONONONONO—

———

Salavar's reality shifted to a plunging dive. He was not in a ship cabin. He plummeted from his pulpit, past the grand chandeliers, down another seventy feet before he popped on the marble floors like a melon. Like a candle kicked, spinning down, down, down to the ground.

———

Roisin opened her eyes. She had blacked out. Nito shook her with a terrified grip.

"Hey! What did you do? What did you just fucking do?"

She was on the floor, cushioned by thick carpet. Rope was all around her, but she wasn't tied up anymore. Two chairs lay on the floor next to her, fine rosewood chairs. Plush seats.

Nito shook her again. His eyes were red-rimmed and crazy. "What was that? Was that sorcery? What the fuck was that?"

The door to the High Priest's office banged with armored gauntlets. "Unlock this right now, in the name of Brother Summer." A lot of armor clanged, a whole squad of churchknights. "I WILL NOT ASK AGAIN!"

Nito panicked. He just watched High-Father Salavar seize up, babble incoherently, then cut their bonds and throw himself over the pulpit. It made a noise like a cow hit by a carriage, echoed through the vast temple. "What did you do?" More armor clanked in the hallway.

"I opened a door," she said, shaking.

18

———

Maharez sat on a rooftop against cool stone on a hot night. He looked down at the marina's end and their mark. A simple inn hunched between two ship-master's buildings, its entrance sank half a story into the street. "Spirits," the sign read. It was another mundane inn, a common place for Maharez the past few years. He'd killed men and women around inns like this. He strangled a fishmonger around an inn like this, turned at the last second to see their granddaughter watching with the purest of fear. The purest of hate.

He looked up at the vast wheel of stars, still shining despite the light pollution of Cruxia and its million candles. A whole economy built around candles. White people, Maharez would never understand them. He wished to be anywhere but on that roof. Wished to Halladar, no, prayed to Halladar that after this death his life would have meaning. That he could help people instead of killing them. This life was a test, it had to be.

But he knew that was folly. Your actions and decisions in every life designated your slot in the next wheel of stars. He stared up at the deep black cut with tiny diamonds. He didn't have a choice, right? Enslaved to indentured. Captured then captured again by the Cazzaraati syndicate.

But you always have a choice. This was the easy way and he knew that. He sighed.

And there was Fatimah, cracking him in the back of the head. "Be silent, we await the fat wizard." Maharez forgot she was there, her pre-job tick of rapping her knuckles on the ground was so common he didn't hear it anymore.

They cased this Nito's bar. It was two hours to dawn, about fourth bell in the morning. So far only a scullery girl came out with the garbage and walked around to make sure there were no homeless in the alley. The proprietor was nowhere to be seen. The place had no constable patrols, which meant they weren't paid up with the Citywatch nor the syndicates. What a rube, Maharez thought, running a business in this city with no grease. He felt disgusted at the thought. He wouldn't have thought that way three years ago.

The work changed him.

"Fati, sister."

"Shhh."

"Oh, we haven't seen him in two bells, he isn't coming anytime soon."

"Hook said to await his signal, we wait."

"He didn't even tell us what the signal was."

"We always know when it happens," she said. Fatimah, only business and nothing else. Maharez worried at her sense of compassion. She was older, after all; the work changed her long ago.

The slave galley changed her, truth be told.

"Fati..."

"Shhhhh!"

"Fati, what if we leave? Right here, right now."

"What?" she almost shouted. They both flinched below the

roof's brick wall at the noise. "What the fuck?" she whispered close to him.

He hadn't started this argument in a while, the eternal argument. "We could leave right now. Those shipmasters are open day and night. We could go put our names on a roster and be gone by fifth bell. Just be done with it all."

"And do what, exactly?"

"Anything. That's a Krodan whaling vessel, they don't care about the color of our skin." He pointed to a slim cutter with three masts. "Or there, that's a Hanrab pleasure cog, you could serve drinks, and I could make kabobs."

She grabbed him by his short, curly hair and yanked him close. Always too rough, Fati. "And do what? Make barely enough money to eat? We'd owe them for the voyage and be stuck there. Indentured again, enslaved again. Here we are rich."

"To do what?" he shouted. She smacked the back of his head, and he came down to a whisper. "We haven't even paid off our debt. Surely a life of labor is better than this one of lies and killing."

He was wrong, of course, they paid up two years prior. Fatimah always took the most lucrative jobs that no one else wanted. The pussies were scared of real danger. As if these white men knew what that was. Fatimah sat on a hoard of two thousand gold. They could do anything, go anywhere on Galea's surface.

But Maharez could never know that. He was one of the pussies. He would try to live a life of peace and prosperity, the fool. Fatimah could bring them millions of gold. Her donkey of a brother had to stay in the dark. She smiled at him, "Maha, think of the life we would live. Think what the Cazaraati would send, people just like us."

"Sweepers." He spit.

"Sweepers as long as we lived, hounded on every continent."

"There's no syndicates with the Krodan, nor the Turra."

"The Krodan would eat you, the Turra would make drums from your skin. Think."

Maharez sighed. He heard the white men's words drip from her mouth. "How many more jobs?"

"This is the last," she lied.

His head snapped to her. "Truth?"

"Janna has'hoom." *True as the gods.* Fatimah lied like it was magic. Maharez lit up with joy and turned back to the inn. "Why did you not tell me?"

"I didn't want it to mess with your judgement. This job," she faked a sigh, "this job is already so out of control."

"Yes. It has never been like this. I thought Polo would have a stroke." He calmed down. He breathed easy. He smiled at her, she smiled back at him.

Fatimah faked a good smile. Maharez you donkey, why did you suggest that? Leave? Flee the Cazaraati? Surprised he hadn't asked again sooner, by the gods.

But if he asked Hook or Polo, then he would have to die. Fatimah paused but for two seconds at the prospect of killing her brother.

Needs must be.

———

Gantry walked to the end of Skelton Boulevard, right by the bay. Ninth bell, at the end of the block by the water. He waited under a lamppost for Theresa. His witness with the flash of red hair. His witness who knew where Roisin the Buea lived.

Gantry stood strong and tall, puffing his chest out like some jock at the University. This was his city. He stood at the edge of a vast conspiracy manufactured by the rich and would take it down with the poorest citizens. This was justice.

This was Gantry Willow.

———

Sariah watched Gantry from the second story window of a shipmaster's building, the same master that built Citywatch patrol vessels. His son owed Sternwood a dozen favors, and she cashed them in for his front door unlocked and no questions asked. She aimed a heavy crossbow at Gantry and the avenue of approach. She glanced over her shoulder at two alternate positions on the east and south wall of the building between masts suspended by chain.

Gantry stood still, she noted. He never stood still. Gantry would sway from left to right, he bit his fingernails, he drummed a tattoo on any surface he came across. He peeled leaves from trees in passing and tore them up as he spoke. But down there he stood still.

Sariah long ago mastered observation, it was the most important tool to police work. She didn't pay more attention to Gantry, she took in details by rote. But she was around Gantry Willow so often, she saw all his details.

Why was she so angry that he stood still? It brought up her blood pressure, it canted her crossbow left and right.

Did she love Gantry Willow?

Impossible.

But she did. It was true. It set her crossbow steady. She breathed deep with that truth.

The gods must be crazy. Because then that red-haired woman came around the corner towards Gantry. He stood at the end of the marina by a basic inn. Its sign only read, "Spirits."

———

Warmth swept through Gantry. It climbed from his cock to his face. Here was Theresa in a sundress of cream, it captured her curves in marble. Bright hair rolled down her neck and around her shoulders. He kept his desire reigned in like a dog.

They needed information. They needed this candlelighter's address, they needed to crack open this case and blast the aristocracy out of the Citywatch and Inquisition. Gantry pushed his lust down. Duty beckoned.

Theresa looked around the alley, fear scampered across her face. Must be Mule-born, she was so poor. Her belt was just a rope. Gantry beckoned her deeper into the alley, away from the lampposts and the street. Right in line with Sariah Sternwood and her crossbow.

"Inspector Willow, you came," she said, her voice husky and low.

"This friend of yours is in a lot of trouble, I won't lie. None of it her own doing, but powerful people want her dead. Roisin could break this whole city in half."

"I know," came back her voice. She leaned in close. "I'm scared."

His duty blasted out the window. He took her in his arms.

Sariah rolled her eyes twenty-five yards away at the sniper's nest.

"Who else knows about this? I don't trust the Citywatch." She kissed him. He seized her tighter. His first kiss in ten years.

"No one," he whispered.

"You're a good man," she said, her voice low like crushed silk. Then it changed, a deep baritone. A man's voice. "Sorry you're such a shit wizard."

Theresa morphed. Her frame shifted from plump to bulky. She grew a foot and a half, and Willow stood in front of Hook. Those baby blue eyes stayed the same.

Hook drove a knife into Gantry's heart and then a second into his throat. Gantry shuddered and shook and drowned in his own blood, it gushed to the pavement. Hook cushioned him as he fell. "Hey, hey. I got you. It's okay."

Gantry grappled at Hook's face with hands losing strength. He started to cry, tried to speak. Blood and snot and tears ran down his face.

"Shh, it's okay, I got you." Hook wiped a tear from his face. "I got you, man."

Someone fired a crossbow bolt, but Hook's senses were keyed up at a job. He raised a palm and scorched the wood to ash with a quick spell.

Gantry died a bloody mess, convulsing in Hook's arms. This poor fuck. The Theresa was a face he wore back during the war, and it took a little bit out of him each time he put it back on. Brought back memories and things he'd done. Theresa killed a lot of men. Men who deserved it.

This little man did not deserve it, the poor fuck. A thought like that crossbow bolt through Hook's mind.

———

Sariah fired her crossbow as soon as Theresa morphed from a red-haired woman to a murderer. He denied the bolt like she would a fly. She screamed as the huge man drove his daggers into Gantry.

She watched Gantry Willow die in red wreckage. Most of her broke.

And then boots crashed through the windows to her left and right, big black boots. Stormtroopers on rappel lines from the roof. Downstairs the east and west doors broke in like an explosion. More Inquisition stormtroopers: they wore blackened chainmail under long coats marked with a red circle on the lapel, heavy rapiers and bucklers at arms. Dietrich marched at their center, his wide hat brimmed over mirrored spectacles. "Inspector General Sariah Sternwood, you are under arrest. By order of the Emperor."

19

Bert woke up with a grunt, his face soaked in stale beer and drool. Where was he, fuck's sake?

He looked around. Nito's joint. Oh yeah. A half-full Fontaigne whisky and a warm Janoe lager sat in front of him. He was the only patron. That made sense. Sun wasn't up yet. He shrugged and finished the whisky. He sipped the stale beer. "Oi, Nito, where you fucking at?" he shouted.

The back door slammed, and Mariah came in all red hair, curves, and attitude. She was in her twenties, a toddler to someone like Bert. "He ain't come in yet, which means I can throw your sorry ass out. Finally."

Okay, maybe she was alright. "I'd like to see you try, missy."

She pulled a lid from a barrel and took a butcher's knife, crossed them in front of her like a sword and buckler. Veridaan's cooch. She wasn't kidding. "Oi, Fireworks, put that shit away. Here," he tossed a gold coin on the counter, "for the night's sleep and a boiled chicken and you keep the rest. Nito ain't need to know. Wait, and one more Fontaigne double."

Mariah looked at the gold coin with wide eyes. Six silver covered his order, that was three hells of a tip. She slipped it into her pocket, sparked the boiling pit to life with a pitch-stick, then put the whole bottle of Fontaigne whisky in front of Bert.

"Fuck yeah, Fireworks. I like you after all."

"It ain't mutual." She marched upstairs to the sailors in their room, fourth bell wake-up. She knocked three times, too loud, then popped the door open banging a pot with her butcher knife. Four Krodan sailors, big leathery bastards from the western continent, laid on the floor and beds, squashed and rank in the tight quarters. The shortest wasn't quite seven feet tall. Mariah wondered how big their cocks were. And how leathery.

The captain grumbled. "I heard you when you knocked, ma'am." He stood and stretched, red-leather skin spotted in black. His snout snubbed like a turtle's, but two others were long-jawed like crocodiles. "We require seven chickens and a dozen potatoes."

"The water's boiling and you're paid up. Give it half a bell."

He nodded. "No longer. We muster at five."

The fourth Krodan had a shell on his back sprouting bone spines. "Hiesta hucha lora tohassi, hon puti," he whispered.

Everyone laughed but the captain. He glared their eyes to the floor, but the spiked one kept chuckling.

"What did he just say?"

The captain sighed. "The big-rump white girl can hit me with that pan."

"I need four more silver for the chickens." Mariah left downstairs, swinging her hips a touch.

Downstairs, Bert took the bottle from the neck, tilted it to the ceiling. The only other man she'd seen drink like that was her papa and he bit it five years back when his liver left him. The old fools. Cruxia was full of Berts, full of her papas. Mariah had no sympathy for them, she'd take every dime they had if she could.

Bert finished his warm lager as the Krodan thundered down

to the taproom. Their taloned feet clicked on the stairs and dust shook from the ceiling with them.

"How ya' been, Jakarth?" said Bert.

Jakarth, the snub-nose captain, stared at Bert for two beats. "Sober. We ship at fifth bell, puta."

"Ayuh, I'll be there. I have to piss." Bert slapped the counter with both hands and pushed to his feet. He stood only to Jakarth's elbow. The rest of the Krodan crowded the tables waiting for their chickens. Mariah already had the backup cauldron going to cook for them. Bert crossed to the alley exit and knocked knuckles with the mustard yellow Krodan coated in bone spines. "How ya' been, Toci?"

He shrugged, his shoulder spikes tapped together. "Much time with these Crusa. Ready to leave."

Bert laughed. "Too fucking right, brother. This whole city is nothing but white nonsense."

Mariah looked up from her cauldrons, Bert was as white as she was.

Bert paused at the door. "Say, Fireworks, you said Nito ain't been back?"

"Black out already, Baldy?"

Bert grit his teeth at that one. This kid was in the right business.

"Forget it." Bert thought back to Nito's questions, he'd gone in search of kax. That was four or five bells ago. Could be Nito was in a bit of trouble.

If Bert hadn't paused, if he had just gone out for a piss, he'd have seen Gantry Willow murdered in front of Nito's joint.

———

On their rooftop, Maharez and Fatimah watched Gantry Willow shudder to death in Hook's arms. Maharez realized why he liked Hook so much. Even in murder the man had grace. Hook cradled the chubby white man as he died.

Fatimah only saw weakness.

But then Hook looked up at them across the block, he raised a bloody hand and formed a fist.

"That's the signal," said Fatimah. "We burn." She pulled out one of the orange capsules and held it to the streetlamp light.

Maharez's stomach roiled. They'd killed before, so many times. Too many times. But they'd never burned down a building. His thoughts stalled on the collateral damage. He swept a view of the marina.

Nito's little bar sunk at the end of Skelton Boulevard surrounded by apartments and shipwright's warehouses. So much wood. Cogs and galleys drifted their masts over the buildings, all docked by rope. This fire left unabated would consume the whole Marina District. Worse; candles lit up in the bar marked "Spirits." It wasn't empty. Figures moved around inside, at least six.

Maharez had never killed six people at once.

———

Bert was piss-drunk. He also pissed while drunk. He chuckled at his stupid little joke. But then his instincts kicked in. Where was Nito? Nito went out looking for kax a while ago. Had Bert suggested he talk to Mama Roeneck?

Shit. Fuck. You dumb motherfucking drunk, Bert. You definitely told him that was his only option. Mama Roeneck ate him, most like. Bert couldn't ship off with Jakarth and Toci if he'd sent Nito to his death.

Bert's piss-stream was a staccato thing. It didn't flow like it did when he was thirty. You had to stand there and wait for the right moment to get out a blast, then wait for the next. A Medicer told him it was the drink that fucked him up, something called a prostate, that dumb motherfucker. Point was, a piss took him a little bit of time. Five, sometimes ten minutes. He stood there, waiting on his cock.

———

Maharez slipped around the corner of the alley with his third and final capsule of fairyfire. Fatimah and Hook set theirs below each window and door frame while Maharez hit the three corners not buried by the street.

"Nine points to the burn," said Hook earlier, "impossible to extinguish." He dragged Gantry Willow's corpse to obstruct the main door. The chubby dead white man let out heinous gas when Hook slumped him there, a shocked red mess with a moon of a face. Maharez hated Hook again in that moment, how casually he treated this murder. He'd been so gentle when it happened. "Once we start this, we dust. And quick. Head back to Ganon but not together. You both know the city well enough by now."

Maharez chewed on that scene as he placed the orange gel at the corner of the building. It reeked of concentrated oil. Inside he heard a cauldron bubble, someone belched. It was an inn, full of life. Maharez's time spent at inns only involved death. Planning to kill, hiding after a kill, casing out a kill. For once he wanted to walk into an inn with his own money, sit down and have a good time. Take a drink, maybe wink at a pretty woman. Across the sea, of course, in Hanrabi where the inns had mosaics of glass enamel. Where they served desi distilled from sweet cane and the dances lasted past sunrise.

Halladar protect, he missed Hanrabi. Perhaps he'd abandon Fatimah after all and join one of those Krodan vessels. He was light and strong for his age, he could excel. Somewhere across the street, he heard windows break but he was too focused to pay it any attention.

But when he walked around the corner with his final capsule, he saw a bald and tattooed white man.

———

Bert stood staring at the sky, waiting on more piss to splash Nito's joint.

No witnesses, Maharez. Isn't that how they got here in the first place?

Bert turned and saw Maharez. They both paused in shock. Bert was drunk. But that kid held fairyfire. Bert knew all about that shit, wiped cities with it in the long, long ago. "Hey, what's that you got there?"

Maharez leapt forward and drove his foot into Bert's throat. Bert backed up, dick out, and pissed a whole lot of gumption all over Maharez. He grabbed at his throat where the air was stolen. Maharez whirled his heel into Bert's temple who flipped into his meager piss pool, unconscious.

Maharez turned and ran the way he'd come, around the two alley corners. He reeked of urine and oil. Hook stood with Fatimah in the shadows of the opposite alley. "Fuck's sake, Maha, what's wrong?"

"A man; there was a man. I took him out."

"Maruth kaba," said Fatimah.

"Is he dead?" asked Hook.

Maharez hesitated one moment. "Yes." Hook noticed the pause; Fatimah did not.

"Just speeds up the agenda, here it is kids," said Hook. He snapped his fingers, a blue spark burned Maharez's eyes.

The burn, now? With them not five paces from the building. "You'll kill us."

"Watch." Hook pointed at the orange gel on the corner of the building, a worm of it about six inches long smeared on the wooden struts. It burned, low and slow. "That will give us about ten minutes. Now dust. Hit the Mule, the constables in this district break Hanrab heads after the lamps are lit. Dust."

Hook walked off, a strong fast pace down Skelton Boulevard, right in view of everyone. Maharez hated him again, to walk through this Cruxia with no fear. It wasn't unique to Hook, all white people carried that magic in this gods' damned city.

"Come," said Fatimah. "We can escape through the night market."

"No, I will find it on my own."

She turned and smacked him in the face.

But he caught her wrist and held it. "Do what you want, Fati, I will return to Ganon my own way. To be safe."

She glared at him. Stupid Maharez, his grip was strong but he was weak.

"You dare?" she hissed. The veneer slipped. Maharez stood in the alley with something that was not his sister. Perhaps he always knew the truth of her, hoped that he could take her away from this monstrosity she'd become. He knew this to be folly. His sister died on that slave galley and this thing that lived in her skin no longer could fake it. Cruxia started it, but Polo's influence tore out the last remnants of her. Maharez almost cried, standing there holding her arm. More weakness, she would think.

He flung her away. "I will see you at Ganon, watch yourself." He wedged between the two apartment buildings behind Nito's "Spirits" and climbed over a brick fence, out of sight.

Fatimah stood in shock. Heat rolled from the orange-gel worm in waves. She glanced at it, but it streaked white lines in her vision. The wood smoldered around it, the first wisps of black smoke dragged towards the night sky, morning a silver beam on the horizon.

Maharez refused her. This was new. This was bad. This worsened her resolve. He would have to die. Soon.

———

Bert woke up again. What the fuck? Face down in piss?

Not again, Bert. Not again.

He stood up and wiped his face off. His head fogged. Too much of the Fontaine. Woke up drunk and got drunker. Something tore at his memory, but it was lost. Fuck. Piss reek everywhere. Fuck.

He struggled to his feet, his hip screaming bloody fucking mercy. That hip went out when he hit forty-two. There was something he couldn't remember, something right there.

Fuck it, he needed a drink.

Bert stumbled by Nito's back entrance where Maria dumped the trash or cleared out the homeless. It smelled like a smoker back there, someone set up some meat. Bert's awareness pricked up. Something he should remember, something. Something, something.

Shit he needed a drink first. Fifth bell couldn't be far off; that meant the Krodan left soon, with or without him. He pushed into Nito's joint.

Maria served up seven boiled chickens and a rack of potatoes to Jakarth and his crew. The giant Krodan bent at the low ceiling and clamored to the largest table. It sat right up next to the bar, the most expensive spirits above it on high shelves. A giant copper still of rum crowded near Toci where he squished into the corner of the booth.

Outside, all nine worms of Hook's orange gel burned slow. They melted through wood and stone, burning all the way to the bones of the bar. Gantry Willow's clothes caught, and his body exploded in fire.

Inside, the Krodan smashed their breakfast since they wouldn't eat for another day or two. No one noticed the burning bulk blocking off the front entrance.

Bert sat down at his bottle of Fontaine and shook his wits

right. This didn't feel like drunk, this felt like that time a mule kicked his head and sent him reeling. Thoughts like clouds drifting on a summer day. Smoked meat outside. Falling asleep in his own piss. What happened, man? Bert did a lot of detective work on himself over the years, heavy drinkers have to.

Then Maria turned to him from the Krodan table, "There he is, Jakarth. Turned up for ship off after— Juno's balls, Bert. What the fuck happened to your head?"

"Huh?" He reached up to his forehead. Black blood caked there and a stinging ring in his ears. "Ah, fuck."

It came back. The Hanrab in the alley, his combustible fairyfire, the roundhouse kick. The hickory smoke stank outside. Oh, god of all fucks. Someone pulled a burn. Here, at Nito's.

"Oh fuck, Mariah, we gotta—" Bert started to shout.

The rum-still caught first, pressurized by distillation. It exploded, dousing Jakarth and three of his sailors in liquor-drenched fire. They screamed, their tough skins melting in seconds. Jakarth died choking on his scorched throat, clawing great furrows in the wood floor.

Toci, the spiked Krodan, flipped his table over. The burned corpses of his shipmates slid to the floor where fire spread like spilled water. The bar caught, bursting all the bottles behind it one by one. Bert stood slack, shocked and concussed. Mariah tackled him to the cover with Toci, damn near broke her shoulder on Bert.

"We must away from here," said Toci.

"Auron's fat cock, what gave you that idea?" said Mariah.

"No time for jokes." He pulled up to a crouch. Black smoke clogged the taproom. He counted more than six points of fire at the edges and windows of the room. This was professional. He darted to the front door, low, and smashed into it. It didn't budge and burned his shoulder. On the other side Gantry's two hundred thirty pounds fused with the door, black and reeking of bacon. It would not budge.

Bert got his wits back, bit by bit. He still needed that Fontaigne double. Liquor, liquor everywhere and not a drop to drink, he laughed with a tinge of lunacy. Toci returned. "The door is blocked, they were thorough."

"We have to try the windows," said Mariah.

"No good," said Bert hacking as the smoke drove further. The front of their oak table shield caught and the heat slammed them in growing waves. "This is a sweeper's burn. They'd hit every door, window, and corner. Fucking sweepers."

"I got it, follow me." Mariah ran to the east wall, ducking as glass and flaming liquor sprayed. The whole front entrance and the marble bar burned completely, but Mariah skirted around them to the stairs and the second floor.

Toci and Bert didn't have time to argue. They both ran after her. "You go first," said Toci.

"Why?" said Bert.

"Just go!"

Bert's hip didn't move like it used to; he hobbled up the steps as fast as it let him. The far side of the balcony over the bar blazed, but the closest inn room hadn't caught yet. Mariah shot into the room and dove through the window, shoulder first. It shattered and she flew out and down the six feet to street level where the bar sloped up with the hill. Her shoulder finally gave out after Bert, the window, and now the ground. It snapped like an oar and all she could see was white.

Bert finagled into the room on his aching hip, his breath choked and hot. The room filled with harsh smoke. He couldn't see. He backed up onto the burning balcony. Toci took the flaming steps two at a time while they collapsed under his weight. Bert stumbled, but Toci shoved him into the room as the whole balcony fell off the wall and burst into cinders on the floor. They sat on the floor of the inn room under the smoke for

one punch-drunk moment, then Toci threw Bert like a sack of
potatoes. He sailed out the window, over Mariah, right into a
fruit cart.

Mariah blinked away her pain. Juno knew Dad broke her
arm enough when she was a wee lass. "And don't you cry over
it," he'd say. She looked up at their escape route, the room
licked fire out to the night, black smoke poured. And that
window was much too small for a Krodan.

Then the frame cracked and plaster rained. The brick and
mortar around the window flexed outward. Finally, the spiked
Krodan burst through the whole wall, screaming a warcry as he
landed amongst bricks and dust. Bert pulled himself out of
apples and strawberries now reeking of oil, piss, smoke, and
fruit. Pretty standard weekend for Bert, actually.

"Toci, you tough son of a bitch. You saved my life," said Bert.

"This one saved both of us." Toci walked to Mariah, white-
faced from her arm, hair full of plaster dust. "Your ingenuity
saved us all. Here, you are hurt." He took her shoulder in a
giant, leathery hand and popped it back into place.

She screamed, but only for three seconds. "Th-th-thanks."

"It was only dislocated," Toci said with a broad grin.

"Look, I don't wanna get in the way of your courtship, but
the three of us caught right outside this building will not be rex
at all," said Bert. "If some constable comes 'round that corner,
guess what Toci?"

"I will be the escaped goat," he said.

"Something like that. We gotta move." Bert took off down
Melchior Way. Bert abandoned many things in his life: boats,
marriages, the army. If it was bullshit, why do it? Toci and
Mariah didn't have his knack for moving on. The two stood
another few moments and watched Nito's "Spirits" burn away
to the night sky.

Nito's was the best family Mariah ever had. Not just Nito
but the regulars and the delivery porters and even the nightly

candlelighters and morning dowsers. Gods above and below only knew where Nito was.

Toci watched the sacred fire. It interred his cousin Jakarth in the inn. It carried his soul up to the heavens where he would be reborn in the great wheel of stars. Of all his family, Jakarth was the strongest and wisest. Perhaps he would ride eternal on the wheel, a constellation stood for a million years. Perhaps Toci would meet Jakarth again, reborn in a new life. *Miquiztli yocoxca.* Ancestors guide his soul.

Toci pulled a snuff case from his belt and took out a tiny pinch of k'axcaldous. He put it to his nose and watched as the spirits of his kin flowed up with the fire. They rode the fire to the wheel far, far above. He reached out and Mariah took his hand, she squeezed.

When she tugged, he smiled down and walked from the burning inn with no remorse. Death was but the beginning.

———

The bar burned another hour before the constables and the fire brigade roared over with bells clanging. The block was on full lockdown by the Inquisition, some clandestine op of blah, blah, blah. Constable General Roary Bullworth didn't give three hells about the Inquisition and the way they gave fuck-all about the damn law. No agency should be above the Emperor. Bastards probably started this fire. Bullworth sighed and rolled some tobacco at the corner of Melchior Way, he couldn't afford the tailors they sold at street shops. He stayed upwind of the smoke and bacon reek.

A young clerk came out of the throng of uniforms that coated this part of the marina. He pushed up his spectacles and saluted.

"Don't do that, Juno's sake, I'm just a Constable."

"Uh, Constable General?"

"Ain't an Inspector, so you can put that shit on the stovetop. Sitrep; tell me the facts, ain't got time for no pageantry."

"Sir, the blaze started from oil-based material. Wizards have pulled out alchemical compounds."

"How bad was it besides the bar?"

"Well," the clerk wiped sweat and looked at his parchment, "three ships caught ablaze, two private barges and a Krodan whaling vessel. All immolated completely. Three docks caught fire, but it was contained by Coastwatch. The winds blew it away from the Shipmaster's guild down to the Mule housing where small fires continue. That's a lot of industry, thank the Siblings it was spared."

"I sure fuckin' ain't. How many dead?"

He flicked through more parchment. "Thirty-nine. No business owners nor guild officers, though. A bunch of immigrants and a few homeless."

Bullworth spit into the lapping water that slammed against Melchior Way and its docks.

"Oh, and one more thing. The Inquisition sent an official edict. This case is off-limits to Citywatch and the Inspector's office. It's their jurisdiction now.

"Juno's fucking anus, Spectacles, why did you tell me all that?"

The clerk balked at the nickname. "Well, well. Well, I wrote it down, didn't I?"

Roary threw his cap into the water and cursed so loud it shot seagulls flying up and down the marina. Justice? Fuck's sake.

20

Nito stood in Montka's office, the curtain to his pulpit balcony drifted. The priest's corpse spattered the floor some fifty feet below in the center of his nave. Outside the bolted door blue-gold Auric Guard smashed away with warhammers. The wood split and splintered. Roisin didn't move, hadn't since she opened her eyes after Salavar's leap of faith. She sweat and shook like one does after a good vomit.

"What do we do now?" he asked for the fifth time. Like a parrot, he couldn't stop saying it. There was only the door with the churchknights and the balcony four stories up. Nito wasn't quite ready for either kind of exit. Roisin stumbled and almost fell to the floor.

But then she caught her balance and looked at Nito with furious intent. Gold motes of light danced around her, but it was just dust. "Past the balcony, we can climb the chandeliers, there's a service ladder. I worked here for months."

"Who in the three hells are you?"

"Just a candlelighter."

Nito walked to the balcony and shifted the curtain. Right she was, a rotten ladder led up the further twenty feet to the ceiling. Six stories above the floor where, oh look, Salazar burst across the floor like a squashed tick.

Don't look down. Just climb.

Roisin put a hand on his shoulder. "It will be alright, I'll help you."

He looked back at her, his fear melting. What changed? Why was she so capable?

The top half of the door crashed to pieces, a spiked warhammer smashed in and wrecked the rest of the door away.

"This is it," said Roisin.

Nito gulped and reached up to the first weak rung.

Oppressive darkness flooded the temple in seconds. It bloomed from under Salavar's body then exploded in a heart-beat to fill every corner of the building. It pierced the Auric Guards' armor and crawled into their eyes and ears and anuses. They died wilting like fruit until there was just gleaming armor full of pulped flesh. It stopped around Nito and Roisin on the pulpit, an aura of reality surrounded by ferrous shadow.

Nito hated sorcery. Everyone hates what they fear most. The birthplace of fetish. Those men didn't have a chance to raise their weapons and now they were gone in a breath. Fuck 'em, but still, no one deserves that. He'd seen this type of magic only once, a long time ago. "Three hells, girl. Just what are you?"

Roisin shook in terror. "That wasn't me."

The darkness shifted and hummed like the sea outside the low decks of a ship. It had pressure. When the voice spoke, Nito thought his ear drums burst. Roisin screamed.

"Candlelighter. Your actions endanger machinations far beyond your comprehension."

Nito bent and sneezed blood. It smoked where it hit the absolute darkness around them. He fell to his knees. He closed his eyes but that took him to the dankest corner of his life. Standing at the grave of his wife while Salavar told him his daughter got orphaned to a nunnery. He opened his eyes, but they stung and teared like someone poured mustard on them.

No, Nito. Not again.

Roisin almost shit herself. The dark pressure pushed and pulled on her eyes, her ears, her rectum. Her nose clogged with scabby blood. But the pressure wouldn't pop. It hovered around this state of perpetual in-between.

It would not pierce their bubble, could not. Something stopped it.

She...she stopped it.

"Get out of here!" she screamed into the void.

And the void shrunk back. But for a second.

"YOU DARE, CANDLELIGHTER! YOU JUST AWOKE. I COMMAND THE AURA OF AN EMPIRE."

The darkness hummed louder, now grinding like steel on rock. Dark spears crackled into Roisin's reality bubble, but she pushed them aside with a wave of her hand. Adrenaline commanded her body, her mind burrowed back into animal panic. Like when she first came to High-Father Alonso after the death of her father.

Stop. No.

Not now.

Too late. The Door returned to her booming and the *swish-swish* crawled all over her. No, no, no, not now, please. Anytime but now.

A black tendril thrust into the reality bubble and took Nito through the heart. He screamed and shit a horrible discharge of blood, shit, and pus. For only five seconds, but to Nito it was a week, he watched his daughter clean lepers and never look his way, refuse to look his way, refuse to admit he existed. Refuse, refuse, refuse. He screamed, a man broken.

"Stop it, stop it. You're killing him."

"I WILL DO MUCH WORSE BEFORE I AM DONE."

Nito's mind ran along a barbed iron wire, the empathetic

sorcery sapped his sanity like a mosquito at the vein. He knew this power. He saw it once before from the sidelines and it almost killed him.

This was the full might of Baron Cazzaratti, the Corpse Baron manifest. He would not live to see tomorrow. But it meant his sweepers fucked up far beyond their means. He took his last chuckle then hemorrhaged brown blood from every orifice he owned.

"Stop it!" Roisin screamed. Raw, cracking.

"GIVE IN."

The voice took her away, back to the pews in Veridaan's Sacrament where she hid like a rabbit. Back to when Hook drove his knife into Father Alonso. Again, and again, and again, and again. She sobbed and fell to the floor, shifting between then and now.

The shadow tendrils let go of Nito and filled their whole bubble. It closed in on Roisin, oppressive, debilitating.

But it wasn't as scary as the Door, she thought with a smile. She'd been through worse.

The darkness flinched.

———

The Corpse Baron's aura filled Salavar's office, poured over Roisin and Nito like oil. The dead churchknights' armor sat in the miasma and slowly rusted then wilted to dust. When the darkness cleared Rosin and Nito were gone, just an empty nave and Salavar popped on the floor below. Vincezzo of the Inspector's Precinct would get a letter detailing the cover-up, so would Inquisitor Dietrich. The case would get swept under the rug. Nine widows and two widowers would cry into the night, bereft of their spouses, bereft of their justice.

Hook stalked the lower marina while Ganon Hall watched him over the short dock houses. Truth was he took a longer route than he had to. Truth was he didn't want to go back to Polo and his cane nor his fury. That little Mole got kicked one too many times as a kid and now he wanted to kick down the whole world. Those types were dangerous, and Polo wasn't getting any better.

Fatimah leapt from rooftop to rooftop out of the Mule towards the Crimson Moor. The orange light of their fire lit false dawn across the southern tip of Cruxia. She licked her lips, the flames danced in her eyes. All that power from her actions. Watch the people scurry like ants, all the simple fucks. They didn't know pain, they didn't know suffering, they didn't know the slave galley... No. That was weakness. Watch the power burn, her power burn. Polo would show her how to burn down this whole empire.

Maharez stood at the crossroads of Cranston Way and Melchior Boulevard. Cranston wound through Little Hanrabi and spit him a dozen steps from Ganon Hall. Melchior took him through the white districts, dangerous, but eventually to the mercenary docks. The captains there came from all over the world; Gaiathor, Vohlkhan, the Krodan Jungle, even Hanrabi. The color of his skin was a detail down there, not a death sentence. He started down Melchior Boulevard, away from Ganon Hall. Away from Fatimah.

Sariah Sternwood, no longer Inspector General, lifted her head as the three men pulled her chains and walked her along the hall like a dog. Her arms were chained, her legs were chained, they even put a metal clamp over her mouth with two locks behind her jaw. The only thing free were her eyes so she could watch the desecration. Her fall. Charged with treason. A puppet trial before three Inquisitors. Dietrich sat above them all smiles under his mirrored spectacles. Now chained and dragged through the dungeon of the palace. Fourteen stories down they pulled her, probably below the sea this deep. Sariah never saw the dungeons, she just sent people to them. That thought laughed in her ear when they opened her cell, three inches of fetid water and a mouse-eaten roll of hay.

Polo waited for his agents to return. The East End screamed with fire brigades and clanged with constables. Their burn went well. Good. But did those cunts have the fucking girl? Nothing else mattered. Nothing else. If he failed the Baron Cazzaraati? Best not to think on it. Polo wasn't always a mutant little sadist, once he was a boy who loved his mother and looked after his nineteen younger siblings. Moles were marginalized in Cruxia, couldn't take a loan nor own property. They had to live in sewers or go homeless on the streets. A job for Baron Cazzaraati would support his whole family. He took the gig, but the Baron was cruel, even back when he was human. He beat Polo, he insulted him in front of company, he... did things to Polo with his cock. And now Polo was the greatest sweeper in all of Cruxia. He paid for this position with suffering and now they would all suffer. Every one of them.

The Baron's presence appeared, not slow like usual, but a sinus-cracking punch of black energy. It went dark as fast as light from a candle fills a room. Polo screeched and bent over to keep his vomit down. "FAILURE WILL NOT BE ACCEPTED TWICE."

"What?" Polo screeched. He cried dark blood. "What do you mean?"

The Baron was gone, light returned in a pop and the apartment was exactly as before. Except Roisin and Nito's paralyzed bodies splayed out on the floor. Polo wanted to laugh and cry. All his problems gone. Poof. Delivered here to him, not his agents. Not Hook and his terrifying magic. Polo had the girl. Polo did. Useless, mutant, ugly, monstrous, stinking, gross, rotting, corpulent Polo; there had been so many names over the years. Too many names. Names like bile in the throat.

Something was wrong, though. The Baron never exhausted his own energies anymore. And when he did, there weren't survivors. Baron delivered Polo the girl when Polo failed to deliver her to the Baron. Why wasn't she dead? It made no sense. The Baron could wreck thoughts right from a mortal's consciousness, why drop her here with Polo the torturer?

Because the Baron Caz couldn't read her mind. Maybe he couldn't even kill her. Polo paced and tapped his cane. This girl was a witness to the Baron's assassinations. He killed the hierarchy of the city loyal to the Emperor and consolidated Parliament behind his syndicate. Polo understood the logic of all that, it was business. But the Baron didn't interrogate this girl, he didn't even kill her. Was he scared of her?

This was more than basic witness removal. She threatened the Cazzaraati.

Polo would use this.

21

Sariah curled in the corner of her cell silent as a stone. She would not weep, she would not scream, she would not howl. She would not give the masked dungeon keepers the joy of her misery. They were cruel ones, coming by every half-bell to rattle the bars with their steel mugs. Only at night so the prisoners wouldn't know sleep. They didn't beat her though. A single grain of respect for Cruxian justice she held onto: a starving patriot.

Harsh-cut stone walls covered in mold and a half foot of stinking water on the floor. Cruxian drainage systems, the Fen's great aqueducts, flowed wastewater through the dungeons before they dumped into the Crimson Moor. A more brutal time, Emperor Juilliette Guivere Cruxia instated the sewer dungeons around the same time he built the Inquisition. Sariah thought back to the three Hanrab teenagers hanging from the palace pulpits and looked at her moldy bread attacked by fat cockroaches. More brutal time indeed.

There was no light but the scattered flicker of a torch thirty feet from her cell, her chamber pot was a crusty hole dug in the floor. Her refuse and the city's ran through the cell down to the sludge river below. The stench was unconscionable. Time crawled.

Sariah pushed past the Gantrys as she called them in her head. An hour spent in the doldrums leads to a day, then a year, then that's all there is. The Gantrys. His name brought a smile to her face, in a way she learned more from Gantry than he did from her. About the city, about Cruxia, mostly about how people ticked. She kept distance from her peers and the citizens, how could she not? Hanrab and alien, only recently afforded rights the gods granted all the living. But Gantry showed her you could still know people and keep your distance. Sariah could analyze evidence and alchemical sciences as well as a medicer, her eidetic memory knew the city better than the oldest Inspectors, she couldn't read a witness to save her life though. Gantry didn't even need to access their auras. He would say something homely and disarming and they would warm or get cagey. Three times Sariah would have bagged the wrong suspect if Gantry hadn't figured out the human element at the last moment.

She sighed.

"You sound like me, Inspector General."

"What have I told you about humor?"

"It's an ostentation of the less educated, as always it's the only thing you're wrong about."

"I was wrong about Theresa. Dead wrong."

"Don't sell yourself short, Inspector General. It was my call and play. You felt something was wrong the whole time."

"How would you know that?"

"Because I'm you. Sorry Inspector General, but this is just your coping mechanism."

"It helps me to think with a partner."

"Eh, that's why you kept me around then?"

"No, no. More than that. You knew people, you were kind

and honest with them. You cared about this job, the people, the city."

"I was a sap. Didn't really grow a pair until the end there. Too little, too late."

"What's come over you?"

"Death."

"That's not funny."

"Imagine how I feel."

She chortled. It was an odd sound from Sariah. It just kind of came out, so impulsive. That made her laugh harder, not shrill and panicking but throaty. From deep in her belly, she laughed like she'd never laughed before. Gantry was right, she was wrong about humor.

She laid back on the floor and looked at the ceiling. She studied the grooves and cracks, she had to get used to this. A whole lot of nothing.

"Gantry?"

"Yes, Inspector General."

She bit her tongue. So coy with your own ego? "You used to talk about your sorcery, how emotions and feelings leave an impact. Like the aura of High-Father Alonso after his death, or the pain left on a city block after a fire."

"Aye, it leaves its mark. Energy transferred."

"Could love do the same thing?"

"..."

"Is this really just from my mind? Is there nothing left of you?"

"..."

She started to cry. "Can't I ever see you again?"

"Maybe we can talk again. Further from the event and the location—"

"What?" she almost screamed.

"Come find me when you get out of here. You know the place."

"What?" she shrieked.

But he was gone. If he had even been there in the first place. Something banged on her door startling her to her feet.

It was the jail keep, pock-marked and sallow. "Oi, oilskin," she grimaced, "you talking to yourself already? Most take more than eight hours to crack."

Eight hours? All the gods, she thought it two whole days. Sariah was not used to standing still.

"Don't you have something more important to do? Probably not, huh? Only the most useless citizenry end up as dungeon keepers."

"Oi?" His eyes lit with fire. She would take them where she could. "How about your sorry ass? Eh, oilskin? I got my freedom."

"And yet, here you are. Ten stories beneath the surface, twelve-hour shifts? No, fourteen. It's not like you have family."

He thrust his meaty fingers into the cell, sausages poking out of the merchant stall. She laughed.

"I'll fucking have you, you little cunt. They sent down someone to see you, big fucking dogface with a hammer. Don't think you're gonna make it past tonight, ya' crazy cunt. Believe you me, I'm gonna fuck your corpse if he leaves any of it outside the pulp."

She kept her composure, but his words were cancer. Dogface was a slur for Turakhan, like how oilskin was a slur for Hanrabs. There weren't so many slurs for white Cruxians. Crusa, puta and puti.

"Here he fucking is then. I'll be sure to spit down there before I slide—"

"Remove yourself from this wing at once." The voice rolled, low. The jailkeep flinched.

"Oi, uh... oi, this is my cell block and uh."

A bit of dust shook from the ceiling as the new voice approached her cell. "Uh, uh, uh, that's all you are. Uhhhh." A Turakhan walked up, his hips eye level with the jailor. He wore burnished platemail, each piece larger than her torso though she couldn't see his head past the cell window. The jailor's face turned bone white.

"I...uh, it's just not usual is, uhh..."

The Turakhan flashed a gold signet coin fused into his gauntlet. The jail keep bowed at once, dropped out of Sariah's sight.

"So sorry, uh, whatever your offices be needin.' So sorry."

"Crawl," said the Turakhan.

"Uh, what?"

"Crawl away. You disgust me. I do not want to see you stand. Go. Crawl."

Sariah giggled as the jailor's armor scraped on the dungeon hall, her first giggle. She liked it.

Then the eight-foot-tall Turakhan swung the door open. Masonry scraped off the doorframe as he bent into her tiny cell. He reached outside the door and grabbed a steel maul two feet taller than Sariah. Sariah backed up against her haypile.

Coated in grey skin and coarse hairs, he was a rhino on two legs. Two horns sprouted from his great helm, eyes the size of her fist behind the slits.

"Am I to die?" she asked.

He lifted his head to the ceiling and boomed laughter. "Oh, poor thing. You are already dead. Lucky for you, no?"

She looked at his ancient maul. Enough platemail to cover a horse. His sad, giant eyes.

This would be better than an eternity of waiting. She closed her eyes. Perhaps, perhaps she would see the wheel of stars her grandmama spoke of. She could know the culture stolen from her. She still remembered her real name, Eadala. Eadala like her ancestors on the wheel of stars. She lived as a Cruxian, but she would die a Hanrab.

She opened her eyes. The Turra stood in the corner with his head bowed.

A man walked into her cell, utilitarian armor with no ornamentation. He had brown-grey hair cut short and his face needed a shave five hours ago. A simple signet coin melded into his left pauldron, the only sign that this was Fox Sentelpidio Cruxis, Emperor of Cruxia.

22

Hook lit a tailor outside the doorway to Ganon Hall. The heat stink from the Moor fought through the harsh tobacco. He sneered. It started to rain, a muggy rain that felt like piss down the leg. It pushed the smoke from the Marina, the storm clouds lit like molten gold above their blaze. The commotion took the pressure off of the criminal districts, at least three dozen Greys down there containing the citizens. Hook used to contain citizens back during the Sia'so, herded was more like. Riot control training was similar, pack them in a line, keep them moving, stop stragglers by any means possible. "Treat them like cattle," his CO used to say. "That's all they are, fucking cattle."

Fuck. Hook was sentimental. He always made bad decisions when sentimental. Married a Hanrab woman while sentimental. Left the army after her village and their child got hit by fairyfire, contained; sentimental. And now he mulled if sentimentality would quit him of Polo once and for all. He gave the decision to the end of his handroll, he was all out of tailor tobacco.

A shadow shifted between the alley dumpsters, silent as the

grave. Hook sensed Fatimah with ethereal perception, felt her aura shift the city's ley currents where she went. Girl was harder to pinpoint than a fucking cat and Hook was shit with auras already.

"Oi," he called.

"Fuck you" she called back.

"That used to be charming. Now I'm sick of it. Where's Maharez."

She stepped into the lamplight on the street. "I don't know, he said he'd find his own way."

Shit. Sentimental, huh Maharez? Hook pretended like it didn't phase him. "That's rex. I'm gonna finish my smoke, I'll wait up for him."

"Do whatever you want. If he can't make it back, he's weak." She stalked inside.

Hook watched her. That was new. Fatimah hated Polo and Hook with a daily venom. But Maharez held her last shred of decency. Sure, she smacked him and cussed at him, but you heard concern behind it. What she just said though, unabashed, raw. She didn't care about him. Had she ever?

Fatimah screamed, muffled by Ganon's walls. Hook flicked his tailor and ran in.

———

Maharez gasped, his feet slapping smooth cobblestones. He ran past shops and cafes, neat little houses packed together tighter than cart oxen.

"Stop!" screamed a Citywatch Grey from thirty feet behind.

Shouldn't have taken Melchior Boulevard, Maharez. Not after burning down a tavern, not with the city in upheaval as the blaze took two ships. Definitely not as a black man. He wasn't familiar with the docks, nor the merchant stalls on the East End. The streets were barren, the sky still lit by their arson. Alarm bells clanged from six different blocks across the shoreline.

You really fucked the elephant on this one, huh, Maharez? His dad used to say that, he'd never remembered that before.

A constable beelined out of an alley and tackled Maharez. He rolled, keeping the man's arm locked so it took the force of their fall. It cracked like wet thunder and Maharez bound away back on his feet. The Grey screamed hoarse until the other Citywatch barreled over him in a sprawl.

Maharez banked right then twisted left and jumped into a rice paper storefront. A small restaurant packed with two enormous grey Turakhan drinking tea through long trunks. Everyone, even the teenage serving girl, paused at the absurdity. Maharez leapt over the Turakhan's dining table, clattered the whole tea set to the floor, then burst out the opposite rice paper wall.

"Get back here, you insolen—"

But Maharez was already away, into the empty garbage alley behind the restaurant row. Drawing in deep breaths and holding them, letting the oxygen revitalize him. He kept up his pace. Above the houses, away from the inferno and the burning marina, he saw the masts of great vessels. He closed in on the Mercenary Docks, so close to another world where he could be an equal.

He crashed from the alley onto a great boulevard split by blue flowers. Sixteen Citywatch in heavy armor greeted him with crossbows aimed.

"First rank, fire!" shouted the sergeant.

Maharez rolled away as the bolts bit the pavement.

———

Polo cleaned his instruments in the foyer of their apartment.

Black curtains hung over the kitchen and living room, like a surgeon's tent in the military camp. His victims slumbered.

Downstairs he heard the Hanrab girl scream. That little one was much too ambitious. Polo depended on it the past three years, pointing her like a lance in whatever direction he pleased. Fatimah wanted more, though; she reeked of it. Her imbecile brother just wanted out, like most. The useless cunts. All his life, a shower of cunts.

But not Fatimah, she wanted the whole city, she wanted everyone to suffer like she must have as a child. Polo understood, he too wanted it all. He suffered more than anyone could know. But he needed to watch her and close. Polo would use his molten lance once more. Until he found a place to bury her.

He went to the door, moved downstairs. Fatimah shook in the middle of the lobby. Hook stood at the door like a donkey. Busted skeletons sprayed viscera and blood on the floor, chunky like spilled soup. Fatimah vomited into the closest mess, pinto beans mixed with human offal.

"Just what the fuck is this?" asked Hook. His nose cringed. The sorcery here was virulent. Too long in this room and they'd all catch the wasting.

"Your failure brought the Baron Cazzaratti upon us, he's delivered the girl and Alistair Nito."

Hook stepped back, shook. "Why aren't they dead?"

Fatimah started towards Polo and the stairs like a windup toy. This was the most wretched sorcery she'd ever seen. It reeked like a dozen dead zebras. Born on the border of the Crystal Wastes and their tyrannical sorcerer-kings, she hated magic.

"What?" said Polo.

Hook shouted. "Why didn't the most powerful mage this side of the Claret Sea kill the pair of them?"

Polo hesitated. He would not bleed his cards to Hook quite yet. "Perhaps to teach us a lesson. Come girl, bolster your resolve. I can't have you waffle like your brother." Fatimah glared venom at him and knocked his shoulder with hers as she passed. Perfect. Dig at her hatred. Make her sloppy.

But not yet, girl. Not yet. Polo still had use for her.

Hook glared over the dozen bodies blended like good chili between them. The Corpse Baron let the candlelighter live to 'teach us a lesson?' Along with the most notorious sweeper to give up the chimney? Get the fuck out of here, Polo. What angle did he play?

Fatimah slammed the door to their room. Good, thought Polo. Her brother wasn't here, maybe dead. She was unstable, Polo would use this. On the stairs, he looked down at Hook and his six feet, four. Finally above him. "I need you in here. We are going to melt Nito."

"Melt Nito? You wanna melt a sweeper?"

"Former sweeper. We are not the only ones in need of a lesson."

Hook stared Polo dead in the eye. Polo always looked away first, what with his fear of magic. Polo refused to break. He bore into the wizard. Hook grit his teeth so hard one cracked. "Rex, Polo. Real rex."

Polo smiled, a hangman's smirk. "You and the oilskin will break Nito. I work on the girl. Alone. Baron Cazzaraati's orders."

Hook swept a quick glance; the pulped civilians, Polo stood above him like a king, Fatimah hooked on his bullshit. "Real rex, Polo. You're the boss."

Hook decided. He would put the magic painkiller on Nito and then dust. Maybe find Maharez and an actual life. Anywhere but here.

23

R oisin opened her eyes to a cheap kitchen in need of a sweep. She tried to sit up, her limbs were full of sand. No rope this time, but she felt bound. Drugs, maybe? Sorcery. The past few hours were a haze, like they happened to someone else. A chapel? Yes, a priest with red eyes and terrible desires. Nito and Roisin tied back to back. Then the virulent darkness, a wasting black mist around them.

Wasting, don't think of the wasting. Don't think of Da'. Don't think of the Door.

The Door. She always returned to the Door. Back at the temple of Auron, when that terrible black sorcery struck at them, something kept it away. Roisin thought it her own will, but when it tore into Nito she broke. They should have died. At the end, as it took her, she thought of the Door. Nothing scared her more than the Door, not even Moles. Nor the black virulence that took those churchknights.

She knew what the Door was. She could run from the truth, chased like back on the bridge. Or she could face it.

The Door was not real. The Door was a construct. Long ago, she made the Door. It buried a memory. She did not want to deal with it, and so it grew to this nightmare in her psyche. Compounded by the constant hunting, the loss of her savings, her desecration to the Crimson Moor. She'd unravel every thread that was Roisin just so she would not have to open that Door.

KNOCK-KNOCK

I know, I know. But it won't make a difference. Just go away.

KNOCK-KNOCK.   *KNOCK-KNOCK-KNOCK-KNOCK-KNOCK-KNOCK.*

Father?

———

Nito awoke on the floor in a drab room covered by black curtains. Curtains over the windows, curtains strapped to the floor, curtains hanging over the doorway. It was stuffy, stifled, lit by a single candle swinging from a vacant chandelier. A kill room. Pretty standard syndicate procedure for torture and execution. Problem was, Nito had never been on this side of the curtain. They were good at this, let him wake up alone. Start feeling despair before they bring out the knives.

He tried to flip onto his stomach and push to his feet. His limbs refused to move. Fucking. Sorcery.

Shit, what about the candlelighter? Nito smacked his head on the floor. Failed another girl like he failed his daughter. Like he failed his wife. His head throbbed. Fucking stupid, Nito. He followed the flicker of the single candle. All those empty spots in the chandelier. Sort of like his life in the long run.

Yeah, Nito, mope. That will save the day.

The curtain moved and Hook stalked in with a grim face. Not the grim-I'm-gonna-kill-ya look but the grim-my-puppy-died kind of face. Now who's moping? Nito chuckled.

"How ya' doing, tough guy? What's so funny?"

"You look worse than I feel right now."

Hook grimaced, a bulldog frown. "Yeah, sure, tough guy. I'm... I'm sorry about this." He brought out hethbara from a belt pouch and took the mortar and pestle from a side table.

"Sorry? Thought you were the tough one, Hook. That's what all the chimneys used to say. 'Toughest sum'bitch to walk out of the Hanrab Rebellion'."

Hook glared at him. "There's a code to sweeping. The shit these days... it's just about blood and body count. No style, no form. Another five years and there will be war in the streets." The whole time he ground hethbara in the mortar, pinching more powders and unguents from his belt. "There won't be sweepers, just thugs with steel doing whatever they feel like."

"Hook, what the fuck are you talking about?"

Hook surged over and grabbed his face in a meaty grip, Nito's molars ground like fingernails on chalkslate. "And leave Hanrabi out of this, rex? I'm trying to be fucking nice here."

Nito spit bloody phlegm to the side. "Fuck you."

"Fucked myself, Nito. Fucked myself." He sat down in a slump next to Nito. "Want a smoke?"

Nito raised his paralyzed neck as far as it would go. "Eh?"

"Ah, here." Hook hovered his hand over Nito, blood blossomed through his torso and arms.

"Ah, fuck," said Nito. He shuddered.

"Hell of pins and needles, tough guy. Your whole damn body's been asleep, like sitting on the john too long."

"Bit worse than that."

Hook rolled two handroll tobaccos with white rice paper. Nito reached up for one as the shakes left his hand. Still paralyzed from the waist down, he dragged himself to half-sitting and Hook lifted him the rest of the way. Hook put the handroll in Nito's mouth and snapped a flame in his bare palm, cupped it so Nito could light up. They exhaled together, the stuffy room soon full of smoke.

"What's going on, Hook?"

"Lots. All above our pay grade."

"I'm not on the take."

"Wish you still were, Nito. Wish you were. More men like you and the syndicates might be what they used to. You know, you were the first sweeper to ever take me on a run?"

"Is that right?" The tobacco settled Nito's nerves. He awoke to the black curtains and expected the worst. He didn't know what was up with Hook, but he'd take the reprieve and the smoke. He felt great, actually.

Hook chuckled. "Oh yeah, hit a sopa lane on the Claret Sea. Fortnight job that dragged into a three-monther. Lost a quarter of the crew—"

"—to a sperm whale. We sailed the edge of a storm out too far and—"

"—Captain drove us into a mating site. Damn female almost dragged us to the bottom of the fucking ocean, we were the biggest dick in the sea."

Nito laughed, raucous and raw. He couldn't stop, Hook barrelled guffaws next to him. Tears streaked by the end of it, two sweepers in a kill room. Two sweepers back on that whaler in the mess hall with nothing but ocean and the promise of sopa and oil in front of them.

"You're alright, Hook."

Hook grimaced again. "I'm just polite."

"What?" The words echoed from miles away, miles above. Hook sat next to him on the floor, looked down as Nito spiralled lower and lower. And lower. Like a tub with the plug pulled, round and round to the end. Hook's face hung above him like a stubbly moon, twisting and twisting. "What...what the fuck did you do me?" His words slurred, pulled through molasses.

Hook's moon face frowned down at him. "I'm sorry, Nito. Real sorry. The hethbara, the kax, the yoldomite."

"My handroll."

Hook nodded. "Yeah, easier on you if you inhale it. Kills the pain."

Nito sank further, the black room spun to a black web. Sticky. Encompassing. "Hook. But we were—"

"We were sweepers, Nito. Not after tonight though, neither of us." He put a fat thumb to Nito's forehead and wiped the sweat away. "You don't deserve this, brother. Hanrabi all over again. How long can a man just follow orders?" His eyes drifted.

Nito sank into the drug jungle. Languid vines of comfort wrapped around him and constricted. His vision spun like a top, but the vines held him tight. He missed this, oh! His whole life of atonement, all for a daughter who refused to look his way. Now the impulse was back, the sweet, eternal galaxy of feeling and enlightenment. The gods were nothing next to a good smoke and a cask of fine ale. Nito denied himself too long. He deigned to call it penance? What a fool.

Hook pulled him up so they were eye to eye. Nito stared past him, his vision tripled and kaleidoscoped. "Nito, I'm real sorry about this."

Nito's consciousness spiked like a rusty iron through his drug jungle. He tried to sit up on dead legs. "What about the candlelighter?"

"You know how it goes in this business." Hook pulled an orange vial from his belt, sighed, then grabbed Nito by the shoulder and dragged him close.

Nito's focus bounced; he saw Hook, the vial of orange, the slow burning tailor on the carpet he dropped at some point. "Hey, hey. Hook." His words came through sand, dry and clumsy. His thoughts dragged a mile behind his words, a furrow in the sand. He could not remember why he was here. Or where.

"Hook, Hook." He pointed, his arm a turgid slug. "That tailor. It's still lit." He pointed real hard, only thing he could focus on. That burning cigar on the carpet.

Where did Nito go? Where did Nito show the go, no? Where did Nito flow with the oh-no ho jojo? He chuckled, nothing made sense. Not even the big wizard and his meaty hands. It was funny. Drugs, huh? Missed this.

Hook took his orange capsule and flicked the cork with a pop. "I'll get the tailor, Nito. Don't you worry about it." He leaned in and poured the thick, orange gel over Nito's face.

"Huh, that tickles," said Nito.

Hook looked away. "It won't after a while. Won't tickle at all."

———

KNOCK-KNOCK-KNOCK-KNOCK.

The Hanrab girl and the ugly Mole with his cane pushed past the black curtains into the kitchen. Roisin steeled her jaw shut and slowed her breathing. In through your nose, out through your mouth. Control within and all that other shit Alonso used to say. She would not give these two her screams, not without some effort at least. The Mole's smile was brown and rotten, the girl's a grin of pearls. Rosin spit a thick wad into her face.

"Owed you for the bridge, maruth' kaba."

Fatimah's face burst with rage. "You stupid little bitch!" She cracked Roisin's face into the table leg. Rosin couldn't move her limbs, tangled on the floor.

"Calm yourself, girl. Ire will do you no good in this kind of room. The little cunt here has run you all ragged for the past day and a half, she won't be threatened by your silly little temper. Will you?" The Mole swung his cane and broke Roisin's nose with a squelch. She sneezed bloody cartilage across the floor and almost blacked out from the pain. But she didn't scream.

"There, hold her now."

193

"Why? She is paralyzed."

Polo stepped on her ankle and pushed. Rosin didn't feel the pressure. "She could be faking. This one's a professional, the run around she gave you." The Mole leaned in close to her with a breath of mustard and old onions. It stung. Tears ran down her face in languid streams, but she did not cry out. Would not cry out.

"I'm a candlelighter," Roisin laughed. "You must think you're so smart. But I'm just a candlelighter and you're an ugly idiot." She laughed harder tinged in hysteria. She knew she would not leave this room alive. Life's tragedy, but when you finally understand that it's comedy. She laughed louder.

Fatimah did not know what to do. She was deflated, impotent. If the victim didn't feel fear, there was no point, right? Lightning struck her, did she only want to cause pain? No, she wanted to cause fear. What was the difference? Oh, where was Maharez? Where was her rock?

Polo stared at Rosin, clasped his hands under his chin. His cataracts caught the two candles in the room and burned with the reflection of the girl on the floor. "A candlelighter? Please. I've been a sweeper long enough to know another. And working with Nito, eh? An ex-sweeper and a young sweeper, what a juicy romance that makes. You're younger than his daughter, you know that? Maybe that's what got his glory going—"

"It's not like that, he—"

Polo smacked her broken nose with his cane. "Do not interrupt me." She sobbed. "You were with him when he acquired the kax supply of Cruxia. You work for the Siegewards, meant to disrupt us from the offset and shift the power towards your dying syndicate. We dealt with the Marlowes and we will deal with you. Now," he hit her nose again and she screamed in pain, "just tell me when I am right. I know I am, but I need you to say it."

Roisin sobbed. She couldn't help it when she breathed through her broken nose. How's that for control Veridaan?

"Girl," said the Mole, "grab the cutter. I'm done asking nice-like."

The Hanrab took out a sawtooth knife and passed it to the Mole. Her pearly grin came back. Rosin didn't know how much more pain she could take, when she would break.

"Now, little sweeper. I will take off your fingers, joint by joint. My partner has a burning agent to cauterize the wounds as they appear until you have nothing left on either hand. Rex?"

Knock-knock

Rosin couldn't breathe, her heart a battering ram. She stank of sweat and had to pee. She really had to pee. Fatimah grabbed her arm and dragged it over the short kitchen table, the Mole spread the fingers out. His touch was soft as cotton, but he smelled like a wet dog.

She wanted to cry and scream, bloody mucus ran down her face in sobs, no sound. She thought she might die of fright. Her heart peeled, a timpani drum.

KNOCK-KNOCK-KNOCK-KNOCK-KNOCK

Oh no. Not now. The Door.

"Not scared, so you—" The Mole backhanded her jaw.

KNOCK-KNOCK-KNOCK.

The Mole took her thumb with his sausage fingers and pinched it below her da's ring. Da's wedding band. Proof that he was an actual thing on actual earth.

The Mole sawed at the joint right above where it sat. Feeling returned to her hands in ragged scrapes, skin flensed like chicken breast. She screamed, absolutely, all reason and resistance torn away by the knife.

KNOCK-KNOCK-KNOCK-KNOCK.

Could she let these killers take her da's ring? She would not. The knife continued, caught the bone like a log and sped up. Halfway there streaming ligament; blood sprayed until it pooled on the table and ran in a river toward the short-legged corner.

"Stop, stop, stop."

KNOCK-KNOCK-KNOCK.

He sawed on until the thumb fell to the table, plop. Roisin stopped screaming, staring at the stump of her right thumb. Her da's ring slid along the bloody half-digit, slumped and tinked onto the table. It rolled in and out of the stream of blood, tracing lanes of red.

Polo laughed. Fatimah looked at the thumb, eyes avaricious. She licked her lips. She did love pain, a revelation like ecstasy.

Roisin hissed and glared at her torturers. Polo took a step back. Roisin's face wore nothing human. She screamed, not in fear but in rage. Polo's eyes turned up to the whites, Fatimah pissed her pants, her ears popped.

"Don't you touch my father!" she bellowed. Far louder than her human lungs should be capable of. Why did she say that? The killers collapsed to the floor and spasmed, the mole cracked his head against the floorboards in a quick beat.

The Door entered her vision, it took up everything, filled the room and pushed her to the ground. KNOCK-KNOCK-KNOCK.

She reached and took the knob, her grip slipped in slick blood. She had to drag up her left arm to stabilize. She wanted her da's ring. Where was it? She looked around in utter darkness. There was no room, the killers were gone. Just the Door and her hand on the knob. She pushed, but this time she kept her eyes open.

INTERLUDE

"*Careful, little Rose, you'll catch the wasting.*"
"*Rose, Rose, don't climb so high.*"
"*Did you eat any turnips? You need to eat two before bedtime or no dolls.*"
"*How many times do I have to tell you, stay off the bookcase!*"
"*I will always be with you, Roisin, always. Always.*"

Everything changed when Da' got sick. Just the two of them crammed in a basement apartment, cleaved from the foundation of the city. Mule sick-water ran right under their building. Cheap. No windows. But Da' raised her all by himself. Mother died so Roisin could live. Da' would never say it, but she knew. Mortia protect. Amen.

Da' made it work, taught at three schools while baby Roisin wore diapers. When she was but eight, he picked up two more schools. The pay was garbage. He refused to work the Promenade nor the Palace district where three senators requested his service. Roisin's mother came from nobility, after all, the fairy tale father told every night. Parliament wanted his education. But he kept the two of them down in the Mule.

"Education goes a lot further with us. High-born don't need advantages, the real Cruxians down here do."

But then he got sick.

Slow at first, coughs in the evening. Long trips to the outhouse, more and more frequent. He dropped to three schools again, then one in less than a season.

Life... changed. There was only Da'. He dropped all his classes after winter. Dropped thirty pounds alongside. All his lessons, all his earnings gone. They didn't have money to start. Nor did he have the weight to lose.

At first, she lit candles in her apartment with no windows. Her da' woke up later and later each day. By the third week, he didn't talk. A white tongue clogged his mouth.

Roisin held him, she bathed him. She wiped the snot and drool from his face. Back then the candles burned.

Hours, weeks, maybe months. Roisin took a wet rag to Da's mouth, his nose leaked. She picked up the water and the bread at her door each morn' to mark time. She took the cold rag to her father each evening. Eventually, they ran out of candles. They ran out of money.

There wasn't light. There wasn't bread at the door (DOOR), nor water.

Time stopped, it spread out. No rules.

There was only the dark and the rag. Reality blistered like her skin.

Roisin obsessed over her sick dad. She kept him clean, he kept her safe. But in the dark, it started. That swish-swish. Light and low at first, but after eternity in darkness, it crawled over him. She had to brush off, then fight off the swish-swish. The swish-swish carpeted his body, but she cleaned it off each hour, didn't she just? Hour on hour on hour, darkness. No days. No nights. Just dark. Hours. Hours. *Swish-swish*. A wet rag to his mouth to clear the *swish-swish*. His swollen tongue clean clean clean cleaned. She is a good daughter. Father father, say something just something just say a breath. Say one breath. *Swish-swish*. Hours on hours. No bread, no water at the door anymore. No light. Just *swish-swish* and the rag wet with gods know what. Wipe wipe wipe the tongue. Wipe wipe wipe the butt. Hours and hours and hours.

Then came a knock. A knock at the door.

No, not now, I still have my father.

Knock-knock. Polite.

She scrambled around her da'.

KNOCK-KNOCK.

Light beat around the door (**DOOR**), light in her eye like a sun.

KNOCK-KNOCK-KNOCK.

A voice like thunder, "Please open up, we've had complaints about a smell."

KNOCK-KNOCK-KNOCK-BANG!

The door (**KNOCK**) burst open. Rosin screamed and held her da', at least what was left of him. The light burned her eyes, even just a torch down here in the basement. She screamed and hugged her dead father as the curtain of cockroaches *swish-swished* off his corpse and the two Citywatch walked in.

"DON'T YOU TOUCH MY FATHER—"

Roisin returned to the black curtains and her two killers on the floor. She gagged, dry-heaved spit. She couldn't remember the last time she ate. Her limbs came back in pins and needles. She did not want to remember her da'. Her mind pulsed, shattered the corners of the kill room. Where did that term come from, kill room? Plaster rained.

From the mind of the mole, it opened like a cookbook in front of her.

She ran from Ganon Hall, screaming. Out a door, down a twist of stairs, past a nightmare room of corpses.

Six blocks later, Rosin realized all this horrifying power was hers.

Somewhere, a god laughed. She laughed too. Nothing could stop her now.

24

Maharez watched from a rooftop as Cruxia fell to fire and violence. He was cold and hungry, the sun cut red past the smoke. Three gashes cut by crossbow bolts crossed his face and arms. The streets on the East End tore themselves to pieces. Citizens smashed windows, lines of Greys frayed and retreated. Fires raged everywhere, far from the marina and their burn. Rebellion took Cruxia.

At a crowded corner, a mob of Hanrabs gathered and cheered around a matron Turakhan shaman. Dreads clumped around her twisting horns. "The reckoning is upon them, they hang our Hanrab brothers from the city walls. Trial with no witnesses, no jury? Where is justice? They burn down Krodan whalers, Hanrab cogs. No investigation into the arson. When do we burn down this white man's city? Where is our Emperor now? Where is he?" They cheered, they screamed. Maharez wanted to join them, wanted to shout their justice to the burning city. But a constable pulled himself over the lip of the roof. "I have you now."

Fuck's sake. Were there not more pressing issues?

"Maruth kaba." Maharez dove off the roof. He caught snapping laundry lines until he landed in a wooden dumpster of horse manure. The constable landed with a thick *clunk* on his neck across the street and never moved again.

Maharez took stock. An alley across the back end of a livery. Horse stables sprawled in a dirty alley, they brayed. A mountain of hay leaned against a two-story apartment. Realization gonged. This was her apartment. The candlelighter, or spy girl, or whatever she was. This was her apartment, the same one Hook took out his dirty onion to read the soul of.

Explosions lit the East End above the buildings. One, two, then three. Dull pops like earthquakes below his feet. Maharez scrambled up the hay to the apartment's window. He paused. There was grey behind the glass.

Odd. Just grey. No color.

He pushed a finger through the grey. Then his fist. When nothing happened, he pushed his head through. Like the few times his dad took him swimming before he died, test the water.

"You fucked the elephant on this one, huh?" Maharez's father said from the past.

————

The apartment remained just as he and Hook left it.

But there was the girl curled in the corner like a cat under the bed. Her eyes bore into Maharez like a spear.

He found her. He found their mark. She was beautiful. He couldn't kill her, he would tell—

And then he sank, the wooden windowsill like grease between his fingers, he sank through into the floor.

What?

————

Maharez's fingers squelched in mud, gritty with broken reeds. He could smell smoke. He tried to stand but slipped. Where did he know this from? Gritty mud, smoke. No, no it couldn't be. He looked around, reeds everywhere, fronds between them full of rice. But the fields were smashed, horse hooves trampled their livelihood to nothing. Fires caught. There were raiders in his village.

He ran to find his mother. Fatimah, Fatimah screamed from behind him, somewhere back clogged on the reeds. His legs were so slow, he was young. He was not fast and strong for his age yet. He paused, Fatimah behind him or his mother still down at the river? He chose the river, crying against the harsh smoke, crying as he abandoned his sister.

The stalks whipped and tore at him. He crashed through a thicket, his face streaked in cuts. At the edge of the briarwood, he hid. Riders out there along the river. The sun cut red and orange across the sky. Horsemen rode in silhouette, swinging tulwars down, slashing his brethren like he would the reeds. He couldn't move, fear choked in his throat.

The riders screamed and rode across the shallow river, villagers scattered like mice through the farmlands. He ran to the river, he screamed for his mother. He screamed for Fatimah. He turned over bodies, so many bodies. Mihir and Kalla and little Rani and all of them. Then he saw it.

There, drifting in the fronds like a log. It couldn't be, couldn't be, couldn't be Mother. Mama, mama please blink. Mother, I will pull the water from your lungs like you did to me as a toddler. Mother no, no no, Mother say something. MOTHER.

He held her close and screeched. He yelled and yelled and begged Halladar to return her from the wheel of stars. He was not done with her, he needed her. Please, Halladar, grant this selfishness. Just let her say his name—

The riders got him on their return, yanked him out of the

shallow water, yanked him from his mother. He screamed and reached for her as the man clubbed him. There was darkness...

Then Maharez's fingers squelched in mud, gritty with broken reeds. He could smell smoke. He tried to stand but slipped. Where did he know this from? Gritty mud, smoke. No, no it couldn't be. He looked around, reeds everywhere, fronds between them full of rice. But the fields were smashed, horse hooves trampled their livelihood to nothing. Fires caught. There were raiders in his village.

Oh no. Not again.

Maharez relived the moment seven times before he broke, for the first half of the nightmare he still had hope for his mother. But he broke, he broke and threw himself-

———

Roisin watched the Hanrab sputter on the floor, shake and spit like those two at Ganon Hall. She was surprised this one found her, returned to the scene of the crime and all that. Why did her room smell like rotten onions? No matter. He flew into her web like a skinny fly. He would pay before she killed him. Three more to go after this.

Her mind was open. When she looked out her window, she could see every aura like tracemarks when you stare at a candle too long. The Mule was on fire, riots and looters stalked the streets in growing gangs hazed by red hatred and white-hot rage. One group had a Citywatch corpse on a noose they carried like pallbearers, he radiated black death while he swung. Anytime they came too close to her apartment, she reached out with her new influence and turned them away. Some got sick, some had a sudden fear of death, others didn't even notice the place existed. She flexed her power like a bicep, wood creaked where the room expanded around her. With a thought, she could detonate this whole building and remain unscathed.

But she wouldn't, right? They were decent people, well the innkeep was a nasty old racist but the rest were alright. She put them all asleep when she got here. It was so easy, most people in Cruxia are tired all the time. She shouldn't kill them though, right? They hadn't hurt her. Power and mania fought over her soul.

They didn't deserve it like this one on the floor. Her grin creaked and so did the room around her. She enjoyed causing this one pain. Pain like he and his sister caused her, caused the High-Father.

"You reap what you sow," she spat at him.

A golden mote of light danced at her window then burned so bright she couldn't look at it.

"Is that what I taught you little Rose?" A voice, warm and gentle.

"Father Alonso?" she asked, hand to her eyes.

"Remember what I taught you all those years ago? Control within begets control without. You must control this new energy."

She snarled. "Control couldn't save you, control didn't save me."

"All of life is a test of the Siblings. You have been chosen by Veridaan."

"Enough!" The golden light flew back, its color dulled. "I know things now, things you didn't tell me. Veridaan is long dead, died fighting Auron after he raped her."

"Little Rose, you know—"

"I read it from an evil shit's mind like it was a picture book. You could have shown up anytime. I've been beaten, starved, tortured." She held up the ragged joint. "They took my fucking thumb. Where were you? Where was Veridaan? Take your control and go. I have all that I need." The mote was gone. Blown out the window and atomized over the city.

She twisted her finger and the Hanrab teenager stood up like a marionette. He screamed for his mother in silence. It roared in Roisin's ears. She ran him through his personal little hell one more time, then flicked her finger. He dove out the window.

25

Hook dodged riot gangs through the Mule. Here he was all sentimental. Finally did it, finally left Polo and his cane and his lunacy. In the belly of this district, he'd find Maharez. His aura wriggled somewhere in the Mule's apartment block. This should be preschool magic, but Hook was shit with auras. Plus, the city brimmed with fire and violence. Streaks of smoke lit like hellfire with the riot's white and red aura. He'd find Maharez and the two of them would exit, stage left.

Fuck if Cruxia didn't look more like his tours with the Corp, the whole burg clogged in smoke. The rioters controlled more ground than Citywatch, children hid in alleys and sewers. Word was it started in Little Hanrabi. The district went up in arms when they arrested Sariah Sternwood, some hero Inspector from Tullawas. Fucking idiots upstairs brought this down on themselves. It gave Hook a screen through the city, but how would they get out once he found Maharez?

He slunk into an alley as a horse rode past with its rider dead and dragged behind. The rear of a livery took up the whole alley behind him. Horses brayed and screamed as smoke rolled in. Too sentimental. He was back at Hurasang, murdering horses so the Turvaali couldn't escape. He shivered and lifted their latches one by one. They thundered out into the city. Hook felt their retreat under his toes for another six blocks. People screamed from their path. Fuck 'em. They should've remembered the horses.

He turned back up the alley, caught Maharez's ocean blue aura up in a window where he climbed. Hook realized where he was, the candlelighter's apartment. Smart kid, he hid in the one safehouse he knew.

Then Hook's awareness keyed up. He brought as much power to bear as he could in an instant. The window flew open and golden dust sprayed out, dulled to brown. It caught a smoke haze from the marina winds and dissipated to nothing. That was that High-Father's essence, discorporeated forever. You know an aura pretty well when you killed the man. That was magic like a god up there.

A bundle of sticks dove from the window to land in a hump in front of Hook. Ah, fuck. Fucking Veridaan's wet clit.

He bent down and scooped up Maharez. The boy's neck stuck out with a bad knot, his head hung at the wrong angle. He wheezed through tears. "Don't talk, Hama, don't talk. I've got you, I've got you." Hook rocked back and forth with the boy. He wasn't in some Mule alley, he was back in Kullada. Fire teams of Mage Corps flew over streaming fire in the farmlands. His daughter Hama had not been evacuated. Nor had three thousand Hanrabs. He found her in a refugee camp, alone and choking on smoke, her throat scorched. No hope. He clutched her in the final moments, screaming his curses to the gods, to the Mage Corps, to himself. He failed her. And here he was with Maharez, failed again. Taught the boy just enough to get him killed. Maharez should have been a hero. He'd die a criminal in the gutter.

Maharez took his hand, looked up in his eyes. He faded,

color drained from his face, his eyes got further and further. "Guh, guh, huh guh."

"Shhh, shh, shhh. It's okay, Maha. Look." He twisted the boy, a bag of broken glass. "Look up at the wheel of stars. Look, you have an eternity of rebirth. Can you see them?"

But smoke overtook the whole sky, there were no stars in Cruxia that night. And Maharez was dead.

He kissed Hama's forehead. Maharez's forehead. This was Maharez. "You made it out of Cruxia, buddy. Most don't."

Someone watched him. He glared up at the window and built electricity around his hand. Fuck if it wasn't the candle-lighter. Mortia protect, did she look rough around the edges. Nose squashed like lox on a bagel. She stared down at him with ancient eyes.

"You," she called, "you murdered Father Alonso."

"Well, you just killed my best friend. Call it even?"

"Hardly." Sorcery built around her like the sun. More power than Hook could imagine.

He held up a hand and let his own magic strike the clouds. "No tricks, let's talk."

"I'm done talking."

"Then listen. I killed Alonso, but you just disintegrated his soul. He'll never return to Veridaan's bosom, he's gone. Exorcised. Kaput."

Her face changed, the girl returned. "What?"

"A couple drops of sand ago, golden light blew out your window. You wield that kinda power and don't know your old step-dad?"

"I didn't mean to do that. I just wanted him to leave me alone."

"What, so you could kill my friend?" She buckled, grabbed her hair. "That's one slippery slope. Look," he pulled out a bag and put it on the ground, "that's three hard in gold. I'm gonna leave it. Get out of this city. Get out before it eats you up."

Radiance returned to her eyes. "You can't buy me off. You killed Alonso."

"About as much as you did, kiddo. I fired the shot. But I didn't string the bow. I didn't forge the arrowhead."

"Make. Sense."

"I can give you the real killer, the one who ordered the hit. The one who keeps you all poor and dying."

The girl's face scrunched up catlike, sinister.

"Baron Alouicious Cazzaraati. The Corpse Baron. He lives at 13 Noctic Lane, manor on the Promenade. Sits right up next to the palace."

"Good."

"It's well guarded, don't die out there. Or do. Makes no difference to me. Peace." He lifted a lazy wave, then picked up Maharez's corpse, a sack of spare parts.

"Wait," she said from above.

"Fuck's sake." Hook turned to her with Maharez draped in his arms. She lifted a hand, power returned around her in a rush. "Hey, hey, fuck you, we had a—"

"—deal."

Hook stood in a vast valley between two sandstone mesas. Night. The air tinged in smells like from the heavens. Roast kabobs, grilled tomatoes, spices on spices. Spices like Hook thought he'd never smell again. Sweeping rice fronds, farmland in neat furrows, a river nearby irrigated through pipelines. A neat village of riads. Warm and arid, Hook sweat. Maharez a bag of bones in his arms, never to breathe again.

He returned to Hanrabi. A vast wheel of stars above them, all the stars in the cosmos. Hook breathed deep. Behind him a cemetery, the east side full of mud-brick mausoleums and great statues carved from sandstone. The west was just sticks in the ground, a sign in Hanrab read, "Here Lies the Lost."

A plot not thirty feet from him, empty with a spade stuck in the dirt pile. Hook took Maharez over and gently laid him down in Galea's bosom. He prayed to Halladar that the boy would run again on this earth, he prayed to Hosiris that the beasts would stay away from his body while he found his way home, he prayed to Terminus so the soul-thief would ignore Maharez on his journey to the wheel. The dirt was easy to move, light and full of sand. He worked until only Maharez's face showed. Hook sat down in a heavy heap. He was out of shape these days.

"Look at that, Maha. Look at all those stars. You made it home, brother. We got you home." He rolled on his back and looked at them. Thousands of stars, millions of stars. Maybe this far from all his sins he too could find his way to the great wheel.

Wind blew across the valley, picked up red sand as it went. Hook followed it with his eyes. No sweepers, no burns, no melts. Just wind and sand and his dead friend. He looked over at the long trail of stick headstones. Something caught his eye.

Impossible. No chance.

Hook jumped to his feet and ran down the grave lanes. He dropped to his knees in front of a mound and cried to the moon and wheel. How could the candlelighter know? He didn't even know. All his sins, all his life of violence and death. He did not deserve this. He was not a good man.

"Here Lies Hama."

He hugged her stone. Perhaps she would guide Maharez along the great wheel. His daughter, Hama. Her soul at peace.

26

Nito's eyes gummed with sleep, he couldn't get them open. He turned and bumped his head on a floor. It made a soft clunk, cloth over wood. Not carpet though, thin like a curtain. Ah fuck.

He rolled over, not paralyzed anymore, but thin rope cut into his wrists and ankles. He creaked an eye open finally, vision blurry. He remembered the drug-laced handroll Hook lit him. Hook and Polo and the Hanrab girl, it all came back like a kick in the nuts. His right eye would not open. He must be beat up pretty good, wouldn't be the first time. Gonna be a hell of a hangover when the cocktail wears off.

The door opened, curtains drifting in front of it. Voices, "I don't care, we'll pull it out of his cock if we have to."

"He's awake." The curtain shifted. Polo stood with the girl. A sore pussed down his cheek like a tear. Both were worn out, beat up like a bar rush does to you.

"She got you, didn't she?" he asked. His voice was slurry and odd, not Nito's.

"Fuck you maruth kaba," said the girl.

"You gonna buy me dinner first?" What was up with his voice?

"Quiet. You will tell us all you know about the candlelighter. How long have you worked for the Siegewards?"

"Ha. Auron's puckered asshole, you let her escape? That's rich. Baron Caz couldn't kill her and you two nitwits can't even hold her. Hahaha. You should cut your losses."

"I said quiet." Polo ground the neck of his cane. The girl looked like a mad dog just waiting for the command 'kill'.

Nito laughed louder. "Or what? I'm dead already, Hook told me last night back on the Moor. Oh, you can hurt me. You can make me scream and cry and sob, I don't doubt that. But you won't get any closer to the truth. Because there is no truth. Stupid fucking dozers. She's a poor girl from the Mule. Some teen in the right place at the wrong time doing her job while you did yours. So go on; hit me, take off my fingernails, stuff glass up my cock. You look like that kind of perv, Polo. Do whatever you want because I win. You failed, so I won." His voice, he didn't just slur his words, he lisped. He drooled as he talked. Gods above, please let the drugs wear off. Nito wanted to sober up before the torture, die how he lived most his life. "You can't take anything from me."

Polo's grinned, brown stumps in rotten gums. "I'm going to melt you."

Fatimah laughed, low. Nito's asshole flustered; saliva filled his mouth like he might vomit. He didn't have a witty retort for that, fear in his stomach like rats.

"Oh wait," said Polo. He took out a hand mirror, "I already did."

He spun the looking-glass. No. That was not Nito. Could not be him. Sorcery. An illusion.

There was no flesh on the right side of his face, just melted bone and fried hair. One of his eyes leaked, an egg yolk. His jaw was a mess of fused flesh and shining teeth. Nito's perfect left eye shone through an island of smooth skin. His nose was gone, two holes leaking mucus.

Nito screamed and screamed. His throat burned, scorched on alchemicals. All the pain came back at once. He vomited white sick on the floor, he shook and rolled and screamed; slammed his head as he went. He bucked and kicked, pulled at his bonds until his wrists and ankles bled and there was nothing left of Alistair Nito.

Nothing left at all.

———

Fatimah could climax, she'd never seen such pain. This was a man driven insane, ripped of all the human trappings and left to congeal on the floor.

"Now what?" she asked. There was pure heat between her legs, if she could ride the thing on the floor she would.

Polo smacked her with his cane. "Focus. We dump him. Somewhere close where Citywatch won't look."

"I want to watch him die."

Polo turned on her. "Fatimah, your brother is gone, fled. Hook too. Probably forever. Power shifts in this city." He'd never called her by her real name.

She hissed, uncomfortable, "So, you are a coward just like them?"

Polo swung his cane but stopped before he hit her out of respect. "The city burns, that buys us space. That candelighter is loose out there. The Baron Caz could not kill her despite all his power brought to muster. She weakens him, but she also threatens us. This one," he pointed at the animal on the floor, "is like a beacon to them both. He is nothing but pain. I've been around these magic types long enough, he disrupts their senses. That grants us cover to move through Cruxia."

Fatimah balked. What was Polo on about? They worked for the Baron. "To move where?"

Polo tapped his cane twice on the floor. The animal smacked its head in repetition. "Our Baron has more enemies than allies. You want to climb this syndicate as high as it will go, eh?"

"Yes. More than anything."

"More than your brother?"

She spit on the floor. "He is weak."

"Indeed. Baron Cazaraati must die. We will take his place and rule through his network of lies." She smiled. "He is weak, like your brother."

Fatimah would scream victory. She did it. She worked from slavemaster fucktoy all the way to sweeper. Soon she would be Baron of a syndicate, Baron of a parliamentary family. Once she killed Polo. He had to die once he consolidated all the Cazaraati families. She would know no competition. Only power.

Yes, good. Very good. Fatimah danced to his words like a ballerina. The dumb little cunt. A shower of cunts, all his life. All of them nothing but cunts. This candlelighter cunt. This mutilated no-face cunt on the floor, who's ugly now? Wait until he took out the Lord of Cunts. Truth be he wanted to move on the Corpse Baron alone. But with the candlelighter out there he needed a shield. Dump what was left of Nito, cover their asses from the candlelighter. Use this oilskin to soak any violence from himself. Polo would know victory tonight if it cost every single life in Cruxia. He hawked mucus on what had been Nito, it dripped down his face alongside the burst eye.

27

Sariah stared at the emperor. The emperor stared back. The Turakhan valet returned to the hallway with his great maul. This was for her ears only. Water dripped and waste reeked from the floor. The emperor's nose scrunched slightly at the smell of the prison cell. "Well, this is awkward."

Sariah slumped onto her hay pile, soaked her butt in dirty water. "This is not how I wished to meet you."

The emperor walked over and took a seat next to her. His fine boots soaked in the sludge, his cloak too. "I am sorry this happened. The Inquisition unravels everything I work toward."

"Then do away with it."

"I can't, not without inviting a revolt in parliament. The families—"

She spit on the floor. "The syndicates you mean. Emperor Cruxis protects the Cazaraati. I get it."

"No!" Sariah flinched. Fox Sentelpidio calmed. "Indulge me one moment. The cold war with parliament fails, but I won't surrender. Our nation warred for two hundred years. The Monticello Insurrection, a Hundred Year war with Vohlkhan, then the Turvaali *Sia-sa.*" He used the true name, not the racist

'Hanrab Rebellion.' "And that war rages still. Three thousand Cruxians bolstered by Hanrab recruits fight Turvaali insurgents as we speak."

"I know this."

"We are a nation of soldiers, we know no other way. After the *Sia-sa,* I discharged half our troops. That's a lot of people inured to violence, many with psychological scars. What do you do with an empire of fighters? What does peace mean to them?"

"I never thought of that."

"Nor me. I hatched a plan, outlawed all narcotics, then recruited more local patrols and bolstered the frontier."

Realization dawned. "So your soldiers have someone to fight."

"Exactly. Half of them fall to banditry while the other half hunt them. Keep all the swords pointed away from my citizens and me."

"Brilliant. If your dragon didn't devour the whole city."

"In the hinterlands, it works. Trade and commerce are protected by local outposts and all is well. In the capitol... I did not anticipate the greed of the syndicates nor how much Parliament dances to their tune. Without war and slaves, they ship drugs. They gnaw the empire's marrow until the bones are glass. I won't allow it."

She chuckled, an odd sound. "If only I'd known any of this. Had you deigned to speak with a black woman my partner might still live."

Sentelpidio slumped. "I tried to get in that closed meeting with you and Dietrich. The Corpse Baron's sycophants filibustered me. Believe me, you were the greatest star in my reign. A gleaming example of progress and civil rights."

"Fuck you." He rocked from the words. "I'm no public relations piece, I'm a gods damned human with feelings and ambition. I climbed that wall of hate by myself. Alone. I'm the example of your so-called progress? There should be a portrait of me at the station next to all the Inspector Generals."

"I am so sorr—"

"Spare me." She stood up and leaned in. Rage was new to her, like humor. "You gave my home voting rights, you named us a province. Why are we the poorest? Hanrabi starves while your Parliament splits it up for trade rights. All those resources needed here in the mainland, all that money stolen from my people. Just like always. You abolished slavery to indenture us."

Sentelpedio looked down at the sewage in shame.

"I don't need a white savior. All I've worked for? Burned. My only friend? Dead. I'm to rot out my days in a cell reserved for those I arrested. For what? Tell me."

The emperor's posture crumbled, her only victory.

"For what? The syndicates worm through your empire and flood the streets with junk. Do you know how many there are? Fitzgerald, the Marlowes, don't forget the Cazaraati. These are just the big movers. You've also got the Lestat and the Siegewards."

"I am the Siegewards." His eyes were closed, his hands clasped.

"Excuse me?"

He looked up. "The Siegewards don't exist. I created them."

"You did what?" Anger surged.

"It's a dummy family in parliament. I disguised the Cloud-killers as their 'enforcers' then hired an actor from Ostia to stand in as Baron Siegeward. Together we've taken out the Lestat and the Marlowes."

"The Cloudkillers? Mortia's cold twat, who knows about this?"

"Me, Oneida out there in the hall, and now you. And the Cloudkillers, of course."

"What... what am I supposed to do with this? Look around,

my liege. Your cold war brought me here. They still hang Hanrab scapegoats on the walls."

"You are to die."

Fear like cockroaches all around her.

"Sariah Sternwood will die so you can escape. Your life is yours again. After you disavow your name and leave this city forever."

Forever? She fought her entire life for this place. Hanrabi was just memories of sand and spice. She belonged to Cruxia. Not the empire; this city. She bunched her jaw.

"What is the catch?"

"No catch. Just a choice. You leave this city without question. But if you want to finish what you started." He passed her a slip of paper. 'Baron Alouicious Cazaraati. 13 Noctic Place, Promenade'.

28

Bert was lost as all fuck in the city he'd lived most his life. In fact, besides whalers he'd never left Cruxia. Hadn't even got off the ships at Gaiathor nor Volkhan with its gorgeous mountains. He hated new things. Outside of Hanrabi the Cruxian ports were nothing but white nonsense. So he spent his time on the sea or at Nito's.

Fuck all, there wasn't a Nito's anymore. Looking around there might not be a Cruxia tomorrow. Toci led them down a twisting alley away from the Mule and little Hanrabi. Earlier, rioters set fire to a cattle-waste processing plant. The methane exploded and took six blocks with it, a mushroom cloud over the apartment lanes. Maria took up the rear guard but kept kicking Bert to go faster away from the fires, his hip wasn't any less stiff. By his mark they were a mile-ish outside the Mule, but clogging smoke and scorched buildings made it hard to tell. Lamplighters worked together knocking down lampposts and street signs.

Toci stopped them at the edge of the alley, they bunched behind a dumpster. The street was clear of rioters, Greys, and fire. But an earthquake rumbled under them, low and growing.

"The sewers may have caught fire. This will be the death of your city," said Toci.

"How could you know something like that?" asked Maria.

"I once set fire to a besieged city's sewers."

Bert looked up at him, "What does it mean for us?"

Toci shrugged. "If you have gods, make peace with them."

He swung an arm to push them back. Horses quaked past. A dozen, no, at least three dozen horses raging like a river down the cheap road. One tripped. Trampled in seconds, screaming as she went. Finally, the surge passed along with the earthquake.

"Anyone want a horse?" asked Toci.

"I'd rather brave a sewer fire," said Maria.

Toci chuckled. A donkey brought up the rear, wheezing.

"There ya' go, Bert. There's one for you."

"Ha fucking ha, Fireworks." The stampede brought a breeze, it cleared the smoke haze off the road. Bert bent over and took a fallen street post, dragged it into the alley with Toci's help. He wiped soot-grit off it: 'Ganon Street.' "Fuck all, we're close to the Crimson Moor. It might be the safest place in Cruxia right now."

Toci pointed. "There is someone across the street. Look, curled like a ball."

"He's dead, keep moving," said Maria. "Wait."

Bert's eyes were fuck all, especially at night. Dawn was close but smoke covered the early rays. Still, he couldn't mistake the too-expensive cloak and stupid leather pants. "That's fucking Nito."

Maria ran over screaming. Toci came right after, pushed past to turn him over. Bert limped over on his crummy hip. He took a step back in shock.

It was Nito's cloak, crimson waistcoat, fine boots, and his perfect manicure. But this could not be Nito. Somebody melted this guy. Took fairyfire and slowly burned his face off. They were good, controlled; scar tissue already formed. He might've lived in better conditions.

Maria bent over sobbing and took him from Toci, hugged him tight on the dirty ground. Toci stepped back and looked to the stars with a hand over his two hearts. A big piece of Bert broke like a mug smashed on the floor. Nito was a friend and a constant, Bert lost too many of those. Maria sobbed until her voice cracked and silent grief ran down her cheeks.

Then what-had-been-Nito thrust out of Maria's arms. It screeched and tore at the road, it vomited chunky blood then flipped on its back and spit gibberish. The trio leapt back. It rolled in awkward circles, caught horse tracks in its fresh wounds, screamed louder.

"We must put this one out of his misery," said Toci.

Maria whirled on him with savage fury. "Fuck you we will, that's the best man I've ever known."

Toci stepped up to her, his face a thing of misery. "He is denied reincarnation like this. He will suffer through every wheel of his stars."

"Don't you fucking touch him." She shoved Toci.

"Whoa, whoa, whoa." Bert walked between. "I have an idea. It's bad. Check that, it's terrible. We don't have to kill him. If he survives the next four blocks. Toci, pick him up."

Toci looked at the spasming man. He liked Nito, the only puta who gave the Krodan a fair shake and price at his inn. Treated them like any other citizen, a stand-up puta. But this man was dead, his soul trapped him in a broken mind. He did not want to lock the soul in this cage across those four blocks. Nito would not make it two.

Bert took a deep breath. "We'll take him to Mama Roeneck's. The Moor is three blocks down. If there's a chance he'll live, it lies with Mama."

29

Inspector Dietrich paced in the foyer of 13 Noctic Place, checked his pocket watch for the sixth time in ten minutes. Blast it all. Those sweepers dropped a ball of yarn, and it rolled through the city, caught on every damn corner until it was more tangled than he could untie. Best to cut the cords or let it burn.

Baron Cazaratti's manse wore black and gold walls with stark white carpet, brutal architecture. A ceiling high as a fortress, furniture that lacked ornamentation, sconces like gargoyles. This was not a house for children, thought Dietrich. Hmph, this is no industry for fathers. Not that he could sire any. Sorcerous vasectomies, Inquisition procedure so they would command no other loyalty.

Two staircases wrapped like serpents to meet at the second floor some thirty feet above. The Baron's personal guard stood up there like statues. Two dozen coated in black and gold heavy armor, three great weapons per squad of six. The Baron commanded the greatest knights in the city, more elite than the churchknights. There were another dozen behind the vault door that led to his tower chamber. Outside six squads set in defensive positions like a warzone. All of them human, all of them white.

The Promenade slept though. Dark with all the doors locked and candles doused. The East End fell to chaos. Insurrection like you heard about in the colonies, not here in the capitol where they knew civilization. On his rush to the summons, he watched from Tonscato Bridge as fires ignited across the districts. A waste plant in the Mule exploded, roared a mushroom cloud that pushed him to the road from two miles away. His valets carried him through the district while people finished their breakfast at cafes. The Baron's guard would not allow his valets entrance, they were conscripted on the streets with the other squads.

The Baron was always paranoid, but Dietrich never saw him scared. Summoning an Inquisitor to his residence? Unheard of. What was with the uproar? It was a fucking candlelighter, gods above. Oh, Little Hanrabi erupted over the executions and his arrests. Nothing new there. But it never took to the rest of the East End, the Mule cared as much for the blacks as he did. What was so different about this? What was so special about this girl?

The gold-cut doors burst open. Two of the Baron's knights dragged in a right vulture of a geezer. "Gah, this is unheard of. I never. Do you two lunkheads know who I am?"

"Hello, Vincezzo," said Dietrich.

"Gah," he squawked. Vincezzo ripped out of the knight's grip and brushed his shoulders off. "Just what this fuck is this? Torn from my house on the night I watch my grandchild. Inconceivable."

"This is Baron Cazaraati's mansion."

Vincezzo's face slumped. He suddenly had to shit. "What?"

The knights clunked out the door as if the two old men weren't there.

"The Baron calls his banners, if you will. I made the arrests, you falsified the evidence, those worthless sweepers fucked it all up. Failed to kill the witness and now the city pays for their mistake."

Vincezzo pushed a curtain to look outside. "What will he do with us?"

Dietrich shrugged. "We are loyal. He brought us here for our protection. Don't mistake his theater and the stormtroopers. You are here because he still trusts you."

Vincezzo scanned the room like a bird of prey. "Where are the sweepers?"

Dietrich chuckled. "Where indeed?"

Vincezzo shook, scared. He had to fart. Dreaded it would be more. Never trust a fart after fifty. Never trust a fart, period. Unless you're home and near the tub. He did not want to be here, he did not want to be seen this close to the Corpse Baron. The risk it invited. The Promenade was protected, he could've sat with his grandchild and read him stories of knights and been safer than manses.

"Have... have you seen the Baron?"

Dietrich shook his head. "No one has."

"What are we to do?"

Dietrich shrugged. "Survive."

Vincezzo stepped back from the window.

"What is it?"

Vincezzo's face drained of color. He looked at Dietrich. "There's a girl out there watching us."

30

Sariah Sternwood squirmed through a pipe of Cruxia's shit. Insects skittered away from her in droves. She vomited into Oenida's cloak for the second time and exhaled to push it out of the hood, into the recesses of the poncho. She did not owe Cruxia this. She should leave after these sewers, go anywhere. Escape. But she had an address and a name. She had her duty.

Fuck duty.

If only, right? Sariah had one last case here in Cruxia. Don't think about what comes after, don't think about banishment. She thought back to the cell and the emperor.

She clutched the paper and its address. "So, this is it? I'm your assassin now? Disavow me and all I've done so you can sick me on political insurgents?"

"No. I gave you a choice. You're dead, officially. Sariah Sternwood died in her arrest. You can do whatever you want, I'm trying to grant you freedom."

"On your terms." She held up the paper.

He stood from the hay roll, his white cloak soaked in brown waste. "No. Your terms. I couldn't free you, but I could kill you. I only give you this choice. Your whole case solved with that paper, but what you do next—"

Boots like thunder down the hallway. Clanking weapons and armor.

Oneida popped his head in. "Hostiles. Black with the red circle."

"Inquisitors? Three fucking hells. Deal with them."

Oneida grinned behind his greathelm. He turned and roared, charged out of their view. Metal squealed, the hammer boomed like wet timpani drums. Men and women screamed, they squelched. The Turakhan returned to the cell window, his rhino-helm covered in viscera. "We all clear, boss. They got one of your runners, though."

"Whom?"

"Yuka. She was nice."

The three of them went into the hall. There was no evidence of the inquisitors, just chunky red splashed like a tidal wave. A hanrab woman, thirty, grasped a scroll in her dead grip. Oenieda tore it out and held the two pieces together.

"The East End falls to riots. Citywatch is blocked by the Inquisition. The Baron drives his spear."

"Gods below, we need to activate the Mage Corp. We need to get her out of here. Now."

Oneida pushed them into the cell, the small hay-bed with the waste water running along the edges. "Stand back."

"What?" said the emperor.

Oneida smashed his hammer to the floor. It cracked with a giant splash, soaked emperor, prisoner, and warrior in shit water. A sewage aqueduct ran below them, four feet across, plenty of room for Sariah. "That will lead you to the edge of the city, right out near Ganon Street."

"I can't breathe down there," she said.

"Of course," said Oenida. "Here." He took out a cloak from his pack, grey-white like the skin of a shark. "This was blessed by Karodoan after he killed the Great White Shartaka. You will breathe water and impurities through it like air."

Sariah stared at the dirty thing. "It's a poncho."

Oneida grinned. "Poncho skinned from a god."

And here she was half a mile down the pipe with the hood pulled over her face like a mask. She could breathe through the sludge, but it would not dull the smell. She vomited again and crawled while the wet sick squelched under her stomach, rancid.

How many yards? How many miles was this? There was no time, there was just the rust flaking on her back and the volatile reek like mustard in her eyes. What did she owe this city? Why did she owe this city? The emperor damned her to banishment with sorrow behind his eyes. Fuck him. What about real change? When would Hanrabs be equal to whites?

She turned a corner, and the pipe dropped thirty degrees. She slid face first. Down, down, twisting and crashing through dirty pipes. Ceramic burs caught on her skin through the poncho, but it held, thank Shartaka. Then she burst out of the sewers into a sea of green sludge. It glowed and burned her skin. She floundered, squirmed. Oneida's cloak protected her from the virulent waste and magic residue, but it still hurt. Sariah pierced the surface like an iceberg near a nail-studded dock.

Why did she seek justice for a city that gave her none?

31

Nito's wreckage sobbed and shook lightly in Toci's arms. Still alive though. A bell echoed seven in the morning far up on the Promenade. No one manned the bells on the East End, smoke covered most of it. "I do not like this idea," said Toci.

"Well, it's the only one we got," said Bert. Fire and clamor cleared the reprobates from the Crimson Moor, but a light flickered behind the cheesecloth windows of Mama Roeneck's shack.

Maria shivered, it wasn't even cold. "I'm with Toci, this place climbs up my leg. I don't like it." She'd never been to the Moor before, she knew a lot of women that never returned.

"You both can dust then, but leave Nito. I still wanna keep the poor fuck alive, rex?" said Bert.

The plywood that blocked off the entrance, Toci couldn't bring himself to call it a door, crashed open. A quilted beast in a burqa stalked out, her giant jade eye rolled across the party on her doorstep. Toci almost screamed.

"What's this tap-tap-tapping outside my window? I didn't

order a pretty man. Oof, not so pretty anymore, eh?" Nito groaned a blood bubble from his desiccated cheek.

"Mama, he needs help," said Bert.

"Yes, did he ask this himself? Hmm, did he say, 'Take me to Mama's to heal my face even though my soul is shattered into a million itsy bitsy shards of glass?' Huh?"

"Um-uhhh—"

"Um-uhh? Yes, that sounds more like what he said." She sighed, a dead man's rasp. "I will help him though. The city is in short enough supply of good dick. But you know what they say about Mama?"

"Always a price," said Bert.

"Very good, hobbled man." Everybody with the nicknames tonight, thought Bert. "All the players are not yet here. We can't start without her."

"Without whom?" asked Toci.

The breakers near their dock crashed bright green against the pylons, they spit something with them. Toci shook his head. For one brilliant second, he saw Sharkata, first god of the sea and dire enemy to his god, Karoadoan. But no, it was a woman in a filthy shark-skin poncho. He did not like the energies this dock merged. Nothing good could come from this place.

"Mortia's tight asshole," said Maria, "who the fuck is this?" She bent down to help on instinct, then paused. Did she want to touch whatever Mama waited for? It was a woman, she could see. Didn't matter anyway, she grabbed Maria's shoulder and hoisted halfway out.

Maria rolled away as the woman, Hanrab, pulled up and over the dock. She ripped off the poncho and vomited sickwater for a good minute, Maria crabbed back to hold her hair. Bert, Mama, even Toci, just stared. She was in her thirties, fit, and drenched in a reeking sweat-vomit blend.

"Ah yes, yes. Joyous gatherings and all that bullshit. Here is

Sariah Eadala, our final benefactor and honestly? The only one of you left with any gumption," said Mama.

"Sariah Sternwood," said Maria, "the Inspector General?"

Sariah wiped her lips and spit. "I can speak. Inspector no longer, nor a Sternwood. I'm dead."

"Hey!" Bert shouted. "This guy is, like, actually dying."

Mama lifted his arm, felt his pulse. "He has a good hour."

"Fuck's sake." Bert pushed past her into the shack. Mama followed. Toci stood awkwardly with the dying man for a moment then went in and left the women outside.

"That's Mama Roeneck," said Sariah.

Maria shrugged. "If you say so."

"She has over four hundred warrants out for her arrest."

"Guess it's a good thing you're not on the force anymore, rex?"

Sariah laughed. "Sure."

"Just what the fuck happened to you?"

"That... that is a long story. Got any tobacco?"

———

Toci stood in the corner. He did not wish to touch anything. The room stretched twice further than its shack should, but that could be the incense burning with different drugs. He smelled hethbara, orsin, and a touch of sopa. He filtered the harsh smoke through an extra flap of skin in his nostrils. This was no time to be high. He glanced over at the window and winced; a jar of fetuses sat not six inches from his face. Mama didn't discriminate; krodan, human, even fen floated around like shrimp. They were still alive, Toci gulped.

Mama cleared a butcher table for Nito when they first came in. He sprawled on his back with arms hanging while she circled him holding a painter's pallet of powders. Bert couldn't look at his face. Nothing but scabs and skull. No lips, no nose.

Cheeks gone, just teeth. Mama rubbed ungents into his arms and legs. "What are you doing to him?" said Bert.

"Relaxing his muscles. He's gone rictus out of shock. He thinks he is dead, so the body follows," said Mama.

"Rex, rex, super rex."

Time went by. Toci watched the women chat outside and throw their tobacco into the green marsh, tiny fireballs.

Bert gripped his shoulder tight and bit it with fingernails. Fuck Nito, why did Bert care about any of this? Did he just want his bar back? I mean, would Nito be slinging drinks anytime soon? Ever? Bert was too sober for all this shit. He walked to the brazier of incense and inhaled, hard. It filled his lungs and brain with sweet amorphia. Too fucking right, that was better. Nito was a pal, that was enough reason to be here in this shack. Enough reason to risk his life. A pal is a pal. Fuck if sobriety always made decisions so hard, so messy. Life was clearer a few deep, huh?

Mama pinched a blue powder from her pallet. "Giiwe, neyaab, biskaabi!" The words blew the powder all across Nito. It flowed through his empty cheeks and exposed nostrils. He sat up like a trap sprung.

"Oh, fuck all the ducks in the pond, oh fuck. Oh fuck, what just... we gotta—" He spun over too fast and smashed to the floor with a splotch. "Auron's fat dick, what is going on? Where am I? Why does it smell like bad salmon?"

"Uh, I think that's you," said Bert.

———

.

"That's a lot."

"Yes," Sariah sighed, "yes it was." She lit another tailor, hadn't smoked since she quit her pipe seven years back. It felt great, blowing heat out of her lungs, though the next day would be one of wheezing pain. Drinkers and addicts weren't so different, just nicer Junktowns. "Fuck it all."

Maria took Sariah's tailor to light her own, it was a day for chainsmoking. Would you look at the fires across the East End? Ganon Way caught halfway through Sariah's story and Ganon Hall finally slumped into the sea off scorched pylons. The fire stopped outside the Crimson, must be Mama holding it all back. "So, what are you gonna do next?"

"I don't know, that's the first time this has ever happened to me. What do I want to do? What do I choose to do instead of being ordered to? I have a name, I have the location. I could kill this Baron and solve every cold case I ever had. Or I could leave, fuck this city and its white people. No offense."

"None taken," said Maria, "this place is nothing but white nonsense."

Sariah snorted. "Too right. I like you, Maria."

"I like you too, Eadala."

It felt good to hear her real name. "Unfortunately, I can't be selfish. At the center of this case is a candlelighter, some teenager. I thought she was the killer, but now I think she's as caught up in this storm as us. A small raft of decency rocked by all of Cruxia's terribleness. So, I think I'm going. If I die, it will be doing what I love."

"Police work?" asked Maria.

"Helping."

Toci pushed his giant head out the plywood door. "He is awake. Sanity seems to have returned."

"Nito?" Maria leapt up and ran to the shack.

"Whom?" said Sariah to the empty dock before she got up to follow.

"Would someone besides Mama look me in the eye? She's giving me the creeps." Nito sat up and ate some beef jerky with a jar of water. No one in the room could watch it all mash together through his exposed cheek. He was healthy, but still just a skull covered in sinew and scar tissue. Mama watched him, licked her lips with a pointed white tongue.

"It's, uh, it's good to see you up, Nito," said Bert.

"Don't lie to me."

"I'm glad you're not dead."

"That's more like it, buddy." He punched Bert's arm. "So, they hit me with a melt. No face? Am I all caught up?"

"That's about most of it," said Maria.

"But I'm not dead." He sat further up. "Fuck, the candle-lighter got away. They dumped me to bait her out. We gotta move." He tried to stand up too fast, struggled on sore legs until he fell to the floor.

Sariah hunched down to help him back to the table. "I agree with you, the girl is still out there and needs our help."

"Who the fuck are you?" asked Nito as he settled back. He'd never felt weak like this, so irrelevant.

"Who the fuck are you?" asked Sariah.

"Fair point. We are in this together, I take it? Veridaan's cooter, how are you, Toci?"

Toci shrugged. "I miss my brethren."

"Nothing but sorrow today, huh?"

Mama clapped, a wet sound. "I gathered all of you here for a reason, for a purpose."

Maria glared at her. "You didn't gather any of us."

"Didn't I, big hips? I have you all, all of you with grief for the Corpse Baron. I want you five to assault Baron Cazzaraati. Kill him once and for all and clear his rot from my city. He declared himself my enemy, I devour my enemies, hahaha."

Sariah sighed heavy. "Everyone is selling me this idea tonight."

"Must be a good one then, eh?" said Bert. "Rex. I'm in. Fuck the Corpse Baron and his extra levy on Krodan vessels."

Maria looked up at Toci. "What about you? You don't owe this place anything."

He smiled down. "No, but I will give you anything you desire."

Nito rolled his eyes, quite macabre in his lack of a face. "Keep it in your tunics. Yeah, I want this motherfucker to fall harder than the Fen. If we move now, we might save Roisin."

"Let's do it," said Sariah.

"Good, good. Yes, your own decisions led you to this particular moment. Free choice and all that mortal film flam. I will send you there with my power. But one little thing. Nito, your wound's cauterized, but you really shouldn't walk around with that face."

"You don't fucking say."

"I have something for it," Mama careened across her shack and returned to Nito. She clutched an iron mask, riveted like the lepers wore beneath Auron's Mercy.

He screamed, he rocked and spasmed. Toci and Bert tried to hold him down, but he flung about in the grip of insanity, kicked bottles of green liquid smashing to the floor. "NO, NO, NO, NO, NO, NO!"

Mama raised her hand. "Sove." He collapsed. Mama gingerly clasped the mask around his skull-face and locked it with a clunk. She looked around the horrified room, "He will be like this for a while, quick triggers and bouts of seizure. Nito fakes his way through life, but you can't fake out of this trauma. His obsession with redeemed fatherhood should shield him from what comes next. Or he will break. Forever. When he awakens you shall go. Kill the Baron. After Mama will pay your way anywhere on Galea's surface."

"Always a price, eh?" said Bert.

"Cruxia's first rule."

32

Polo crept through a fine alley with red brick roads and painted lamp posts. Everywhere smelled of good flowers and cinnamon, even the garbage lane of this cafe. It was enough to make him retch. Cruxia wore fine perfume and makeup this high up the walls, but here was the true evil of the city. Polo was but a weapon, all these fine mansions and apartments housed the arm that wielded men like him.

Fatimah ranged in front of him by two blocks, checking the streets as they slunk ever closer to Noctic Land and the Baron Caz. An odd mix of excitement and fear shook her heart, tinged in something else. Something that made her feel weak and distracted. Sadness? Yes, sorrow at the loss of her brother. She glanced over the walls of the Promenade where the East End fires burned smoke-wash against the palace itself. No way he made it out of that, not without her to correct him when he acted like a donkey. Oh, Maharez, she missed him but now she had no restraints. She was Fatimah in full, untethered. She squashed the sadness down until it popped like a pimple.

Emotions, who had time for them? She tripped over something rusty and wet.

Polo watched Fatimah stumble, then hold back a shriek. He shuffled over fast as he could on his cane. The girl armored herself to the work, but there were soft spots. If she lived through this, Polo would toughen her up. Easier with her brother gone. "What is it now?" he whispered. She pointed.

Blood and gore soaked the street in front of them, splashed up the storefronts, gunked in the cracks between the bricks, it ran like a river all the way down to the next intersection. Rusted armor floated in the viscera like logs in a swamp. Polo flipped over a helmet with his boot, but it flaked to dust. "These are the Baron's personal guards. The cunt beat us to it. Watch yourself."

Fatimah vomited into the gore. The sight of it was nothing, but the reek. It smelled like good bacon.

———

13 Noctic Place, right inside where twin staircases ran around the room to a balcony thirty feet up. Dietrich rushed across the Baron's foyer and grabbed Vincezzo by his shoulder. "What did you just say?"

Vincezzo pointed again outside the window. "It's her, it's her. The candlelight—"

Dietrich dashed away, too late. His muscles seized, ropes lashed around bone. Vincezzo tried to scream, but it caught in his throat like a bad cough. Dietrich's legs wrenched in front of him no matter how hard he tried to stop. Vincezzo was old, his hip broke with the first forced step. Agony like lightning. Still, he walked on, a marionette. No screams. Dietrich cantilevered up the west staircase, Vincezzo mirrored him on the east one. Pain in white stripes across his vision, the hip grinding bone flakes into his blood.

The main door opened, slow and squealing. In walked the

candlelighter. The fucking candlelighter, Dietrich stared down with utter hate. She had sandy hair matted in blood, filthy clothes, and a brown-red bandage around her hand. Polo took her thumb. Good. He laughed. Then all his teeth fell out.

"I can hear you," she said. Her voice was monotone, lifeless. "I can hear everything you are. I can hear everything you've been."

Dietrich gummed his teeth and watched them fall from his mouth in little groups. Click-clack. Vincezzo spit over the balcony. "You do not know anything, child. I will—"

"Silence." Vincezzo's lips sealed together on a molecular level. "You are in my way."

Vincezzo took Dietrich in his arms, movement jerky, controlled. From his belt, he took out thick rope and tied it in a noose. Vincezzo's eyes were all the way open, bloodshot and full of terror. He almost broke his jaw trying to open his mouth. They still had control of their faces.

Dietrich could only look at his teeth. Like spilled change on the floor. Harsh rope ripped across his neck. He turned. There was Vincezzo the vulture with no mouth, no lips, just bugged eyes and a nose. The rope pulled taut, he lifted a leg to the balcony rail.

"You both are guiltier than the killers."

Dietrich's hands pulled his small-knife out from its belt sheath. A paring knife meant for fruit, he used it to cut off eyelids and fingers. He lifted his other leg to the balcony, sat on it like a swing. Vincezzo tied the noose to the railing.

Dietrich brought up his paring knife, slow-like. Tears ran down Vincezzo's face, the pain, the terror. Who would watch his grandson after tonight? The paring knife came into his vision, the only thing in his vision. He clenched his eyes shut but it cared naught, pierced the bunched flesh, hovered at the cornea, plunged into the iris and pupil with a burst of liquid. It bit his brain. Vincezzo seized and shoved Dietrich over the balcony. There they died. Dietrich swaying on the rope, red-faced and toothless. Vincezzo shook on the thick carpet with a knife in his eye and no mouth to scream.

———

Sariah gripped the brick between her fingers and vomited onto the fine street. Behind her Nito stumbled into a wall, his iron mask gonged like a bell. "Fuck," he said.

There was the quick reek of burnt chemicals and a low thump. Maria and Toci appeared next to Sariah and Nito showering blue sparks. Toci bent down to help Sariah up. "First time in teleportation?"

"First time in any fucking sorcery, I don't like it." She wiped spittle from her chin. Maria stepped awkwardly with a dopey smile.

"Sweet Veridaan, it was full of light."

Nito stepped up. "You really shouldn't open your eyes in there, things in the Jaunt feast on mortal eyes."

"Buzzkill," said Maria.

"Oi, fuckheads." Suddenly.

The four looked up, there was Bert atop the roofs. "Mama fucking missed, man. I don't fancy climbing down on this leg."

Toci shouted up, "Then reconnoiter. Where are we?"

"Uh…" Bert walked out of their vision to check. "I have no fucking clue, brother."

Nito smacked his iron forehead. Same old Bert.

"I know this place," said Sariah. "That's Wharth Lane, the central bank is about three blocks north of here." Hanrabs aren't allowed in this district, she didn't say. Nor did she point to the three-story manse with iron-spiked gates. That was her first home here on the Promenade before her stepfather's fall from grace.

"Where do we go from here?" asked Toci.

"Noctic Lane is only a block past Wharth." She glanced around. "It's quiet." The sun pushed to mid-day, it cut shadows deep in the alleys and roads of the Promenade. The palace loomed blocking the light from the east.

"Lockdown on the East End, they've been shuttered like in wartime. Plus, the Baron's bribes move this city," said Nito.

Sariah took stock of her team, hard to call it that. Nito wore a brace of knives, but his balance was akilter from the four pounds of iron on his head. Maria swung a nice short-sword willed from her father and wore a pickle barrel lid for a shield, Mortia's sake. Bert was on the roof and probably stuck up there, which was good. He looked like a brawler, and this would be a fight of steel. Toci she would depend on; seven feet of spiked-shell and bunched muscle, he wore a lionskull shield and a short spear taken off Mama's wall. "A Turra weapon, one to respect." Sariah missed her Inspector's gear: short sword and rapier, small steel buckler, whip and garrotte. She took two light swords and a crossbow with one bolt from Mama. This would not be a night to reload.

Bert monkeyed down a fire escape and dropped in a clunking fury of curses. Fuck, Sariah really didn't want him in this fight.

"Auron's cock-fucking-beard that hurt. Shit, shit, shitloaf."

"What did it look like up there, Bert?" said Sariah.

"Pretty fucking wretched, Grey. Don't turn that corner, let me tell you. Bad sorcery out there tonight- What did I just say? Fuck's sake."

Maria squealed. Toci rushed to her side at the alley's end where she peeked. His green face went white. Sariah joined them.

It wasn't a boulevard lane with nice flower beds splitting it in twain, it was a butcher's table. Rusted armor floated in thick red gore, offal, and the occasional intestines stuck out like barbs on a wire.

"Someone killed a lot of men in armor with some terrible sorcery," said Toci.

Maria turned, shook the horror from her face. "What was it you said about saving the wrong girl, Inspector?"

Sariah walked over to view the charnel road, "Don't... don't call me that anymore."

————

Polo watched Fatimah's big ass flex and climb above him and felt nothing. Baron Caz's penetration of his teenage frame choked any sexuality out of Polo long, long ago. Noctic Lane was coated in dead, so they took to the rooftops. Fatimah secured rope to each gutter before her leap to the next. Polo crawled along them like a silkworm. But here they were at the main attraction. 13 Noctic Place. Only a fool would approach at ground level. So they climbed.

High up on the tower window of the east wing Polo felt fear. He hated fear. Almost as much as he hated the Baron. Stripped of his family and dignity, fucked in every corner of this manor house, he needed the artifact to die for real this time. Fear gripped his heart, dragged sweat from his temples.

Fatimah took out a crowbar forty feet above the road. She snapped out the iron bars then broke the window. "We are here, what comes next?"

Polo wiped dank sweat from his brow. "The future, Fatimah. Whatever that proves to be."

————

Sariah knocked twice on the double door of 13 Noctic Lane. Toci smashed through like it was paper. The team moved in, Bert and Nito stumbling low and left, Mariah and Toci in the center. Sariah aimed her crossbow all over from the right.

Marble floors and ebony furniture, two spiral staircases running along the east and west to meet at the top. At the second-floor balcony, a man hung next to a slumped corpse with a knife in his eye.

The candlelighter sat on the balcony next to them, double doors to the inner sanctum behind her.

"You shouldn't have come here, none of you. And you're late."

Nito stepped up. "Roisin, you don't have to do this."

She lifted a hand, and pure force pushed them all back a step, held them there. It rang in Nito's helmet.

"This has nothing to do with any of you, all of you good souls. I can see by your candles— auras. I meant auras. I came for vengeance," she pointed at Nito, "not redemption," then to Sariah, "nor justice." She looked at the motley rest, paused. Maria had no fucking idea what was going on. Toci was used to situations veering out of control.

"Nor comradery," said Bert.

"I only ever had the one friend, and he left Cruxia. He was smart."

"Enough of this bullshit, Roisin. What would the High-Father say to all this?" Nito shouted. "Is this how you want to go out, this how you want to be remembered? Just come down from there, let us handle—"

Her eyes shined bright blue, energy cascaded electro-shocking her hair into static. "Handle what? Get us arrested then captured and lose your face again? Please. This is real power."

"But from where?"

Another pause, just a split second, but did Nito get through?

"Eventually you'll have to pay for all of this. Debtors collect, especially the gods."

"Enough." Her power flexed and the wall of force evaporated. Toci and Sariah took a clumsy step forward as the tension lifted.

Nito's head cracked back into the manor wall and showered marble dust. "Ugh-amugh-a-ugh—" He slumped to the floor, drool pouring from his mouthpiece. Eyes wide open.

Mariah shrieked, "What did you do to him?" She wanted to charge up the stairs to the little bitch, but she was scared. She'd never seen any sorcery, ever.

"I took his mind. Just for the evening. Tomorrow he'll return to the broken addict that he is."

Sariah glanced at Toci and touched her rapier, he nodded. The two broke east and west charging the girl.

"I can read your minds," she said. Rosin raised a hand. The double doors behind her burst open and a dozen heavy knights clanked out. The eyes behind their visors were cloudy and white, their movements jerky. Puppet like. "I didn't want to hurt you good people. I already killed one good man today. Sometimes…" Toci and Sariah were almost at her on both sides with blades raised. Roisin flicked a finger and the two meteored down the stairs in a tangle of weapons and armor. "Sometimes the needs must be as your enemy drives."

With that she turned from them as the Baron's knights closed the distance with sword and shield ready. Sariah and Toci recovered and pulled the crew into a circle around the gibbering Nito.

———

Fatimah took one last stock of Cruxia from this angle. High up here on the Baron's manse. 13 Noctic Lane, she could see every part of the city besides the palace. Even the Promenade crawled up to the emperor like all of the rest of the East End. A whole city, whole nation, sucking the cock of the wealthy. Pathetic. But there was Polo with his cane, smack. "Focus."

"Of course." Oh, he would die soon. She hated that cane, hated a smack to the back of the head. Even before the slave galley when her mom did it with an open palm. Always with control issues, eh, Fatimah?

Who said that? Who thought that? It sounded like something Maharez would say. But he was dead. She didn't know how she knew that, she just did. She readied her rope on the broken bars and got ready to drop. There was a lush hallway below. The wealthy deserved to die.

She let herself down the rope and dropped the last few feet into complete darkness.

Wait.

Complete darkness and she landed on wood. That made no sense. There was thick carpet in the hallway. Not hardwood. Not hardwood that creaked. No, no no no no.

She stood on the deck of a ship. The sway of the waves, the salt stench, the creak that came so often you didn't hear it. She could not be here, would not ever be here again. Then came the boom-boom. She ran on instinct.

The deck slapped beneath her feet until she ran into railing. Boom-boom. Boom-boom. She looked down into black water. She looked up into black skies. Impossible. A nightmare of her past. Boom-boom, boom-boom, BOOM-BOOM. The slave drummer beat, the ship picked up speed.

"Hey, you oilskin," called an apparition out of the dark. A score more joined him. Dark figures closed in on her, slow.

"No!" she screamed. She ran back to stern, dodged the hulking shadow slavers, felt a meaty grip run down her back and miss by inches. She rolled. She would escape. She tried so many times in her past. In her present. Oh no. Where was Maharez? He rowed on the second deck, two steps up from the chainroom and the slaves for delivery. She beelined into a staircase as the drumming stopped and the alarm horn blared.

Down staircase after staircase, too many for a ship this size, farther and farther down into the nightmare. She found the row deck, eighty slaves in chains and rags pushing and pulling oar lanes. A whole row of eight for each giant oar. The eternal push and pull her brother suffered. There he was, row three, two deep. He looked up at her with a smile. His face was nothing but skull and eyeballs. "Sister? When will you learn?" she screamed.

Back upstairs to the deck, the furtive slavers hunted like tigers in silhouette. She ran to the stern, up the stairs past the castle. Behind her was the same. Just black. Black sea, black sky, black deck under her feet.

Footsteps like thunder. Five slavers up atop the sterncastle with her. The muscly fat one up front stepped forward. "Alright, ya little sandborn. You know the drill. You don't row, then you suck." He dropped his trousers. She leapt over the edge, dove into the dark sea, praying it would break her nec—

—she landed on wood. That made no sense. There was thick carpet in the hallway. Not hardwood. Not hardwood that creaked. No, no no no no.

She stood on the deck of a ship. The sway of the waves, the salt stench, the creak that came so often you didn't hear it.

And over, and over, and over, and over, and over, and over again. And there she would remain for the last forty years of her life.

———

Polo watched Fatimah hit the floor as the candlelighter opened the hallway door. The rest went as expected. No one planned like Polo, just look down there. All this shit and who still stood? Not Hook, not the Hanrabs, but fucking Polo. He crawled over the roof to the Baron's personal suite. Fatimah played right into his scheme, soaked the candlelighter so he could hit the main attraction.

Polo smashed the windows with his cane and tied the fine silk rope like Maharez showed him. He lowered down, but his weight was too much for his arms, dropped the final six feet to fall in a slump. How disrespectful?

The Baron's suite was a pipe-dredging system coated around a hospital room. Copper filters ran around every corner, curled around the room like a thousand worms. Giant pumps behind glass filled bellows and released them into the pipes. Polo pushed to his feet and walked through the surgical drains, shifted the hanging cable with his cane.

"YOU SHOULD NOT BE HERE," came a voice.

"But here I am."

"I WILL FLENSE EVERY PIECE OF YOU."

"Then do it." Polo stood on his dare, expected oblivion. The bellows surged faster. Polo moved through the machines, smacking his cane as he went. "But you can't, eh?"

He moved deeper into the suite, past the machines and life support. To a bed shrouded by hanging sheets. A crumpled form lay beneath. "You can't hurt me because of the candle-lighter. I gambled." He pulled the sheet away with a theatrical sweep. "And I won."

A corpse in rictus fetal position claimed the bed. A skeleton with a starch of yellowing skin and fine white hair around the scalp. "You are nothing without your power and the Candle-lighter nullified it. Do you feel it? The helplessness?"

The Baron screeched through his machines. The bellows fluttered, all the copper pipes filled with whatever ran through them. Polo gripped the bottom of the bed and flipped it. The Corpse Baron rolled to the floor like a dead bird. A sudden surge of power, Polo fell to his knees.

"YOU WOULD DARE."

Polo sneezed black blood. Oh, he overextended.

"THIS IS MY MANSE, MY PLACE OF POWER."

The words echoed and Polo had to crawl across the floor,

his bones shuddered. But then he saw it. The Baron's bed ran copper wire to a glass pump, but instead of bellows, it held a brain. A big pink mass with nerves connected to gold wire, a million wires connected to the pumps and machines. A whole suite stuffed with pumps to keep him alive.

Fuck that.

Polo crawled, he spit and vomited black sick on his way.

"YOU ARE NOTHING."

"Likewise." Polo lifted himself, pushed every bit of consti- tution he had left. He shouldered the glass container. "Unnngh." The brain chamber lilted, rolled back, then crashed to the floor in a flood of glass, embalming fluid, and the Baron Caz.

"AUGHHHH-IGGHHHHHH-egh—"

Polo sneezed red blood with the psychic fallout. But the Baron was dead. The monster was dead forever.

Then the doors crashed open and in walked that dumb little white girl, the fucking candlelighter.

"Thanks for clearing the way."

———

Sariah blocked a puppet-knight's downswing with shortswords crossed. The force of it pushed her back to the wall, stumbling over Nito. They were slow and predictable, but it was so much power, so much armor. This was the sixth sword fight of her life and four of those were in Citywatch days. She wasn't twenty anymore. To the left, Mariah and Toci kept four of them boxed against the stairs. Toci caved one of their helmets and screamed a warcry. The knight fell, smearing blood on the marble in a din.

Swish. Sariah stepped left to avoid a claymore. The puppet- knight bullied her into the corner. Her knee buckled, older now. There he was with the killing blow ready. She thrust her rapier into his neck, past the chain, through the top spinal column. He collapsed.

She took a beat to breathe.

"Nice kill!" yelled Toci through a grin.

Crunch. Someone hit her shoulder, crushed her to the marble floor. Her head bounced like a ball.

"No," screamed someone. Mariah?

Her vision fluttered, spiked. She was on the floor. Flip onto your back girl, like a turtle. Haha. But you can't get up on your back. Screams, shouts. She looked up at the ceiling, rolled her head, Toci smashed his back and bone-spines into a knight. Impaled him. Good. Oh no.

Sudden tunnel vision. The puppet-knight with a greathammer stood above her with it raised high. Not raised, falling. Oh no, indeed.

Gantry, be seeing you.

"Fuck you!" Bert dove from the staircase and tackled greathammer into a sidestep. Smash, the marble exploded a foot from Sariah's head. She stood up, still dizzy. The knight dropped its weapon and took Bert's shoulders in both hands, lifted him two feet to eye level.

"You don't listen so well, eh, fuckface?" Bert smashed his forehead into the slotted grill of the knight's fullhelm. The knight took two steps back, almost dropped Bert. He smashed his head into it again, a mallet to an oyster. The grill bent. "UAAAAAGHH!" He smashed a final time and crunched the steel into the knight's nose and brain. The force split Bert's skull like a pumpkin. They both clattered to the floor.

Sariah staggered over to him. He still breathed, his exposed brain shone in the flickering chandelier light. "Hey, Grey."

"Hey," she sat next to him and took his hand.

"That felt good, didn't it fuckin' just? Got that bastard."

"Why did you do that?"

He shrugged and grimaced. "Eh, you have to help a pal in need. Simple as that."

Toci and Mariah fought the final two knights against the stairs, pushed them back. Sariah looked back to Bert, he smiled. "Plus, elephants good boat muck." One of his eyes went lazy, the skin stretched off his split skull like ripped canvas. "Fuck, sorry about that. Stroked out maybe."

"It's okay."

Toci threw a puppet-knight off the top balcony head first.

"Ha," Bert gave a thumbs up, "fuck that white nonsense, huh, Toci?"

Toci grinned down at him.

"Don't talk," said Sariah.

"Fuck that, Grey. You gotta move, go save that girl. It feels good. Living for something besides myself."

"Yeah," said Sariah.

"Real rex. I could get used to—"

Toci and Maria joined them as Bert died.

———

The candlelighter stalked towards Polo. He stood in a hospital room designed by a madman. Copper tubes and beakers all over. A mummy and a brain lay on the floor in a mess of broken glass and stinking green fluid.

"Of all those involved in the High-Father's death, you are the most evil. Your candle is like the wasting, it blackens all those who come close to you."

Polo tapped his cane. "That's a whole lot of words from some Mule wench."

She grit her teeth. "I read."

"An understatement. The king is dead, may the peasants rejoice."

"Then let me hang the chancellor."

She opened up her power, drove her tentacles into the brain matter of this mole. Same as she did with the Hanrabs, same as she did with the pervert priest. Her mind expanded, it hurt but only for a second. She saw all of his memory like a picture book. But something was different. There was so much hatred, hatred built up like fortress walls around his mind. She fell into the black.

Polo's face above her, like she rolled down a drain and he was the water. What?

"Foolish girl. I was raised by the Baron, raped by the Baron. Do you think your newborn power compares to his? Do you know what real fear is?"

She gushed down a waterfall of horror, grasping at jagged memories. The Baron pushing child-Polo to the floor of a washroom, in the confessionals of Auron's temple, in a torture chamber deep in the dungeons of somewhere.

Rosin was a virgin, sex terrified her.

"Stop it, stop it, stop it, STOP IT."

She cracked at the bottom of the waterfall, soaked in memory and the abyss. Hands took her shoulders, flipped her to her knees.

"His psychic terror breathed down my shoulder every night while his cock filled my asshole. You dare to threaten me?"

Utter darkness and cold water rained on her. The hands on her shoulders forced her to the ground inch by inch. Something pulled her pants down, a cold, strong grip. She cried.

"You live my memories. They are but a shield to me now."

Roisin could not take this anymore, a stinking laugh behind her, the impossible grip pushing her down, the air on her bare bottom. No, please, no no no no no no.

THUNK. A wooden noise to dissipate the nightmare. Roisin was back in the Baron's hospital-bedroom, face on the floor with her buttocks high but no one held her down. The Mole stalked in front of her like a drunk, pointed and tried to speak.

A crossbow bolt stuck through his eye, out the back of his head. Blood pooled at his chin.

Rosin turned back to the entrance. A woman slumped against the doorframe with a heavy crossbow. Red streaked down her forehead.

"Was that the Baron?"

Rosin burst into tears. She screamed and cried like her eight-year-old self did when someone took her doll. She cried like she never had when her da' died, like she'd suppressed for years, 'not some Mule wench.' Sariah rushed to her in a stumble and held the girl tight.

"I didn't want to do it. I didn't mean to. It's too much. I know too much. I want to die. I want to die."

"Shhhh, shh. I have you, I have you."

"I want to die. I want to die. I WANT TO DIE I WANT TO DIE I WANT TO DIE."

Roisin's control collapsed in full, her psychic control blown away in a maelstrom. In one horrific moment, Sariah absorbed all the memories. The murder of the High-Father, the savage hunt, even the Door and her da's death. She held the girl tighter, her collar soaked in tears and mucus.

"I want to die," Rose sobbed, weaker.

Sariah kissed her forehead and stroked her hair. "It's over. It's over and you are okay. I have you, I have you. You're safe now."

Rosin hugged Sariah tight, like you would a mother.

33

Kaveh snuck through the reeds, mud squelched between his toes. The warm river water washed over his feet and took the mud away in an odd, comfortable way. He bent lower. Across the river the big man sat with a small knife working at something, Kaveh couldn't tell what from this distance. Two hundred feet or so. Dragonflies whirred by, a crane bit the water, the sun dropped blood orange behind the Mehrdad Mountains. Kaveh crept closer than he ever had, the big man's senses were like Hosiris, god of beasts.

Something grabbed his shoulder and growled. "Uga—" he started to shout then caught himself. Stealth, Kaveh, stealth.

"Hehehe," she laughed. His baby sister covered her mouth, stupid little Shirin. "I got you," she whispered.

He put a finger to his lips, and she giggled. How was she so quiet, Halladar? How?

"What are you doing?" she whispered.

"I'm following the outsider. I don't trust him."

"Well, yeah, he's white. Gran says all white men are the work of Turvaal."

He wiped his face, exasperated. "That's why I'm following him. I know he's up to—"

"Would you two just come out of there?" the big white man shouted over the river, "The homara snakes mate with the full moon. I'm safer than those reeds."

"Eep," said Shirin.

Kaveh stood up to his full five feet four and pushed out his chest. "What are you doing with that knife?"

The big white man lifted something in the distance. "I'm making toys."

Shirin looked at Kaveh with delight. "Toys?"

"Could be a lure," said Kaveh.

But Shirin was crashing through the shallow river. Kaveh ran after her, but he was bigger, the river pushed back harder. When he broke the opposite shore Shirin sat on a stump next to the big white man. Kaveh tried to look large like when a cheetah gets too close to the village.

"Whoa there, hunter." He lifted his hands and dropped the knife.

"Look at all his toys," Shirin said with a handful of them. Little wooden figures with felt clothes; a farmer, a priestess, even Hosiris with his bird head.

Kaveh frowned. "Who are you?"

The man had a square jaw on a big face, it grimaced. "Just the gravedigger, son. Nothing more, nothing less."

Shirin's face lit up. "And you make these? Can you make me one? How about Veridaan? Please, could you please? Could you, could you, could you?"

He chuckled. "Sure, I can make her."

"Enough," Kaveh said. Too loud.

"That is if the village guardian says it's ok. Eh?"

Village guardian? All the elders ignored the threats of Turvaali and outsiders like this one. Even if this one wasn't so bad. For a white man. "Can you make a soldier?"

The big man's eyes went dark and rolled over the graveyard. It stretched far back to the dunes where the nameless dead rested.

"No, I don't make killers. How about a farmer, or a fisherman? I have priests and gods, porters, builders, anything but soldiers."

"I want all the gods," said Shirin. "Halladar, the Siblings, Hosiris, even Terminus."

The big man chuckled. "I'll get started right away. Terminus is a killer, though."

"No," she said with a stomp of her foot. "Terminus is a soul-thief. He steals from the dead."

The big man sighed. "Ok, I can make Terminus."

"But who are you?" said Kaveh.

The white man looked over the dunes again, shifted his gaze to the river and the village across. "You can call me Carver."

———

Nito awoke. Stinking sweat and the rough stench of iron. Ugh. He shifted his shoulders and dipped his head. It clanked.

Fuck.

He hoped the last day was a fever dream. But here he was. Healthy and sane. Double fuck.

He touched the iron mask with his long fingers, it was real. He probed through the eyehole, rubbed at his exposed cheek. The lolling tongue. He tried not to scream.

All real. Well, fuck you in the skull, Nito. You're ugly. Hideous even. Deal with it.

As if he could just do that.

He looked around the little cell. Hard stone and flickering torches. A moment of panic. He knew this room.

Auron's Mercy. Home to the terminally ill and the lepers.

Across the room wrapped up on the cot like a mummy was Munson. Fucking Munson and his lack of limbs. It made sense. Iron mask and uninhibited insanity. Nito would have thrown his ass in the quarantine dungeons also. But would he ever get out? He thought of the church complex coated in blue-steel knights with gold cloaks.

"Hey, Muson, how have ya' been?"

Munson shrugged. An iron mask on a torso with no limbs.

"Yeah, same. Hey, what do you say to a man with a two-foot cock?"

Munson shrugged and laughed snot from his mask.

"Ok, but can you split it between the three of us?"

Munson guffawed a mist of snot. Nito leaned back on the stone and moss bed they left for the lepers. Was this so bad? A roommate with a sense of humor. Three meals a day. A life of peace, eh?

Rex.

The cheesecloth door swished from the frame. In she walked, there she was with a warm sponge and bucket of soapy water. He froze, for once in his life Nito had no words. She bent down and removed the mask. She looked him in his remaining eye with a sad smile. Warmth then soapy water on his desiccated face.

"Hello, dad."

———

Constable Roary Bullworth leaned over the rail and glared at the cold, black saltwater. The Claret Sea, a trip across was death to any Citywatchmen's career, they used to laugh over mugs of dark beer. Constable once Constable General, shit. He threw his cigar stub into the water. He bought cheap fare on this Krodan whaler with his own commission. The crown didn't pay your way this hard down a demotion.

He rubbed his moustache. Cruxia's East End burned long into the next day from twelve good miles behind. Someone had to take the fall for it. The Inquisition moved in and pinned it on the first Watchmen they could find. Nevermind his report was signed off after no guild ships caught flame. Once rebellion flared in the depressed districts, they needed a fallguy. Not fucking rex. Not one bit. The price of honesty in the Watch.

He reached for another cigar as the harsh wind caught sails and the deck spilled him over. "Juno's rotten taint," he cursed. The cigar sank into the wine-dark sea. He couldn't afford many more.

Someone took his shoulder, a grip of stone. He stood up on the rail with help. "Here," she passed him a tailor-rolled tobacco like they sold at markets. She lit it for him on a pitch-stick then her own.

"Thanks, long time until a trade post."

"Uh-huh," she said.

He tried to look over the waves, but she was just so pretty. Skin like coffee with a dash of cream. Don't look, just follow the breakers, Roary. Veridaan's sake.

"Where are you stationed next? I can always spot a Grye." She smiled.

Roary melted. Forty-seven, overweight, but man alive did he have hair? It wasn't oiled right now though. Too expensive. "Gred. Just finished twenty years as Constable General on the Merchant Quarter." Dammit, Roary. Less is more.

"Retired?" she asked.

"Eh, something like that." What an absolute duff. Admit to a discharge in disgrace.

She sighed, a sound like the warm summer breeze. "I'm somewhat retired myself. Taking the longest holiday." She chuckled.

"Wait a bit. I know you."

Her soft smile hardened. "You must be mistaken." She turned to leave.

"Didn't mean to offend you, just, you're the woman with the stepchild. The Ostian teen that helps down in the hold. I just said stepchild what with, uhm, her red hair, that usually coming from Ostia, and, you know," oh, Roary, keep digging that grave, "what with you and your black... hair."

She laughed into the cold sea air, took his arm. "Yes, yes. More of a ward than my stepchild. She's had a tough time in the city, I figure a new climate will help."

Roary looked back to the smoke haze drifting off the East End and all the burned-out burgs like rotten teeth on a jack-o-lantern. A Hanrab woman and some Mule kid, he didn't need to pry what they ran from. "Off to Gred then, is it?" he asked. "Figure the cold fresh air and pines will get all that coal smoke out of her soul?"

"No, we're going to the end of the line on this one. Gaiathor, the western continent. Mabura to be specific."

He whistled on high down to low. "That's a long journey. That's a lot of whales between us and Tuura lands. Those Krodan will hunt every single one of them to the bottom of the ocean along the way. You sure that's best for you and your ward? Sure it's safe?"

She parried the question. "Why do you care?"

"Well, she's a hard worker down there and just so polite. Seems like she'd do well up in the old Gred. Also." Did he dare? "It sure would be sour to lose your company, what with this great rapport we've developed." He dared.

She laughed deep, roared it to the sky and all its stars. He laughed too, but nervous-like.

"You know what, you remind me of someone I knew a long time ago."

Aw, shucks. It worked. "Name's Bullworth, Roary Bullworth." He put out a chunky hand.

She took it. "Eadala, we didn't use surnames down in the Mule."

"A fine pleasure, Eadala. I look forward to the next two months where I convince you to stay in Gred."

They were easy friends and even easier lovers. But to Roary's chagrin Eadala and her ward stayed on two months later when he got off the ship at Gred.

———

Violet was bored. That's what she had to call herself now, Violet. It reminded her of her father in a good way. Violet and Eadala, refugees from the great Mule fire. That was fine, it felt good to be away from the city. Just too much memory, those that came from her and those that came from others. She shivered. Bored was lame, but it was better than-

It was better than the last few days.

Bored, bored, bored. She laid on a lemon crate, the least smelly thing in the creaking hold of the whaler. Toci and Mariah were no help, clogged in their tiny room for hours and hours on end. Bumping furniture, Garvis used to call it. A big part of her wanted to stay when they made it to Gred, see if she couldn't find her old brothel slopper buddy. She knew a lot of people in Gred. But Sariah was right, the farther from Cruxia the better.

The past days were foggy. Memory rainbowed through a prism. After that horrorshow hospital room, she blacked out. Saw things no mortal should. The death of gods, the birth of realms.

When she awoke, she was in a burnt-out alley with Sariah. The scorched bones of buildings ran down the wharf but all the ones north were spared. The clean buildings with a brush of scorch compared to the desolation that ran south for three miles. Like a lightning bolt surged across all the East End.

She was tired and her head hurt. She trusted this woman. She'd seen her whole past and present. The gods still clashed when she closed her eyes but most of the power drifted away. "Why are we here, where are we?"

Sariah looked around the burnt crossroads. "We're waiting for someone before we leave."

"We've been here for hours," she guessed. Time was still elastic, memories breathed in and out of her mind.

Sariah looked around the burnt street as it slumped to the sea, looked at the bones of Nito's inn. She sighed. "He's not coming, let's go." *So long, Gantry.* A thought like someone else's in Roisin's mind.

And now here Violet was a day later in the hold of this whaler. With each mile away from the city she felt her old self return. Boredom, angst, desire, the whole teenage bag. She spied around the room to make sure she was alone. She was.

She closed her eyes and counted. Forty-three little auras running around the hold. Tiny brown things. Auras was the word pulled from Polo's head. She liked to think of it as candle-light. Each bright little soul had a Door. Smaller animals had smaller Doors. Once she found the key, the Door would open, and she saw their candle.

This was her third attempt. Last time she managed twenty of them, but this time she stretched her mind and breathed in through her nose and out through her mouth. Control within begets control without. She flicked open all forty-three Doors and brought their candles to her. Forty-three mice lined up on the rafters, ready for her whim.

Her power fleeted, but it wasn't gone. She would have it all back. Maybe not the memories. But the power. Exercise it like you would a muscle; no matter how long it took, how hard it got.

She wondered what color the gods' candles were.

———

Mama Roeneck swirled a cauldron of dead turtles and cackled. Oh, how sweet? Oh, how absolutely delicious? All of her machinations ran together like carbon and iron, a plan forged to steel. Oh, hehehe indeed.

She was born a Mama, but not Roeneck. Veridaan was her true name. Sister Summer and goddess of birth. Not dead, only mostly dead these past, what was it? Two thousand five hundred thirty-six years. Who counted, eh? Hehehe. Mama to all mortal creation on Galea's surface. Fen, Krodan, Turakhan? Those were her in the long ago. Then her jealous fuckstick of a brother raped her because she loved Halladar. And oh, the priests lied, lied and lied. Covered up the whole matter to keep their myths squeaky clean.

Imagine if history was taught? Imagine if Auron was the God of Rape instead of Life? How different would the planet be if they carved the real images, Veridaan with her sword through his heart while his gauntlets crushed her skull. Teach these women that you fucking kill your aggressor. No, just fairytale statues of him in armor, her in flowers. Fucking mortal twats.

A Sibling can't die for real, at least she hoped. So, her primordial slug crept long across the ocean's bottom those two millennia ago, slimed and dragged across three thousand plus miles until she ended up at the tip of a peninsula. She grew like a fungus, full of hatred and bile and vengeance. Oh so full of vengeance. Birthed humans in that fit of hatred. The Citadel grew around her, eventually it was sacked and called Cruxia. She watched the Fen rise and fall, the humans follow. Her hatred and foulness bled up into the city over the years, decades, centuries, millennia. Shaped in her new image, hatred and stinking chemicals. Exploitation and moral decay.

Auron flourished, too. He took much of her essence when

they died together in a thermo-radiant explosion. Took more from her with his thumbs last penetration. Turvaal he called himself now. God of Chains, god of rape and slavery. Veridaan became Mama Roeneck, Auron became Turvaal. Times change but they don't really.

Auron-now-Turvaal would fall. Yes, yes. She altered Cruxian politics to dig at her fuckstick brother. Fought wars over centuries with his cultists. Her endgame now closed to the decades.

It was an easy thing to take out the hit on Alonso using the Cazzaraati. The hard part was lining it up with that damn girl's candlelighter schedule. The little virgin saw such trauma as a child she made for the perfect seed. After that, it was a matter of leading her down to the Crimson Moor psychically right as Mama gave all of Cruxia's kax supply to Nito. Dodging that dabbler Hook and suppressing the soul of Alonso were middling difficult. Why did all of her priests have to be such wankers? Cruxia was better off without the old High Fuck. Roisin the Beau made sure of that. Hehehe.

The East End burned, an enema required every century or so in Cruxia. She cared naught for the Baron Cazarrati and his syndicate. After all, she had someone sequestered down in Leper Block B of Auron's Mercy if she ever needed another crime lord. She was a fan of irony and Nito was not, which made it extra delicious.

Her seed ranged across the sea to Gaiathor. Towards the weakest of the Gates. Roisin, now Violet, would accept her role as the new Veridaan. Daughter Spring, goddess of memory. Already the seed worked back power after Mama toned her influence down. Couldn't burn out the shell too early. Mama Veridaan had plans. Mama would crack this planet in half, dig into the other realm to kill her brother, then rewrite all of creation in her own name.

Wouldn't she just?

October 26th, 2021

ABOUT THE AUTHOR

Carter Reynolds started writing at age 12 and never lost the bug. He is a father, husband, an avid painter of miniatures, and a stalwart defender of love. Candlelighter is his first novel and there are a handful of short stories besides. He doesn't plan on leaving Cruxia and Galea anytime soon.

———

To learn more about Carter Reynolds and discover more Next Chapter authors, visit our website at www.nextchapter.pub.

Candlelighter
ISBN: 978-4-82414-083-8

Published by
Next Chapter
2-5-6 SANNO
SANNO BRIDGE
143-0023 Ota-Ku, Tokyo
+818035793528

10th November 2024

Milton Keynes UK
Ingram Content Group UK Ltd.
UKHW030152051224
452010UK00010B/515

9 784824 140838